LYING IN A
WHIRLPOOL OF BLOOD

I took off my shoes and socks. I left them in a pile by the floor as I sat at the edge of the pool. I first tested the temperature—it was somewhere between warm cider and cauldron stew—and then dipped my feet into the water.

A fan came on—that must have been Jack's doing—and the fog lifted slowly. I closed my eyes, trying to preserve the peace of the moment. Jack said, "Oh my God." I opened my eyes. Jack's scruffy face was all twisted. I followed the path of his eyes, and for the first time, I noticed that the color of the water was as red as wine. The jets forced even darker streams of burgundy fluid to the surface. On reflex, I drew my legs out of the water. My big toe hit something hard.

I fought a wave of heebie-jeebies. The top of a man's bald head bobbed in the water, rising out and sinking back into the red soup. Jack seemed paralyzed by the sight. I feigned superhuman bravery and said, "Waiter, there's a man in my whirlpool."

Books by Valerie Frankel

FICTION*
Deadline for Murder
Murder on Wheels
Prime Time for Murder
A Body to Die For

NONFICTION (WITH ELLEN TIEN)
The Heartbreak Handbook
The I Hate My Job Handbook

*Published by POCKET BOOKS

A WANDA
MALLORY
MYSTERY

A BODY TO DIE FOR

VALERIE FRANKEL

POCKET BOOKS

New York   London   Toronto   Sydney   Tokyo   Singapore

Dedicated to Wanda's fans.
May you all be happy, stay healthy and become big-shot
Hollywood movie producers someday.

———————

This book is a work of fiction. Names, characters, places and
incidents are products of the author's imagination or are used
fictitiously. Any resemblance to actual events or locales or persons,
living or dead, is entirely coincidental.

An *Original* Publication of POCKET BOOKS

POCKET BOOKS, a division of Simon & Schuster Inc.
1230 Avenue of the Americas, New York, NY 10020

ISBN: 0-671-79520-1

First Pocket Books printing July 1995

10 9 8 7 6 5 4 3 2 1

POCKET and colophon are registered trademarks of
Simon & Schuster Inc.

Cover design and illustration by Tom McKeveny

Printed in the U.S.A.

1

~~~

The Fully
Naked City

I was standing on the Brooklyn Heights Promenade, peering at Manhattan's famous skyline. It was hard not to be impressed with the view. Search beams streamed heavenward like Bat signals from the heliport on top of the World Trade Center. Bright taillights formed giant red snakes as traffic zipped across the Brooklyn Bridge and then up the FDR Drive. Strands of white and yellow bulbs hung from the masts on the tall ships docked at the South Street Seaport. Manhattan looked more like a floating carnival than the crime capital of the world.

The sounds of waves and laughter drew my attention to the Booze Cruise churning up the East River. Drunk passengers danced on deck to a mariachi band. Above the tinkling of glasses and the tickling of guitars, I heard the high-pitched squeal of a woman being pinched on the ass. She didn't seem to mind. After the boat chugalugged by, I returned my complete attention to the couple I'd been tailing. They held hands while leaning on the railing and pointing like dorks at the Chrysler Building and the Empire State. The smells of sex and Brooklyn Queens Expressway exhaust filled the air.

I took a hearty whiff and hid behind one of those owl-faced binocular machines otherwise found on the tip of the Grand Canyon. My luscious red curls were tucked into a black beret that made my ears look big. I wore a black jacket (lightweight, mid-length), black knee-highs pulled up to my thigh, but not quite reaching the bottom of my black bike shorts. I'd never worn the black tank top without a bra before. I made a mental note to unpack my underwear box. I felt a wave of self-consciousness, and pulled the jacket over my chest. The whole outfit was the result of my lazy unpacking practices. But the idea was not to dress like myself. Ordinarily, I'd never look like such a geek.

I put a quarter in the owl-head, and turned the viewfinder toward the couple. He looked rugged-yet-sensitive in jeans and a Marlboro T-shirt. Not the kind of guy who'd ever fantasize about what life would be like on the wrong side of the law, but I was sure he had something of an indecent heart, at least when in the sack. He had long red hair, sparkly green eyes, good bones and big muscles. And tall—have I mentioned tall? Attractive though he may be, she was the one I wanted to examine closely. Her aerobics instructor body was not hidden in floral leggings and an orange tit shirt. I was happy to note that my breasts were significantly larger. But so was my ass. An overworked soulfulness filled her brown eyes. She clearly wanted something, a favor. Money. Sex, maybe. When the breeze blew off the river below, long strands of yellow hair swept across her throat like a corn silk broom. The man, Max, my boyfriend, said something to make her laugh. The woman, Leeza, Max's ex-girlfriend, cupped her hand shyly over her mouth like she was self-conscious of her breath.

In an effort not to be too conspicuous, I scanned the rest of the Promenade. Another couple sat on a bench farther down the strip, smoking cigarettes and talking eagerly about something political no doubt. As soon as I saw the smoke, I desperately craved one. A few joggers blurred by and I made myself think about lung cancer. An old man with a white beard had climbed over the fence to the municipal playground. He pissed in the sandbox and went over to nap on the slide. I turned back toward Leeza, the aerobics goddess. Her back was to me now.

I kept the line on Max's face. He seemed uncomfortable, which made me happy. Leeza started waving her hands around, impassioned, making a point. He tried to calm her down and put his hands on her shoulders. She took the opportunity to slide her arms around his neck. My heart sank to my ankles as their heads inched toward each other. I heard a click. The viewfinder went black. And me, fresh out of quarters.

I peered over the top of the binocular machine. They were walking again, this time toward me. They were still hand in hand. Damn, I cursed. I missed it. I turned toward the railing to avoid being noticed. They seemed to be pretty distracted by each other, so I felt enraged, but safe. Inches from me now, I'd practically leaned all the way over the railing so my head was completely in the shadows. When I turned to check if they'd passed by, a dust swirl from a speeding eighteen-wheeler on the BQE (which runs directly below the Promenade), blew the beret off my head. It floated dreamily to the highway and was immediately crushed like a roadkill.

I never liked it anyway. My fluffy red curls spilled onto my shoulders. There goes my cover, I thought. I dared to look. But Max and his ex-slut hadn't noticed a thing.

If they kissed, I had to know. I wasn't satisfied with hand holding. That didn't constitute infidelity. I felt in my pocket for my spare beret. I took it out and fumbled with it in the rush to get it on right. In a sudden moment of self-consciousness, I asked myself, what's your fucking problem? I knew the answer already, so I counted to ten—they were about fifty feet away—and set off to follow. I hoped she didn't have a car.

"Hey, aren't you Wanda Mallory?" The voice came from behind me. I turned to look, annoyed. I didn't recognize him. He wore a sweaty pink T-shirt and blue running shorts that gave him a banana wedgie. I ignored him and kept walking.

He jogged after me, this time shouting my name. "Wait. You're Wanda Mallory, I saw your picture in the newspapers. Wait. I just want to talk to you for a minute."

"Shut up, you idiot," I hissed, jamming the beret on my head.

Too late. Max heard and stopped in his tracks. He turned around and saw me. His face flushed red with anger—matching his auburn locks quite beautifully. He grabbed the aerobics chick by the arm (above the elbow) and tugged her down the Promenade, out of sight.

I turned toward the jogger and said, "Thanks a lot. You probably just cost me the love of my life."

"Jeez, I'm sorry," he said.

"Get lost." Another bungle in the asphalt jungle. Max and I had just moved in together two days ago.

We were going to see how things went, and decide if we should get engaged. But that was probably off now, considering that he'd never speak to me again. Leeza, his ex-girlfriend, was in town for some fitness convention at the Jacob Javits Center. She was his date for the night. When she called to say she'd be in town, he asked me if I'd have a problem with them going to dinner. I said no. And I was fine about it, until she showed up at the apartment looking just like the type who'd go to a fitness convention. I knew Max had once asked her to marry him. This was years ago. Four of them. She said no. They broke up. He got over it (or so he says). I didn't believe him, partially out of paranoia, partially because he hummed in the shower. We already had plans to do some serious work around the house between shots of tequila and taking turns jerking each other off.

So I decided to follow them. Quite naturally and smartly, I applied the skills of my trade (detecting, that is), to my personal predicament. If Max had a problem with that, he can jerk himself off from now on.

The jogger tapped me on the shoulder. "Are you okay?" he asked. "You look kind of sick." I sneered at him. I needed a plan. Okay, I'd throw some stuff into my purse and go to Santina's for the night. Santina Epstein was a half-Jewish, half-Italian beautician who was my former landlord and permanent surrogate mother. It'd be swell. She'd cook me pasta, chide me about my weight, tell me to beg for Max's forgiveness. On second thought, fuck Santina. I'll ride the subways all night, risking life and limb. Later I'd tell Max he drove me to it. That'd show him. I started marching in the direction of the Borough Hall subway entrance. It's times like these that I wish I hadn't quit smoking.

I was stopped in my tracks when the jogger grabbed my wrist. "I'm sorry if I've offended you in some way," he said.

I wretched my arm back. The guy smelled like he'd just run back from California. Not that I mind manly male pungents. In fact, during and after sex, I like it fine when Max works up a healthy glisten. But this guy wasn't glistening. He was flooding. I took a step back and said, "I make a rule of not talking to strangers who have visible body odor."

"Male sweat is full of pheromones," he said and smiled like a goon. "Pheromones are supposed to attract women."

"I'm not a woman," I said. He looked confused.

"I know you're a woman," he said knowingly. "I read all about you on Page Six." This couldn't help but raise a smile. Finally, after years of hoping and praying, I earned a mention on Page Six, the *Daily Mirror*'s gossip sheet. It happened when I solved a big murder case on the set of a TV game show. (Long story—246 pages, in fact.) The Page Six item—with flattering photo (thank God)—hangs framed on the wall in my Times Square office.

"Did you like the picture?" I couldn't help asking.

"Oh, yeah. It was great. Nice smile. Very nice."

I reappraised this stinky jogger. He wasn't hard on the eyes. Around twenty-six. Good legs, too hairy though. His nipples poked at his shirt like turkey thermometers. His sandy blond hair was darkened with sweat. The hazel eyes were outlined by long, girly lashes. The overall look was scruffy, like a dog or a kid after playing touch football. And he was hitting on me. "Not interested," I said. "Take your banana wedgie somewhere else."

He blushed and rearranged his shorts. "I think

you've misunderstood me," he protested. "I'm married. While you are an extremely attractive woman, you're really not my type."

But I was every man's sexual fantasy. Surely he knew. "And what type might that be, asshole?" I asked.

"Well, you know. Someone who works out."

"You think I don't work out?"

"Do you?" he asked, shocked.

"As a matter of fact, I do." I burn a million calories a day, lifting crumpets to my mouth. And chewing. Melts fat like crazy.

"I'm sorry," he said. "I have to stop offending you. This just isn't turning out the way I wanted it to. I wanted to come up to you, say that I saw your picture, and then, well, you know."

"What, jog off into the sunset?" I asked.

"Hire you," he said, shyly.

"And you just happened to know that I'd be walking along this stretch of pavement at this particular hour on this Tuesday night in June?"

"It was a spontaneous decision," he said. "I saw you, and the answer to my problem was suddenly clear." He paused, crossing his arms over his chest. "It's my wife. I think she's cheating on me. With a bald guy." His brow furrowed with the confession. Genuine or not, he seemed concerned. I hadn't taken a case since the big TV caper, and my funds were nearly depleted. I'd planned to start looking for work as soon as I could get my belongings unpacked in my new apartment with Max. That particular project was moving as quickly as continental drift.

"Who's your wife?"

"Ameleth Bergen," he said proudly.

"Is that supposed to mean something to me?"

"You haven't heard of Ameleth?" he asked, surprised.

"It's a big city. I don't think we run in the same circles."

"I just run along the Promenade."

"Who is she, Jack?"

"How'd you know my name was Jack?" I didn't, but shrugged mysteriously. "Either you're an incredible detective"—natch, I thought—"or a tennis fan." He searched my eyes, hoping.

"Love all," I said.

He smiled modestly. "Oh, I've won my share of trophies, but I guess you know that already." Max followed tennis. I made a mental note to ask him about this guy, Jack. Bergen? Didn't ring a single, tiny bell. Maybe he had another last name.

"Ameleth didn't change her name," I bluffed.

"Why should she? She's her own person," he answered defensively.

I waved him off. "I'm sure she is." Like I needed a lesson on being your own person.

"She's got a profession, you know," he said. "She has business contacts. If she changed her name, they'd be confused." Sounded to me like this was a sore spot for Jack.

"You've been married for a while?" I asked. At least long enough for her to go elsewhere for action.

"Two years. Ameleth owns and runs the Western Athletic Club on Pierrepont Street. Right around the corner. Four clay courts. I'm the head pro." Wonder how he got the job. The Western Athletic Club was the place where downwardly mobile Brooklyn Heights yups gathered to inflict pain on themselves and discuss it later over a carrot cocktail by the natural juice bar. Max toured the place a couple weeks ago and signed up on the spot. The club was one of the reasons he agreed to move to Brooklyn from the Upper East Side.

"I've heard of the place," I said. Max's year membership set him back $1,200, plus another couple hundred for a one-time-only initiation fee. To me, it seemed like a lot to pay for the privilege of lifting heavy metal objects. This Jack must be rolling. I said, "I take three days' fee up-front, and you pay expenses."

"Starting when?"

"Right now."

"You'll start the investigation tonight?" he asked, obviously pleased.

"You've got an ATM card, don't you?" Why not, I figured. My other options were going home to an irate boyfriend and two cats who hated each other (the meeting of my black she-cat, Otis, and Max's fat tabby, Syd, did not go well), a night riding the subway, or listening to a bouffanted beautician scold me for taking a second helping of garlic bread. "My fee is fifteen hundred a day," I started. "But I like you, kid. I'll tell you what I'm gonna do. I'll offer you my services for one thousand dollars a day. Bargain basement. Take it or I leave." A highball. I'd settle on three hundred.

"That's an awful lot of money," he complained.

"It sure is." He frowned. I guess tennis pros don't make so much these days. I shrugged and walked away.

I had to go about ten paces—I almost buckled after five—when he finally said, "No, wait." I smiled deep inside. I turned around. "My wife keeps some money in the safe at the club," he said. "It's just around the corner." Hook, line, he was sunk. One day's work would cover my rent for two months. All from having my picture in the paper. I couldn't wait to tell Max. I felt a pang. I should have trusted him. Maybe I would have, if Leeza wasn't so—what's the word—*toned?* I hated her tone. For all I knew, her perky, firm body was astride Max at that very second. And he was making those tiny, birdlike noises he does with me when he gets really hot. A flash of green exploded behind my eyes.

"Are you okay?" Jack asked. "You look kind of sick again."

"Shut up." I took a breath. Do the Zen thing, I prodded myself. Visualize that day in the future when Leeza will lose her girlish figure. Just like I had. Okay, I'll be brutally honest. I never had a girlish figure. I've been womanly since the sixth grade. I wondered if agonizing about Leeza would burn off a few pounds.

Only one thing could cut through my jealousy: money. "Let's go," I said to Jack and we split like Russian gymnasts for the Western Athletic Club.

I didn't mind the walk through the North Heights. Brooklyn, that is. The old limestone and brick brown-stones had iron-work patterns on heavy wooden doors. Inside arched windows, I could just make out some fancy wall and ceiling molding. Chandeliers. I'd bet on maple inlay floors. And hanging from the windows and sitting on the stone stoops, were the most ambitious flower boxes I'd ever seen. Begonias, impatiens, those orange ones that look like fireworks and the white ones that look like mushroom clouds. I wondered if I'd have to learn the horticultural lingo to make friends in my new neighborhood. Like I needed friends. I had loads of friends. Three of them. We passed an old-fashioned gas lamp on the corner of

Pierrepont and Henry Streets. Jack said, "I hope Ameleth didn't go to the club tonight. I'm supposed to be doing fieldwork, so she won't be expecting me."

"Maybe we'll catch her in the act, in which case, my hourly rate will go into effect."

"We won't catch her tonight," he said, fairly certain. "The man she's doing it with is away for the day."

"You know the guy?" I asked. We were approaching the blue awning above the entrance to the club.

"I suspect. That's why I need you." We stepped toward the building's blue welcome mat. The insignia with the letters *WAC* hung on the door. Just looking at it, I felt fitter.

"Who is he?" I asked.

"I'll tell you inside," he said and shooshed me.

The club was built into the hollowed shells of two brownstones. Ameleth had, apparently, gutted the prewar buildings to construct the ultimate exercise and fitness space with state-of-the-art Soloflexes, Genuflexes and Nexusplexes. She'd gotten Stair-Masters, LifeCycles and ButtMashers. Pool, tennis courts and a spa. After Max toured the place, he raved for so long I had to seduce him to get him to shut up. The feel was very eighties, though construction was completed just last year.

In Max's opinion, the club was the greatest thing since spliced atoms. Ameleth had left the original brownstone facades. Still, the club was pretty conspicuous on that quiet block. No other building had a white-gloved, blue-capped steroid monster in blue bike shorts and a muscle T stand in front to open the door for you. I smiled and mentally measured his thighs (forty-five inches, which I found freakish), as the doorman admitted us to the club.

Once inside, I was bombarded with reflections of myself. Every wall, even in the inside corridor, was mirrored. It was a three-quarters view nightmare. No wonder the clients were obsessed with their bodies. The next thing I noticed were the smells of chlorine, baby powder and the slightest notes of Ben-Gay. For an ex-smoker, my olfactory sense was remarkably keen. It's helped solve a few jobs for me, in particular, the Case of the Cheating Boyfriend and the Litter Box Caper. Jack smiled and said, "You get used to the smell. It's refreshing though, isn't it?"

If refreshing smelled like moldy menthol, then yeah, sure. We walked along the mirrored corridor. I stared straight ahead the whole time. Along the way, Jack and I passed the pro shop, called Cut Me. Sporting goods, health food and supplements were for sale. Jack waved at the people behind the counters. They waved back. Everyone wore workout clothes. A woman walked by in a pink leotard G-string and shiny orange tights. Another passed in a green body stocking that hugged her sinew so tightly I wondered if Lycra could fall in love.

We reached the reception desk. An early twentyish woman in a spotted workout getup smiled from behind the console. She had one ponytail on the top of her head. Strands of blond hair streamed down her shoulders. She had some knockers. "Hi, Jack," she said and smiled brightly while stretching her leg muscles. "I didn't expect to see you tonight." I noticed that there wasn't a chair behind her desk.

Jack said, "Change of plans. Ameleth around?"

She eyed me suspiciously. "She's isn't here. Should I call her?"

"No." Jack waved her off. "I just have to run upstairs. I left something in the suite. Janey, this is my new friend, Wanda Mallory." I nodded. She nodded and checked me out.

"Mark from Cut Me needs to talk to you," Janey said. "Like, right away." Must be another sports bra emergency.

Jack sighed and said, "He probably wants to ask about the sneakers shipment. Wanda, wait right here?" I shrugged affirmative, and he left.

Janey smiled at me. I smiled back. She said, "I guess you'll be joining the club."

I nearly laughed out loud.

"It's really the right decision," she said all-confidential-like. "It's never too late to start exercising. How old are you? Like, thirty-two?" I was, like, twenty-nine. I ignored her, not caring if I was rude. "No wedding ring," she observed. "Our singles memberships are on sale this month." She shifted legs, and stretched with vigor. Out of the corner of my eye, I watched her examine my head. Finally, she asked, "Is that your real hair color?"

"Are those real silicone implants?" I asked. "Maybe I should just ask Jack when he comes back. I'm sure he'll have an opinion. Unless that would embarrass you, of course." Finally, that ended our conversation.

Jack returned moments later and we walked past Janey toward the elevators. I turned to look at her butt and caught her checking a load of mine. Satisfied that my butt couldn't be more genuine, she turned back around with a smirk on her face.

"You fucked Janey," I said to Jack.

He seemed shocked. "I've been completely faithful to Ameleth."

"Except for that time you screwed Janey," I prodded.

We stepped into one of the two elevators. Most

brownstones don't have them. Ameleth must have spent a million pretty pennies installing these. The elevator car had a spongy floor, like a gym mat, and the walls and ceiling were mirrored. The buttons were big rectangles with words on them. From the top down, the buttons read: aerobics; free-weights, nautilus; racketball, tennis; lobby, shops, restaurant (where we were); pool, spa, locker rooms. Five floors. Only one seemed remotely tempting to me: the spa. Maybe Jack could get me a free massage.

Jack reached into his pocket and pulled out a key chain. He fit a cylindrically shaped key into a slot on the elevator control panel. He turned it, and the car took off. We zoomed like a vertical express train past the tennis and nautilus levels to a floor not listed on the panel. The car's stop nearly flattened me. The mirrored doors slid open with a *kerchunk*. Jack stepped off. I followed. We walked into the first room of a suite. Behind, the elevator doors whooshed closed, the car dropped with a whistle. I was trapped. Just me and Jack and a CyberRun treadmill in the center of the room. A well-stocked silver and glass bar was built into the rear wall. I headed straight for it. A few round white stools with stilt-like legs stood in front of the counter. I was hoping for a soothing shot of tequila. The hardest stuff I found was Tabasco. I took a shot. A few hairs grew on my chest. I made a mental note to pluck them later.

The floor was carpeted in white and the walls were a bluish gray. The room smelled of sweat and industrial cleanser. Jack said, "I knew you were some detective, but how on earth did you figure it out about me and Janey?"

How could I not? She seemed livid that Jack would take another woman—furthermore, an extremely attractive one—to the suite when Ameleth wasn't around. She had to have cause to be so openly rude. Ergo, she was jealous and they fucked. Probably only once or twice because Jack was tolerant when he didn't have to be. A combination of regret and guilt. I said, "Elementary, my dear Watson."

He laughed charmingly. His bangs dropped cutely when he said, "You already knew my last name was Watson, so I won't be impressed this time." The name Jack Watson did sound vaguely familiar. "But really. Janey must have told you something."

I shook my head. "I don't discuss my psychic powers. So few believe."

He poured himself a Perrier and took it over to the exercise equipment. He hopped on top of the CyberRun and placed his drink in the built-in cup holder. He put it on Light Stroll. "I only did it because of Ameleth," he said, his T-shirt swaying as he strolled. "I was jealous and I wanted her attention. That's normal, isn't it? I wasn't in love with Janey. I guess there's something wrong in cheating." Could he not go without exercise for five minutes?

"Look, Jack, shrink service will cost you extra."

"Of course. The money. Just a minute." Jack leapt from the machine. He excused himself and walked into another room, out of sight. I'd assumed he was headed for the office portion of the suite. I gave the front room a quick sweep. No real business happened in here, I thought, looking at the treadmill and the gym mats on the floor. The distraction of the juice bar was just too tempting. I spotted a door next to a well-grown rubber tree. The tiny glass window in its center was steamed over. I walked toward it. As I got closer, I heard the level hiss of steam. A faint gurgle sound escaped from under the door.

"I've got it," Jack announced, emerging from the other room. He waved a fan of greenbacks. He walked over to me and placed three thousand dollars in my hand. I pocketed the bundle. My insides were suddenly warm and cozy.

I said, "You don't happen to be a smoker?" The texture of money excites all my senses and I craved one.

"You want one?" He nodded.

"A jock-strapping young man like yourself has a cigarette for me?" I couldn't believe he smoked. He seemed to brim with all that was good.

"Ameleth doesn't know," he confessed. "It's my biggest secret."

"Besides Janey."

"Besides Janey," he agreed. "Ameleth is so busy all the time."

I hate when men blame women for their own mistakes. "But not too busy to screw around on the side herself," I said. "You can tell me about the guy now."

Jack suddenly looked sad. I felt a pang of guilt for my meanness. But Jack hadn't hired me for absolution. I'd give it, don't get me wrong, but it'd cost him. "He's owns Cut Me, the health store downstairs. We rent the space to him and get three percent of his profits. It's a good deal for Ameleth and me. Cut Me does very well, so everyone's happy."

"Except you."

"I see the way Barney looks at Ameleth when she wears her turquoise G-string bodysuit. It's disgusting. Like he can see through her clothes." There couldn't have been much to see through. I let it pass. "He makes me nervous. They spend so much time together. And they're so flagrant. I don't know how many times I've found them here in the Jacuzzi. Laughing and sipping beet juice. Of course, she says it's completely innocent. Not trusting her is what gets to me the most." Jack's eyes were damp, though his shirt had dried. It draped over his chest nicely, and for a moment, I was distracted.

"I trust they were wearing bathing suits?" I asked, thinking of hot wetness.

"That's not the point. They were, I don't know, frolicking." He puckered in thought. "It hurts me to think about them together."

I shuffled my feet. I get uncomfortable when people get serious on me. And all this talk of Jacuzzis made me want to soak in one. "I guess the scene of the crime would be a good place to start," I said. "The Jacuzzi?"

Jack pointed at the door behind me. I turned around and punched it open. I assumed my cocky-for-clients strut, though the fog in the room was so thick Jack might have missed it. I reached into my purse for my glasses. They were steamed before I arranged them on my nose.

Jack entered the room, waving his arms through the fog. "The Jacuzzi should be off. Damn, Ameleth! She never remembers." Jack walked past me into the room. He groped for the light switch and hit it. The ceiling was suddenly dotted with yellow orbs, shimmering through the fog.

I took off my glasses and walked forward on the wood-planked floor. I made out the border of the circular Jacuzzi. It was the size of a birdbath for pterodactyls. The gurgle was loud, comforting, like the boil of tomato soup. I spied Jack's outline across the room, fiddling with what I assumed were the Jacuzzi controls. I hoped he'd turn on the vent. The steam was making me sweat.

I took off my shoes and socks. I left them in a pile on the floor as I sat at the edge of the Jacuzzi. I first tested the temperature—it was somewhere between warm cider and cauldron stew—and then dipped my feet into the water. The swirling jets and hot bubbles tingled, and I thought briefly of the days when I'd masturbate by positioning myself just so in the Jacuzzi at the home of one of my ex-boyfriends. He wasn't as good as his tub. I was sad to leave him, but I knew it'd never work when I found myself begging off sex for some alone time in his bathroom.

A fan came on—that must have been Jack's doing —and the fog lifted slowly. I closed my eyes, trying to preserve the peace of the moment. Jack said, "Oh my God." I opened my eyes. Jack's scruffy face was all twisted. I followed the path of his eyes and for the first time, I noticed that the color of the Jacuzzi water was as red as wine. The jets forced even darker streams of burgundy fluid to the surface. On reflex, I drew my legs out of the water. My big toe hit something hard.

I fought a wave of heebie-geebies. The top of a man's bald head bobbed in the water, rising out and sinking back into the red soup. Jack seemed paralyzed by the sight. I feigned superhuman bravery and said, "Waiter, there's a man in my Jacuzzi."

Jack must not have heard me. Not even a puke sound from him. One of us would have to be a man about this. As I watched Jack's frozen stare, I realized it would have to be me. I took a deep breath and grabbed the bald man by his ears. I flipped him over so we could see his face. His cheeks were pruned and bright red, almost cooked. Patches of skin on his nose were peeling off. He must have been cooking for a few hours at least. He was completely nude. I shuddered to think what damage the water had done to his dick.

I let go of his ears. He sank to the bottom of the deep red pool. One jet must have gotten underneath him and his body momentarily rose again to the surface. Sticking straight out of his gut (which, by the way, had more definition than the dictionary), was the carved wooden handle of a kitchen knife.

"Just when you thought it was safe to go back in the Jacuzzi," I said. "Pass me one of those towels." I pointed at a stack near where Jack was standing. He tossed one over and I wiped my legs of the clinging droplets of bloody water. Without thinking, I raised the towel to wipe my brow and noticed spots of pink. I felt slightly sick at the sight, but not as sick as Jack, who had begun to vomit politely in the corner.

"Let me guess," I said when the retching was over. "This is the guy your wife had been sleeping with."

Jack straightened himself. I touched the corners of my mouth to show him where to wipe. He used the bottom of his pinkish T-shirt. "He's the guy."

"You can stop worrying, Jack," I said. "It's all over between them." I picked up my shoes and socks. I nearly slipped on the floorboards as I walked out of the room. I picked up the phone on the wall by the elevators and called the cops.

2

Dead Man's Float

Once I was sure the cops were on the way, I walked toward the room's only comfortable place to sit: a white couch with mushy pillows. I checked to make sure my legs were free of bloody water. They were, but felt dirty. I made a mental note to shave.

Jack flopped down next to me on the couch. His legs were unshaven, too. He said, "I'd wished Barney dead a million times." His eyebrows arched upward on the insides, like the roof of a house. "I wished it, and it happened."

"Cigarette?" I asked.

"In the office," he said, jerking a thumb over his shoulder. "Bottom desk drawer."

I didn't have much trouble finding the office, the place where the business of staying fit went on. The room was lushly decorated with a large red leather couch and arm chairs. The walls were painted a deep green, the carpet gold. Rasta colors. Unlike the crisp whiteness of the front room, this space was a bit sloppier. Bottles of Gatorade lay empty on the carpet.

Heaps of clothes were strewn all over the desk and chairs. A pair of sweats were draped over the back of the red couch. Must be Barney's stuff, I thought. He couldn't have walked into the suite naked.

I wondered why Jack hadn't mentioned Barney's clothes when he came back here to get the money. He must not have noticed them. I gave them a quick rifle. In the back hip pocket of the sweats, I found Barney's club photo ID card. He was an attractive fortyish guy with bushy eyebrows and a wide smile. His front tooth was chipped—a charming imperfection. He was bald as a tire. (I wondered if Max would ever go bald.) I slipped the ID back in the sweatpants pocket.

I hunted some more, but didn't find a wallet or date book in any of Barney's other clothes. I found no notes written to himself that read: "Meeting with_____today. Hope I don't get stabbed in the heart." Clueless, I left the gear where I'd found it. Then I searched the desk. It was a gorgeous hunk of oak supported by skinny wrought-iron legs. The desktop was immaculate—the sign of an organizational wizard or someone with too much time on her hands. I've always found that if one is hyper-organized on the outside, one's psychotic on the inside. My guess: Ameleth Bergen was psychotic.

I decided to forgo searching through her Power-Book, sticking with superficials for the present. A desk photo in a large gold frame showed Ameleth pumping iron with the Mayor of New York. Another recorded Ameleth's tennis game with John McEnroe. There were no photos of Jack. The oak slab had just one drawer—a thin little pencil compartment. No cigarettes. Could Jack be mistaken?

Maybe he meant another desk. My nicotine homing mechanism led me toward a cork partition. Painted hunter green, it sectioned off a small square of space. Behind the temporary wall was an elementary school teacher's desk. There wasn't much space in the cubicle. I had to edge my way around the corner of the desk. I had to struggle hard to pull open the bottom drawer. It was stuck on something. After a good fight, I managed and hit pay dirt. A soft pack of Marlboro Mediums jumped into my palm. I removed a few and replaced the pack in the drawer. The sparkle of brown liquid caught my eye. A closer look in the drawer revealed a flask of Bajan Sugar Brandy. I hated brandy, but took a large swig anyway. I closed the drawer and stood up. A framed photo of Jack and Ameleth at their wedding was prominently displayed on the desk. I took another shot. The brandy was as smooth as my legs.

Jack had poured himself a Virgin Mary. He was jogging at a good clip on the treadmill when I returned to the exercise room. I dropped my treasures on the bar. He said, "Do you mind not smoking until I stop?"

I minded. I hadn't had a cigarette in months, and the sight of a dead body was like a trigger. Max said he wouldn't consider getting engaged to a smoker. That was not why I quit. I did it on a bet—no other motivation short of cancer would have been sufficient. For seventy-four days, I've only smoked when I was on fire. (That had only happened twice.) I held the butt in my hand and studied the wrapping. My lungs clinched in expectation.

"Emphysema, cancer, bad breath, a thousand dollars a year," I recited my mantra. Didn't work. I picked up a butt from the bar, letting it fall between my fingers.

Jack slowed down to a traipse and stepped off the machine. His shirt was damp again. His nipples were hard. "You know, Wanda," he started, "it's pretty lucky we were together when we found the body. I don't know what I would have done if I were alone."

"You'd have called the cops, just like I did." I've seen dead people before, some in worse shape than baked Barney. That's not to say I've gotten used to it. Poor Jack chugged his Virgin Mary and shivered in his damp shirt. "This helps, Jack," I said, and handed him the bottle of brandy. He drank greedily—not the chug of a novice belter—and passed the bottle back. He smacked his lips. "Yeah, Jack," I said. "Sure is a good thing we found the body together. If only this gave you an alibi."

"What do you mean?" he asked, concerned. "How could I have killed Barney if I was with you?"

"From the look of him, he'd been in the drink for a few hours. And if my short-term memory serves, we hooked up less than an hour ago." Jack's mouth dropped wide open. I could have flipped a few matchbooks in there. "And you were dripping wet when I first saw you. With sweat, maybe. But I can't imagine a murderer stabbing someone in a Jacuzzi and not getting soaked."

"You've been right all night, Wanda," he said gravely. "But you're wrong now."

"And your shirt. Pink with bloody water, or did you wash it with new red jeans?"

"What red jeans?" he asked.

"The point I'm making is that tracking me down on the Promenade—or lucking out and finding me there—is not going to do a damn thing for your alibi. In fact, if I were a cop"—a horrifying thought—"I'd put you on top of my list." Jack's jaw slackened. He stuttered a bit, which didn't flatter him, but his face and body took care of that anyway.

"Here, have a cigarette while we wait," I suggested. We both lit up. My first cigarette in months. Disgusting, but swell.

Jack huffed and puffed, panicked. "After giving you three thousand dollars in cash," he said, "I'm surprised you'd threaten me like this."

"This isn't a threat, Jack. I'm giving you fair warning to get yourself together for the cops." I took a drag. "They should be here any second." I had no idea what I was trying to do. I'd never give him an alibi for free. I didn't think I would for money either, definitely not for a measly three grand. I suppose I was looking for some clue that Jack didn't wield anything more fatal than a tennis racket. I reminded myself that it was I who had pressed him to come up here tonight.

Jack sighed. "I'll understand if you want to leave. I hired you to find out about Barney and Ameleth. And as you said, I don't have to worry about that anymore." His lower lip held firm. "So I'll take that money back now, if you don't mind. Keep a couple hundred for your time."

I considered it. Bolt now, pay in the next lifetime. Before I could make up my mind, the elevator whoosh drew my attention away. I dropped the cigarette in the empty Virgin Mary glass and turned to face the symphony. The doors slammed open. The crowd inside the car included Janey, the plastic wonder from downstairs, and about five cops, uniform and brown bag. I wondered who was minding the club, but then, the building was probably sealed. The entourage flooded the suite.

A female detective seemed to be in charge. "Body?"

she asked, flashing her wallet badge. Her ghostly voice spoke of many cigarettes long gone. Her skin was sallow, her hair wavy and thinning but a nice shade of brown. Her body was as dumpy as a truck. She hovered near forty years. Jack and I pointed toward the Jacuzzi door. She directed the uniforms to guard the entrance.

Janey bounced to Jack's side. Her Lycra uniform seemed vacuum packed. "I called Ameleth at home," she told Jack.

"Was she there?" he asked.

Janey nodded. "What's going on?"

The cop with the skirt cleared her throat as loudly as possible as she exited the Jacuzzi. "I'm Detective Falcone," she said, shaking all our hands. "Eighteenth Precinct. Homicide. I'm in charge here. Are any of you related to the deceased?" We shook our heads.

Jack and Janey explained who they were. Falcone asked who I was. I gave her one of my brand-new business cards—the one with the Uzi and roses design.

I said, "Mallory, Wanda Mallory. I'm working on a case for Jack Watson." I pointed at Jack.

"What case?" she asked.

I tsked. "Client confidentiality, Detective, private dicks are like priests or shrinks, you know?" I went on to offer her information on the hour we arrived; Barney's role at the club; my relationship with Jack; his relationship with Barney. My relationship with Barney. I'd seen the man naked, after all. I didn't mention that Jack's wife was screwing the mook.

Meanwhile, Janey freaked. "Barney's dead?" she shrieked before sobbing on Jack's already-soggy shoulder.

Detective Falcone took notes by punching letters on

a little Newton keyboard. She had lightning-fast typing fingers. If I could type that fast, I wouldn't have to do this for a living. Mid-key punch, Falcone stopped and stabbed at her own eye with her thumb. She fiddled adroitly for a moment. "Contacts—pain in the ass," she said, like we could relate.

"Wear glasses," I suggested helpfully.

"And distract attention from my stunning figure?" she asked. I laughed. She didn't, but I was reasonably sure she had meant for me to do so.

Janey, from Jack's side, wiped a tear as she said, "We have a discount at the club for city employees, Detective Falcone." She managed to pry herself away from Jack and fix herself a drink from the fridge.

"I'll keep that in mind, Ms. Johnson," Falcone said pleasantly enough. I was desperate for Falcone's first name. She looked like a Martha or a Mildred. She fished around in a giant pocketbook and came up with a pack of cigarettes and a lighter. She fired one up, inhaling the smoke like fresh mountain air.

"There's no smoking in the club, Detective." That was Janey, sipping an orange concoction with a straw.

Falcone smile politely and took another drag. What was Janey going to do—make a citizen's arrest for smoking?

"Mallory," Falcone graveled. "Take a walk with me." She pointed toward the Jacuzzi door. I followed her inside. "I've heard of you. Do It Right Detectives, right? You solved that TV game show case last fall."

"It's a glamorous job, but somebody had to do it," I said, immediately regretting it.

"How unfortunate for you," she retorted. If I didn't hate her on principle, I'd probably like her. Still, it was my job as a private dick to despise all public units. Falcone and I walked into the steamy room. Barney had been fished out of the Jacuzzi. He lay on his back on the wood-plank floor, his body magenta and pruned. The knife had been removed. His chest, especially around the wound, was blue from bruising. I knew squat about this kind of thing, but I'd guess whoever stabbed Barney had killer upper body strength. This narrowed the field not at all.

Falcone tapped a long unpolished fingernail on her tiny Newton screen. She stared moonily at Barney's head as if she were having a telepathic gabfest from the dead zone. A chill spread across my shoulders like an oil spill. Falcone shook her head, and then seemed to break her contact with the world beyond. She smiled politely at me. I faked it back. A couple cops milled around the body, pointing here and there at whatever they found notable. Barney's penis, in case you're interested, wasn't visible from where I stood. A cop in a uniform took samples of the Jacuzzi water.

Detective Falcone said, "What's the story you're not telling me, Mallory?"

"You know everything." Like I'd give away information to a cop. I said, "Just my dumb luck tripping into this."

"Something tells me the word *dumb* doesn't have anything to do with you, Mallory," she observed correctly.

"You're a remarkable judge of character," I responded.

"And your client's character?" She tapped her Newton. "Seems to me he's innocent," she said matter-of-factly. "Until proven guilty, that is." Was she taunting me?

"In Turkey," I noted, "it's the other way around. God bless America."

"If you're working for him, I assume you'd lie for

him." Falcone glared at me. Through the puffs and folds around her eyes, the light of conviction beamed from behind her contacts. A female dick with a badge and a hard-on for justice. Just what I needed. The cops turned Barney over onto his stomach. No visible marks. The knife hadn't cut clear through.

"What's your first name?" I asked.

"Detective," she answered.

I said, "I'd really like to stay and dance around the issues, Detective, but somewhere out there, I have a life. So, if you're done with me, I'll split."

"Why don't you hang around for a while?" she said.

"What's in it for me?"

"Not casting suspicion on yourself for leaving the scene of the crime for starters." She had a slight Southern accent—maybe Maryland or Washington. It added just enough lilt to her cigarette scratch to charm. I smiled and took the hint. I turned to leave and wait with Jack in the white room. "Oh, Mallory, one more thing," Falcone called after me. "You dance around the issues divinely."

I walked out, wondering if Falcone was flirting with me. It wouldn't be the first time I was hit on by a cop. My stomach growled. Police investigations always lasted at least two meal periods. I'd missed dinner. Breakfast would be next. I ignored the rumblings. It was a struggle at times, but I try never to let my clients see me sweat (metaphorically, I mean).

I wiped my dewy brow. Jack and Janey were huddled together on the couch, comforting each other. I needed to talk business with him alone. "Hey, Janey, go take a hike." I thumbed behind me at the treadmill. She clung to Jack, but he nudged her away. She actually went over to the machine and started hoofing. These people were like robots whose batteries constantly needed recharging. "Jack," I said, "Falcone wants to nail you."

"Oh, God! For murder?" he asked.

"No, for being too damn handsome," I joked. Jack seemed concerned. His face got slightly red. His jawbones clinched and released. I thought he might bite his tongue.

"This is horrible," gasped Jack. "If Ameleth thinks I killed her lover, she'll never talk to me again!"

With a sudden whoosh and *kerchunk,* the elevator doors flew open. I couldn't help but look. A woman stood in the center of the car, her wild brown and gray hair frizzed out from the humidity. She wore white cross-trainers, a sports bra and brown leggings. Ameleth Bergen couldn't have been more than five-foot-óne. The proportions were sublime, but in miniature. Her gray eyes scanned the room with a wild panic. "What the fuck is this?" she asked no one in particular. "Cops at the front door. No one at the front fucking desk." She spotted Janey on the treadmill and glared.

"Ameleth," Jack almost begged. "Barney was murdered, but I didn't do it." He didn't mince meats. Nor words. I liked that in a client.

Ameleth's tan face froze. Except for her lips. "Bastard," she snarled. To one of the uniforms, she said, "Where's Barney?" The man pointed toward the Jacuzzi room. She sprang at the door and flung it open with a tiny grunt. I jogged gracefully over to the open doorway to watch. I didn't see much. Ameleth walked over on the wet wood planks and stood over Barney's corpse. He was still on his stomach. Despite the protests of the cops, Ameleth flipped him faceup. His shiny head lulled to one side. His mouth hung open.

"He loved to sit in the Jacuzzi for hours," Ameleth

recounted. "And he loved when I rubbed his head with energizing oils. Now, he's dead. Fuck." Ameleth began to cry.

"Mrs. Bergen, why don't you step outside?" asked Falcone. She stood at my side in the doorway. Jack was behind me. I hadn't realized we were gawking. Ameleth looked up. Her gray eyes settled on Jack.

"Step outside?" Ameleth asked. "Are you calling me out or something? You want to start a fight with me, *broad?*" The double meaning was intentional. Falcone took the insult like a man, but I could tell it bothered her. I wondered if Ameleth wouldn't rather scrap with me. Regardless, she didn't step outside. Instead, she gently rubbed Barney's cheeks like she wanted to know if he'd crumble or flake. Her leggings were straining against her knees from kneeling so long. Her tiny thighs began to shake slightly. Suddenly, she jumped out of the kneel and began stretching her legs. She leaned to one side.

"This stinks," she said while touching her toes. I didn't know if she meant the situation or the body. She shook out each leg and then pushed past Falcone and me in the doorway.

Jack waited just outside with a fresh Virgin Mary and arms outstretched for a hug. I found it to be a particularly inappropriate beverage choice. Ameleth agreed and threw the drink across the room, decorating the white carpet with a spin art splatter of tomato juice. As for the hug, she wasn't interested. "How much attention do you need?" she asked Jack. "You must really miss the big time, don't you, Tennis Star?"

A low blow. "Now it's just us two, Ameleth," Jack said. "It's just me and you again, honey."

I heard a tsk in my ear. Falcone revved up her Newton and started punching keys.

I said, "Jack, can I talk to you for a second?" If he was about to confess, I needed to know right away. Not for any technical reason. I just like to be the first one to learn these things.

"We talked already." Jack stared at the object of his attention. She gave him the finger.

"I've got a train ticket, see, and I have to get to the *railroad.*" I make stabs at subtlety.

He looked confused. "So go catch your train."

Ameleth had taken the opportunity to sob alone behind the juice bar. She rummaged in the fridge for something other than a Virgin Mary. I took the opportunity to calm Jack down and try to shut him up. He said, "I think I'm dehydrated. I need something to drink. Excuse me a moment." He actually tried to go to Ameleth again.

"Look, Jack," I said. "You're blowing this. You're acting guilty."

"Ameleth talked about it all the time," Jack said, the most testy he'd been all night. "She never said who, but I heard all about the sex in repugnant detail. He liked her to put on pink cotton panties. Not white. Not red. And pink cotton ankle socks. With ruffles. That man was sick. He was disgusting. I'm glad he's dead." Jack's boyish veneer beamed raw hurt. Falcone watched him, but didn't appear to be listening. I recalled that jocks weren't generally known for their massive brainpower.

"You kill this guy, or what?" I asked in a whisper.

"You don't mince words, do you?"

"Just tell me the truth."

"If I'd killed him, I'd have drowned him," he said thoughtfully. "That way, there'd be no evidence. But I didn't kill him. I found him. Thank God, you're on my side." Ah, the appreciation of a desperate man. I learned a lot about this in my early twenties. Those days were long gone, and I had no plans to return. But Jack—he seemed honest. I believed him. If he was guilty, I'd eat a bag of doughnuts, then my beret.

"Ameleth hates me," he said coldly.

I countered, "It's more of a twisted psycholove."

"You're right." He nodded his head as if that were better.

The paramedics finally arrived. I checked my watch—over an hour since I'd called the police. Good thing Barney was already dead because he wouldn't have lasted that wait. The guys in white entered the Jacuzzi room and wheeled the body out in a green plastic bag. It was a long day's gurney into night for Barney. For the first time all evening, I got that sick rush of panic and dread. A life had been snubbed out like the cherry on a cigarette. I grieved briefly for this stranger.

"He'll never eat a Dorito again," I said to myself.

"He never ate Doritos anyway," Jack—who had rudely eavesdropped on my conversation with myself—shared. "Neither do I. They're pure fat and salt."

"But crunchy," I added. Fat and salt: two of the four basic food groups. The other two being nicotine and NutraSweet. I had a flash craving for french fries with brown gravy on the side, a large Diet Coke and a cigarette after. My mouth watered. I wiped the corners with the beret. I wondered if the Greek diner on the corner would break a hundred-dollar bill. My stomach growled like a rabid dog. I put a mental leash on it.

Ameleth clung to Barney's body bag as the paramedics maneuvered the gurney into the elevator. She wanted to stay with him, but the paramedics and Detective Falcone wouldn't allow it. Ameleth began crying again. She sank into the fluffy white carpet and sobbed quietly. Her face buried in the cushions, her frizzy hair matched her body's tiny shakes. Jack, seeing his big chance, tentatively wandered over to the quivering fitness queen.

Janey smartly intercepted him. "Don't, Jack," she implored. "She's in pain." She took Jack's hand and led him away from his wife. Janey and Jack then pulled up stools at the juice bar.

"As soon as the lady detective tells us we can go," Janey stage-whispered, "I want to take you home with me. I want to help, Jack. Let me take care of you." Lady detective? I supposed that made Janey a lady receptionist. Jack seemed to respond to her offer. He let her stroke his fingers suggestively. Ameleth didn't notice from her face plant on the couch.

We all waited for whatever came next. One thing about Detective Falcone: She didn't let anyone rush her. She'd wrap this investigation when she damn well pleased. All we could do was sit in that room for the three (three!) hours it took her to supervise the dusting, the spraying and the photographing of the crime scene. Every half hour or so, she'd have a few questions. "Besides the fire escape in front, is the elevator the only way to get into the suite?" she asked after the body was gone. A unanimous yes resounded from the married couple and Janey.

After the suite had been dusted, she asked, "How many people have keys that bring the elevator to this floor?" The answer turned out to be four: Ameleth, Jack, a spare at reception, and Barney. When Ameleth supplied that information, it was obvious that Jack didn't know Barney had a key. (I figured this out because he said, "Wait a minute—you gave Barney a key?" Ameleth ignored him.)

Falcone wandered back toward the office area. She

found Barney's sweat clothes on the floor. Ameleth identified them. Falcone asked her if she knew he'd be in the club that evening, and Ameleth said, "I had no idea. Jack told me Barney was out of town. Unlike other men I know," Ameleth continued, "Barney was unpredictable. I never knew where he'd turn up, and I never wanted to know. Does that help?"

"Not at all," Falcone said diplomatically. Poor Jack was being beaten like the eggs from a roost of ripe chickens. Could love really be this blind, even the twisted psycho variety? I will say one thing: Ameleth's treatment of Jack—and the way he swallowed it all—gave him the sex appeal of a Q-Tip. I figured Janey must dig diminutive men. She sat practically in his lap, protecting him from Ameleth's blows with her impenetrable shield of saline.

While the cops drained the Jacuzzi in search of skin and hair, Falcone asked, "Did Barney have any enemies?" A logical query. Only one enemy Ameleth could think of: Jack, her jealous husband.

Falcone's last question of the night was, "Who came up here between the hours of five and nine o'clock tonight?" The cops taped off the Jacuzzi room door. So they'd estimated that the body had been dead for up to four hours before I made the call. I flashed to how he'd looked when Jack and I found him, bobbing in the bubbles of bloody water. The image of tiny fish pecking away at a bigger, dead fish came to mind. I had no idea why. I swallowed hard. I wondered if there were any calories in bile.

Janey said she wasn't sure who used the elevator—as far as she knew, the spare key hadn't left its peg at the reception area all day. "I don't regularly make a list of people who visit the club or anything," she said.

"Jack hadn't been in all day. Ameleth left the club well before five."

Jack turned to Ameleth and said, "I thought you were going shopping in Manhattan for equipment."

"I lied, Jack," Ameleth said from the couch. "I lied because I didn't want you to know where I was. Okay? I didn't want you following me around."

Falcone asked, "If you met Barney here this afternoon, Ms. Bergen, I'll have to insist you let me know what happened."

"No," Ameleth answered succinctly. "I have nothing more to say until my lawyer arrives." The tiny powerhouse then excused herself to call her lawyer from her office. Then Jack did the same from the wall phone. Janey asked to use it next. I didn't know any lawyers; I didn't make any calls.

Falcone, visibly annoyed by this string of stalls, announced that she was going to the hospital to see if the coroner had come up with anything. In the meantime, she expected us to make statements in the morning and she knew where we lived. "And I'm keeping this, Ms. Bergen," she said as she held up a cylindrical key. The one from the reception desk, I assumed.

We all piled into the elevator. The cops, everyone. Jack turned out the lights as we left. I felt an eerie sensation—a cross between hunger and depression that could only be cured with a date with my Swedish friend, Haagen Dazs. The doors opened.

"Get out of the way," Ameleth demanded as she motored past the crowd. She tooled outside, not looking back once.

We followed her to the street. She made unhappy trails. A police sign blocked off the entrance of the club, and a couple of uniforms loitered outside. Falcone instructed them to let no one inside until they heard from her. Then she got into one of the police cruisers and drove down Pierrepont Street toward the station house.

Jack insisted Janey go home by herself. I guess her sex appeal diminished when Ameleth wasn't around. She left, and Jack walked with me down Henry Street.

Jack said, "I put the knife in your pocketbook."

"You what?" I asked.

"It's wrapped in a towel—it won't ruin your stuff."

I couldn't believe what I was hearing. He must have done it when I was looking for a cigarette. "You realize if I don't take this to the cops I'm as guilty of stealing it as you are," I said.

"I don't think Falcone should have the knife." He quickly added, "It's not my knife, Wanda."

"But you recognize it."

"I don't," he insisted.

"You lie like a rug."

"I thought it would help your investigation. Give you the edge over the cops."

I couldn't believe what I was hearing. "Solving murder isn't like playing in a tennis tournament, Jack."

I peeked inside my purse. It had felt a tad heavy. Sure enough, there was a towel shoved in there. Tiny red drops dotted the white terry cloth. This would give me something to work with. The murder weapon is usually a pretty major clue.

"What the fuck am I thinking?" I asked myself out loud. No wonder Falcone hadn't asked about the knife. I took a look at Jack. He was a cutie. Whipped, but cute. "I know you didn't do it because that'd be too obvious."

"I swear to God, Wanda. I did not kill Barney." Jack's blue eyes beamed into mine. "If Ameleth did, though, we should know before the cops."

"Not smart to take the knife, Jack," I said.

"It was an impulsive mistake. I don't know what I was thinking. When I pulled it out, blood spurted from the wound. It was horrible. I lost my sense of reason." He seemed sincere. And scared.

I thought it over. "I'll find the killer for you," I offered.

"Why?" he asked incredulously.

The money. The curiosity. The glitter of it all. "I hate to see an innocent man railroaded for a murder he didn't commit." And Jack was right. I didn't mind going up against Falcone. A chick detective. My first. "But if Ameleth is guilty, no special treatment."

Jack and I agreed to meet at my Times Square office the next afternoon. That'd give me a chance to tell Alex Beaudine, my partner and former live-in flame, what happened. It'd also give me a chance to examine the knife more closely. I got a vibe. A sudden flash of ken that told me this was too big—that if I didn't walk away, my life will change forever. Whenever I get that feeling, I usually do walk away—about a week later with lots of money in my pocket. The higher the risk, the bigger the potential gain. Or loss. But I never lose, I reminded myself quickly.

I told Jack I knew a good all-night liquor store in the neighborhood. He looked pretty bad for the healthiest man I'd ever met. He shook his head. "Thanks, but I want to be alone," he said solemnly. "I'll just go for a run." And on this note, he hopped off like a big rabbit. His lithe legs carried him quickly, and he disappeared down the dark street in a few seconds. I checked my watch: 2:00 A.M. The night was still young. I went in search of a belt (of tequila) and a burrito.

I found both. I had to go into Manhattan to get them. I ended up taking the subway in the middle of the night after all. Knowing the knife was in my purse was strangely comforting. I didn't have to use it once.

I made it home by four. I splurged on a cab back to Brooklyn. My street was dark at that hour. Most of the other streets in America were, too. I entered my new resident brownstone (which was pretty much like my old brownstone in Park Slope), and quietly unlocked my second-floor apartment door. Otis dashed outside as soon as I opened it. The faint waft of cat piss snuck up my nostrils. Have I mentioned that my cat had developed a slight bladder control problem? Max, who despised Otis, insists she was doing it out of spite or because she hated Syd, Max's tabby. I think Otis acted out of jealousy: She just didn't like Max's spending more time in my lap than she did.

So Otis ran out into the hall. I let her go. Some lonely time in the stuffy hallway might make her think twice before she squatted on my carpet again. I adore her, but even I didn't want my apartment smelling like the F train.

The light from the hallway made a wedge of yellow in the blackness of my living room. I pushed the door wide open and took a step inside. I closed the door behind me. I breathed in the darkness. Just as I reached for the light switch, a sticky palm covered my mouth. Another flew over my breast, lifting me off my feet.

"Oh, Wanda. It's you," Max said from behind me, dropping me. He sounded relieved. "Where the fuck have you been?" His anger caught up.

I punched the light switch. My knees were shaking a

little. I had no idea Max was so powerful. I guess that's what you get from working out at the gym. My heart was racing. I took a few deep breaths and said, "I'm very turned on. Let's go do it."

"We'll get to that. I want to know where you've been." He kissed me on the mouth. It was all tender-like. He leaned back and said, "You know you're in big trouble with me."

"Trouble is my business."

"Then you've brought your work home." Max led me by the elbow to the EIK (eat-in kitchen). He sat me down at the table (seats six). He reached into the refrigerator and pulled out a doughnut with pink icing and multicolored sprinkles. He placed it on the table in front of me. I studied it. Admired it.

"Look at that," I said. "My second favorite kind of doughnut." No sooner had I gotten out the words, did he drop a chocolate-frosted, chocolate-filled one next to pinkie. I smiled at my honey. "It's not that I don't trust you to go out with your ex-girlfriend," I tried to defend myself. "It's just that I'm a naturally curious person. I seek mind-expanding knowledge. I crave new experiences. You knew this about me."

Max poured himself some Lactaid and sat down next to me at the table. He started eating the pink doughnut. I watched his jaw move under his pale skin. A piece of his auburn hair dropped into his mouth. With a long, thin finger, Max pulled at the hair and resumed eating. "You've probably never spied on a boyfriend with his ex-girlfriend before," he said. "It was an opportunity for a new experience. You couldn't pass it up."

He knew me so well. "Exactly."

"You expect me to believe you've never spied on a boyfriend before?"

"I haven't," I said.

"What about that story Alex told me with you staking out his apartment?" Have I mentioned that Alex, a talented detective and wizard chef, also had a big mouth?

"Alex and I had broken up by then, so technically, I was spying on my *ex*-boyfriend with his new girl-friend. It's an entirely different situation." I bit into my chocolate circle. "This doughnut—is it a peace offering?"

"If you want to call it that."

"I'm not sure I should eat it," I said and put it down. That burrito and sour cream had been plenty. "I've been feeling fat lately."

Max smiled. I have two complaints about Max: First, he whines when I don't depilate weekly, and second, he waits for me to complain to him about my weight before he says, "I didn't want to say anything, but yes, you have put on a couple pounds." I react by dieting solid for six days and losing at least five pounds of water weight. I feel less bloated and, as a reward for all that self-denial, I pig out on the seventh day.

Max said, "I didn't want to say anything."

"I hate you."

He laughed. "Let's go do it."

"No. I still hate you."

Max sighed. "Okay, I'm sorry. But you hurt me tonight, and I haven't heard you apologize to me yet."

"I don't have to apologize," I said.

"Why not?" he asked.

"Because I've already suffered from that mistake."

He puckered his red lips, which he sometimes does when he gets confused. "I guess that was pretty humiliating for you—getting caught acting like a jerkoff," he said.

I shook my head. "No, it's what happened afterward." I told him as much of the story as I felt comfortable with. I loved Max and he was my boyfriend. But I did have some confidentiality to keep for my client. "And then, as we're standing outside the gym, Jack hands me this." I reached in my bag for the bloodstained towel. Max's face glowed like a torch, had been the whole time I was telling the story. A murder at his gym—that was excitement close to his support cup.

I put the bundle on the table. I unfolded the corners of the towel to reveal the shiny silver blade with a white wooden handle. A layer of blood had dried on the metal. I wrapped the towel around the handle so I could pick up the knife and look at the other side of the blade for a designer logo or company name. I held it aloft for the best light. Max moved away slightly, to get a clearer view.

"NO!" screamed a female voice from inside my apartment. In that half second of confusion, I wondered if Syd had learned to talk. Then someone strong was pinning my arm—with the knife—behind my back. I felt (and heard) my shoulder pop out of the socket. A wallop of agony blinded me. I'm not ashamed to admit I screamed like a girl. The knife fell out of my hand and clunked on the floor. Max leapt to his feet. In a moment I was free. I fell from my chair in pain, just missing sitting down on the knife. Through the stars in my eyes, I looked at my assailant. It was Leeza, the shoulder mashing, aerobicized ex-girlfriend.

Dim though she may be, she could tell she fucked

up. "From where I was standing in the bedroom doorway, it looked like you were going to stab him," Leeza whined. "God, I'm so sorry."

Max helped me to my feet. Before I could demand that he get me to a hospital, he gripped my back and slammed my shoulder against the palm of his hand. My knees collapsed and he had to hold me up. He tried popping the bone back in again. The stars in my eyes had become whole planets. On Max's third try, my shoulder popped back in. It felt better immediately.

"You'll be all right," Max said. "A couple of aspirins and you'll be better by morning."

I bit back the last remnants of pain. I looked up at my attacker. I said, "Just give me a bullet to bite and I'll be fine." She wore a T-shirt and cotton underwear with little yellow duckies on them. Her tummy was flatter than an iron. Her legs looked well-depilitated. To Max I said, "Leeza just came out of our bedroom, honey."

3

Jack in the Box

Leeza covered her semi-naked body with her skinny white arms. "You had me scared to death," she said. "I thought you were trying to kill him."

"You were just a bit premature," Max said for me.

Leeza's baby blue eyes glanced from Max to me and back again as if she couldn't remember what she'd just seen. It reminded me of goldfish—they're so dumb that they can't retain a memory for longer than three seconds. That's why one shouldn't feel sorry for fish in tanks. Each swim through a plastic skull is like their very first time (I picked this up on the Learning Channel).

"You don't think that Max and me . . ." Leeza said aghast in my direction. "Nothing happened, Wanda. I swear. I got sick at the restaurant. Max said it was all right."

I turned to Max. He said, "You don't trust me at all, do you?"

"I guess I was right," I said to Max. "That makes

me feel an iota of happiness underneath this mountain of anguish and betrayal." I sighed. "Being right all the time is such a burden."

"I don't know how you stand the strain," Max responded.

Leeza fidgeted. "I think I better put some clothes on." She pranced through the kitchen and living room toward the bedroom—her butt didn't jiggle once. Then she stopped and said as an afterthought, "Max didn't see me naked at all tonight."

"Comforting," I said as she disappeared in the bedroom.

Alone again, Max gathered me in his arms and kissed me, his lips like lightning bugs buzzing along my neck and collarbone. I could tell he was hot. For one thing, he was denting my leg. He also made tiny chirp sounds that remind me of birds. He breathed in my ear, "Nothing turns me on more than your trusting heart and understanding nature."

"Spare me a tire," I said and pushed him away.

I picked up the knife. Little black cat hairs clung to the red smears. I placed the weapon back in the towel for a closer inspection when I could see straight. I turned to Max and belted him one across the kisser. He recoiled from the force of my blow. "You cheating bastard," I said, to the point.

Max recovered quickly. I'd left an angry red mark on his chin. It looked like it hurt. I felt a twinge of pity. Max said, "She ate a bad oyster. She got sick. I never even went into the fucking bedroom after she did— I've been pacing between your unpacked boxes for the last five hours waiting for you to get home."

"How come the lights were off when I came in?"

"I didn't want the light to bother Leeza." The living

room light did filter into the bedroom. I wasn't convinced.

I asked, "Why was she eating oysters?"

"You'll have to ask her—she ordered them."

"Because she wanted to get revved up to seduce you."

Max said, "I guess that would explain why she also ordered Spanish fly, rare steak, peaches with cream and figs for dessert." I could tell by his twitching eyelid that he was being ironic.

My paranoia was showing. I considered the possibility he was telling the truth. As a detective, it was my obligation to see things from more than one angle. I felt the blood settle in my veins. My breathing slowed. I looked at Max. His nostrils flared slightly and his green eyes were squinty with concentration. I was often surprised by how much my words and actions affected Max. "You're beautiful when you're angry," I tried. I shouldn't have slugged the lug.

"You look like shit when you're apologetic."

"You know I look adorable."

"That knife on the table really adds to the appeal, Lorena."

I smiled. When the abused wife, Lorena Bobbitt, cut off her cheating husband's penis, the women of America rejoiced. Anyone named John Wayne deserved a (cut to the) quick lesson on how to be nice to women anyway. Too bad for him he had to get his education at the expense of his unit. Lorena Bobbitt should have cut off his fornicating head. "What'll you give me to put the knife away?" I asked, happy to wheel and deal.

"I'll go down on you for an hour," he traded.

I accepted. Leeza, meanwhile, had emerged from

the bedroom fully dressed. She clutched her gym bag strap in her fist and announced she was leaving. "I'm intruding," she said. "I feel much better now, so I guess I'll go. I've got to be at the convention in a few hours anyway. Maybe I'll get breakfast. A nice, hot, three-hour breakfast." She looked anxiously at Max. She seemed pathetic. I didn't mind.

"Have a nice meal," I said.

"You don't have to go, Leeza," Max offered.

"No, it's okay," she said with a smile. "I'll see you around anyway, Max. At the club."

What club? my eyes asked Max. A light of recognition flicked in his brain and he exclaimed, "Holy shit, that's right. You're going to be working at the Western Athletic Club. Wanda, Leeza's going to be working as an aerobics instructor at the gym. Maybe she can help you." I nearly punched his ribs. Like the world needed to know about my case.

"Are you looking for a personal trainer?" she asked me, appraising my body. An inside source wouldn't be a terrible idea. I could make something of this if I played my cards right. I relished any chance I got to exploit others. I should really ask her to stay. Be hospitable. I had my own selfish needs to consider.

I smiled big and said, "Don't let the door hit you on the ass on the way out." I can be both near- and short-sighted at the same time. One of my little bar tricks. I'm also good at sucking a cherry through a straw.

Leeza split. Max crushed me against the fridge and we kissed. I felt a flood of dread for a second that he'd smell the cigarette on my breath. But when he pulled back and said, "Whew, Cuervo," I knew I was safe. We jogged into the bedroom and he dove underneath the covers. I did a little striptease action and joined

46

him. Max slipped his arms around my thickish waist. Leeza's was small. I could snap her in half like a twig. Max lapped my neck. Compared to Leeza's ropy throat, mine must have felt mushy. I pushed Max away—not something I do often. I leaned forward and wrapped my arms around my knees. "Honey-bunny," I said, my back to him. "I'm fat."

"You're not fat, Wanda." He sounded exasperated. Off in the distance, I heard Syd puking. She pukes constantly in the summer. Hairballs or bulimia, we'll never be sure.

"How can you be attracted to a woman like Leeza," I asked when Syd finished, "and then be attracted to me?"

"You know this story. I went out with her because she liked me. We were compatible. Everyone drummed it into my head that I was lucky and that she was beautiful. I was also twenty-five at the time. I wasn't exactly a fully-formed adult. Now I know what I really want, and I want you. Right now. So please shut up already."

"You proposed to her," I reminded him. "You must have loved her."

"What difference does it make?" he asked.

He proposed to her; she's skinny. He hasn't proposed to me; I'm soft and voluptuous. "Nothing," I said quietly.

Max sat up in bed. "Nothing, huh?" he asked. " 'Nothing' usually means I don't get any sleep—not that I have all night anyway."

"Excuse me while I dab a tear from my eye," I mocked.

"Look, Wanda, if you want to lose weight, why don't we fuck it off?"

Max, dear bunnyhead, was full of bright ideas. The

only exercise I got was in bed with him anyway. I said, "Deal. Where should we start?"

"We can start by strengthening our tongue muscles."

"The tongue doesn't have muscles. It is a muscle."

"Correcting me is not a turn-on, Wanda," Max said. "Do you want to talk, or do you want to burn calories?" I wanted to talk. Just kidding. We proceeded to tongue-lash each other clean in a very dirty fashion. When I came, a flash of blue exploded behind my eyes.

Afterward, I did some math while Max snored. There are 3,600 calories in a pound. The average sex act burns about 150 calories (I learned this on "Oprah"). My sex with Max, however, was extremely energetic so I'll jack that number up to an even 200. Therefore, eighteen bouts in bed will burn up one pound of fat. But—the big *but*—one load of Max's mighty fluid contained approximately 60 calories (from *Cosmo*). Ergo, if I blow him and swallowed once every three sessions, I'd have to have sex with Max about twenty times to burn one pound of fat.

If we had sex twice a day, every day, it would take three months to lose the necessary ten pounds without having to strap on some Lycra G-string leotard. (Or give up my tequila and/or one-Snickers-a-day habit. Not an option.) Inspired by my new sex-weight loss plan, I poked Max to wake him up. He wouldn't budge, so I started sucking on his dick. That got him up all right. Three months, and counting.

Alex Beaudine doesn't walk. He sidles. He sways. If you couldn't see his bright orange Chuck Connor high-tops, you might think he was on wheels. I'd called Alex after Max left for work and told him to meet me at the office with any info he could scrape together about Jack Watson. When Alex rolled into the Do It Right Detectives office that Wednesday morning at around eleven o'clock, he brought two cups of iced coffee, a cup of ginger tea for me, and some decent vibes. It was a pleasure to watch Alex settle into the plush arm chair I have for clients. He stretched out his legs and deposited his rubber heels on the corner of my desk. He smiled at me—gummy, with a hint of teeth—and said, "This place is a sty, but you look well plucked this morning."

Sty, my eye. The Do It Right Detective Agency wasn't neat—that much I was willing to admit—but what's a few dust bunnies and a full garbage can between friends? The square-shaped office was on the fourth floor in a nearly deserted office building over-looking fabulous Times Square. I had an orange carpet with decorative cigarette burns and wrap-around windows (when the soot wasn't too bad, I had a great view of the 100-foot Sony TV on the *Newsday Building*). The big oak desk with one wobbly leg was the command center. Everything I needed was within my reach: the telephone, answering machine, a bottle of Amaretto in my bottom drawer, a stockpile of tampons, a change of clothes, a bunch of matchbooks to flip into a hat and the hat. I used to keep a carton of cigarettes in my top drawer, but I don't anymore. Like a phantom limb, sometimes I still reach for them.

Alex stirred his ice coffee with his middle finger. He wiped it off on his jeans. I said, "You know where the vacuum is."

"Let me ask you this: Would straightening up harm you in some way?" Alex asked. "Really, I'm curious. Would it cause an allergic reaction? Maybe temporary blindness or might you grow hair on your palms?

Because I would never want you to suggest an activity that could jeopardize your health. You mean too much to me."

Smart guy, that Alex, has a problem with dirt. He'd never call himself compulsively anal. That's what he's got me for. I said, "I'll clean up later."

Alex laughed and sipped his coffee. "I'm not going to fall for it this time, Wanda. I can sit here and have a meeting and not be distracted by that overflowing garbage can, for example. Or the inch of dust on the filing cabinet. Or, what is that mess on the carpet?" He pointed over my left shoulder.

I was afraid to look. "Forget the mess, Alex." I briefed him on the case: Jack Watson, dead Barney, wild Ameleth and rubber-made Janey. Alex had heard of Ameleth. He had also found out a thing or two about the ill-fated tennis career of Jack Watson.

He said, "About Watson—I called my buddy Estoban at the Upper East Side Racquet Club. I've got some hot gossip," he said. "Very hot."

"Hotter than a tamale?" I asked. Alex rarely disappointed me.

"Steaming hot. Sizzling hot."

I almost broke a sweat waiting for him to start yapping. Have I mentioned that my office doesn't have an air conditioner? "Spill already."

"Okay," he started, rubbing his palms together. "Little Jackie Watson was a tennis prodigy. By the time he was fifteen, he was New York State champ. When he was seventeen, he beat McEnroe in a minor tournament. McEnroe threw a temper tantrum and spat in Watson's face after the match. But still, Little Jackie—that was his nickname if you haven't gathered by now—"

"I gathered."

"Little Jackie persevered. After being baptized by McEnroe effluvium, he went from being a comer to having arrived. Almost arrived, anyway. He kept up good play for a few years, but he never quite made it to championship level. He was still young, and he just might have become the next great American tennis champ. But tragedy struck."

He sipped coffee. Examined his fingernails. "Will you get on with this?"

"I was pausing dramatically."

"Like anyone cares, Alex. Just tell the goddamn story."

He stared at me while mentally counting to ten. I could practically see the numbers roll by. Alex hated to be told what to do. It was one of the reasons we broke up. "As I was saying," he started, "after winning a Wimbledon match against some low-ranked French scrub, Jackie attempted to leap over the net to shake his opponent's hand. He'd done it a million times before, but on that day, his ankle didn't quite clear the net. Jackie came tumbling down like London Bridge. He broke his right arm in ten places. By the time it was healed, he'd taken himself off the circuit. The official reason was that his arm hadn't healed properly and that he'd never regain the strength he needed to play for big money. By twenty-one, Little Jackie's career was over."

"Stop calling him Little Jackie. It gives me the creeps."

He rolled his eyes. When he finished, his brown pearls settled on whatever mess was on the carpet behind me. He fidgeted for a second like he was waging some internal battle. Then he calmed down, sipped his iced coffee and continued. "According to Estoban," Alex said, "the real reason Watson dropped out was because he didn't have the balls to pick himself up and get back in the race."

"That's life, as Frank would say."

Alex nodded. "So Watson moved back to New York. After a few years in seclusion, his money ran out. He took a job at the Upper West Side Racquet Club last year to give tennis lessons to yups. He'd been off the circuit for a while, but his name still had some cachet. He insisted that he only instruct the beginner classes, and he never really played any hardcore matches. He just lobbed a few easy shots and nobody got hurt. Including him.

"Then, last September, when the U.S. Open Tournament was being played, the manager of the Racquet Club decided it'd be a good gimmick to have the staff play a round-robin tennis tournament of their own. The club members could bet on a staffer for free lessons—the money went to some charity—and the winning players would get trophies. The manager thought it would be a good promotion for the club. And it was. Everyone covered the tournament— including the *Daily Mirror*. Of course, Watson was the odds-on favorite, even though he protested his participation to the last minute. In the first round of the tournament, Watson got his ass stomped by a five-foot-one, forty-year-old female massage therapist. He ran out of the place in tears and never came back. Not even to pick up his last paycheck."

"I don't get it," I said. "Why would he lose on purpose?" Maybe he threw the match because some Mafia dude had bet against him.

"When I heard this story," Alex said, "I immediately wondered if some Mafia guy bet against him like in old boxer movies." Among his many talents was Alex's ability to read my mind. If only we played bridge. "But this wasn't any big-time tournament," he explained. "There weren't any cash prizes—just lessons, free facials and massages. It was for show, not for bucks."

"Maybe some don had a severe case of blackheads," I prompted.

"When Jackie—Watson—ran out, he also lost his contract to teach tennis. So he was again out of luck and out of money."

"But I still don't get it. Why would he freak out like that?"

Alex shrugged, not really listening. He was staring at the full garbage can. I smiled, inside. I'd give him five more minutes before he'd break down and start cleaning. "Estoban gave me his theory about Watson," Alex said finally. "Jack had a mental block and forgot how to play tennis. Kind of like when Eric Clapton got in that bad car accident and forgot how to play guitar? Jack knew he was supposed to know what to do, so he would walk through a few lessons. But when it came time to actually play a match, he choked." The whole story was so sad, it made me want to help Jack more than ever. I wondered if women have taken care of him his whole life. There was something about him that was just so helplessly boyish. Even I felt an obligation to protect him.

"So what caused this mental block?"

"You're the detective," Alex said, rising from his chair. He stretched. Then he began circling the room. It took every fiber of strength in his body not to swoop down on that wastebasket and clean.

I stood and said, "Bathroom." My bathroom is down the hall. I left the office to take a leak. I'd give Alex his privacy. For him, cleaning up is an intensely personal experience.

The bathroom was intended to be communal, except none of the other offices on the floor were occupied. I did my thing and crept back toward the office. I peeked inside and caught a glimpse of Alex on his hands and knees, vacuuming. Dear, predictable, reliable Alex. If he'd been ready to commit and I'd been easier to live with, we might be married right now. Then I never would have met Max. I perished the thought, and barged inside.

Alex continued vacuuming without acknowledging me. I sat down at my desk. When he got to that area, I waited for him to ask me to move my feet. Finally, he said, "You take terrible advantage, Wanda."

"What of it?" I asked.

"You're a slut and a whore," he said. We smiled at each other.

"For a neat freak, you sure talk dirty."

Alex rubbed the large attachment under my desk. "I've got a brilliant idea—not that all my ideas aren't brilliant," he said over the sucking sound. "I volunteer to go undercover. I will wear gym shorts and a T-shirt that shows off my bulging pectoral muscles. I'll wear tube socks and cross-trainers. And, I'll wear sweat bands on my forehead *and* wrists."

"Yeah, but what's in it for you?" I asked. Alex rarely does anything without an ulterior motive. "Like you've got bulging pectoral muscles."

"We'll see how the ladies of the club feel about them," he said, revealing his motive.

"Fine with me," I said. "The last thing I want to do is surround myself with impossibly toned women in skimpy outfits all day long. Like I need that kind of ego boost."

"Boost?" Alex asked pointedly. I wanted to slug

him. "I'll work out with Max. I'm sure he can show me a thing or two. He can point out a few of the more compelling attractions. About exercising, I mean."

That comment knocked around my brain like a ricocheting pool ball. Alex sometimes makes me so mad. I said, "How come you get jealous of Max all the time, but he never, ever gets jealous of you?" I regretted my retort immediately. I'd much rather ignore the weirdness of the situation—still working with Alex, I mean. We broke up two years ago for Christ's sake—and he dumped me. The room was silent for a moment, except for the klink of the vacuum sucking up a few stray paper clips. I allowed myself to think about how jealous I got about Max and Leeza. Then I pushed the guilt from my mind.

"Okay, you'll pretend to be a new member at the club," I agreed. "We should probably pay for the membership. Jack doesn't need to know every move we make." I generally hated to lay out my own money as expenses, but I didn't have a choice in this case. Besides, I wasn't completely convinced of Jack's innocence. I liked the idea of having one up on him. I'd rather have two. I wondered if Leeza would even think about helping me. Probably not after the way I treated her.

"Okay, Alex. Max does get jealous of you," I lied. "But only because you're a slut and a whore."

"You wish," he said, smiling. I felt a lifting of tension. The vacuuming now done, Alex put the machine back into the bottom drawer of the file cabinet. He then pulled out the rag and can of furniture polish.

I got his attention by taking the murder-knife-bundle out of my purse. I was surprised to see the stacks of hundred-dollar bills underneath it in my bag. How could I have forgotten? I snapped my bag tightly shut and put it on the floor, under my chair. I dropped the knife towel out on my desk and unwrapped it. The blade shined brilliantly in the office light.

Alex began lovingly dusting my desktop as if a genie would rise from the top drawer to grant him three wishes. He asked, "The murder weapon?" I nodded. "Plunged through the heart, right?" I nodded again. "Poor bleeding bastard. Any fingerprints are long gone, right?"

I nodded. Maybe Jack did know who owned the knife and had purposefully destroyed evidence. "No logo," I said about the knife. Ergo, I had no way of finding out what store the knife might have come from.

"Fuck logos," Alex said. He stopped dusting to come inspect the knife more closely. "I think, yeah. White wood handle. Deep seration." Alex ran the edge across his thumb. "Sharp as the point on your head. It's the Bjornskinki bread knife. I've got a whole set."

"The what?"

"The Bjornskinki. From Ikea. I'd know this knife anywhere. I had to special order it from Sweden." Ikea is a Sweden-based discount furniture/housewares chain. For some reason, New Yorkers have found the two nearby stores (one in Hicksville, Long Island, the other in Elizabeth, New Jersey) to be the new consumer-mad Meccas. I'd never been. I get most of my furniture off the street. No matter how inexpensive, Ikea can't be cheaper than free. But millions of others go every weekend to one of the stores, via the buses out of Port Authority or the train from Penn

Station. I guess I'd have to go out there to investigate this knife. I was secretly glad for the excuse. My sleuth's curiosity made me wonder what all the hub-bub was about.

"I ordered at the Elizabeth store," Alex announced. "I've be happy to go back and check this out." He was practically panting. Alex was primarily a domestic animal. Housewares turned him on. We'd had some fun, actually, with his honey spool.

"Do all wizard chefs do things like special order bread knives from Sweden?" I asked.

"They do if they're serious about slicing bread," he responded.

"And if I said that you can seriously slice bread with a two-dollar knife from the neighborhood hardware store, you'd probably tell me I just don't understand."

"Why even have these conversations, Wanda?" he asked.

"Maybe the killer special ordered the knife for the sole purpose of slicing Barney."

"The killer would have been better off with a two-dollar blade from the hardware store."

"Unless the killer stole it from someone," I suggested.

"A frame?" he asked.

"No, a knife."

The phone rang. I cradled the receiver on my shoulder and said, "Do It Right Detectives. If you've got the dime, we've got the ear." Alex took the opportunity to polish the answering machine.

It was Jack. "Wanda—I've been arrested. You've got to help me."

I stood up. Not sure why, I sat back down. "Take it easy, Jack. Where are you?"

"In prison. In Brooklyn Heights."

There was no prison in Brooklyn Heights. A holding tank or two, sure. But if you want prison, you'll have to venture to other boroughs. Queens, for example, had Rikers Island. Manhattan had the floating prison barge on the East River. "Did they take you to the courts?" I asked. The court building for all of Brooklyn was at Town Hall right on Cadman Plaza in the Heights. It was in those courtrooms that John Gotti was sentenced to life.

"Yes, yes, you've got to get over here," Jack cried. "And bring the money."

I hung up. Alex had a questioning look in his eye. I said, "Our client has been arrested for murder and he wants me to bring his money back."

"Does he know we don't give refunds?" Alex asked, as aghast as I.

"I guess not." I bit a pencil. I usually think better with things in my mouth. "Alex, as a man who cheats regularly on his girlfriends, do you ever have any feelings of remorse?"

Alex said, "I'd rather talk about the money."

"Spare me a quarter."

"I never cheated on you."

I scoffed. "I know for a fact that you cheated on me at least once."

"Is that a Wanda fact, or an actual fact?" he asked. "No, let me answer. It's a Wanda fact which means true as long as you think it's true. My dearest heart, not once did my jade stalk enter the gates of another lucky locust during the entire year we lived together. And if you think that Max is cheating on you, you're even more insecure than I thought."

"If Max was cheating, I'll have to kill him," I said. "And you'll have to help me as a penance for screwing around on me all those times while we were going out."

Alex sighed deeply. I wondered if he'd sprung a leak. "Call the club," he instructed when he'd tired of my little game. "See if they're open today."

I dialed the number for the Western Athletic Club. I don't think it was Janey who confirmed the fact that they were indeed open. I supposed the upstairs suite was blocked off, but otherwise, why shouldn't the club be open for business? I asked if the Cut Me store was also open, and I was informed that it was, despite the fact that its owner had been stabbed to death the night before. Heartless, but convenient for us. Alex would need workout gear.

"I'll spring our client if possible," I said. "And you'd better get yourself some decent exercise clothes." Alex's jeans and faded T-shirt didn't quite measure up to the high-style elastic-wear I'd noticed people strutting around in at the club yesterday.

Alex sighed again. "I'll stop by my apartment and get some running shorts, or won't that do?"

I wanted company on the subway ride. "That won't do. We'll go shopping in Brooklyn Heights. Client expenses. And I might pick up a few things for myself."

All settled, we closed up the office. Alex and I took the stairs to the street. A breeze carrying the scent of boiled hot dogs mingled with the odor of hot tar. Exhaust billowed from buses and cars on Broadway. Spilled garbage glistened in the June sunshine. Times Square was at its most pungent in summertime. It was also at its slickest: posters of ice cream in storefront deli windows seemed to melt right onto the asphalt, bare shoulders dripped tiny streams of sweat and air conditioners rained down from on high, drizzling reconstituted water onto our unprotected heads. A cool drop splattered on the back of my neck, oozing down my back. It felt swell.

The three thousand dollars Jack gave me was now nestled safely in my underwear. The knife went back in my purse. Alex and I rode the Number 2 train out to the Clark Street station in Brooklyn Heights. The ride took about twenty-five minutes. I was convinced that some of the passengers had X-ray vision the way they stared at my lap. Not to be daunted, I returned the stares.

Alex, a Lower East Sider, wasn't one of the majority of Manhattanites who thought Brooklyn was some far-off dark continent. He even knew something of the neighborhood. I liked not having to point him in the right direction when we got out of the subway. We walked the three blocks to the Western Athletic Club. I left Alex about a half block away. I didn't want the steroid experiment doorman to see us together. It was possible he had a brain. Alex promised he would be careful and take all the necessary precautions. The last thing he wanted was a pulled muscle.

I power-walked all the way down to Court Street. It's called Court Street because that's where the Brooklyn Municipal Courts were. The precinct was also located under some scaffolding by the big marble and limestone City Hall building. As I approached, a handful of cops in brown uniforms emerged from the building. Brownies (aka the Shit Patrol) are responsible for dispensing parking tickets. The one time I'd been inside the court building was to contest a fifty-five-dollar parking ticket I'd got on a rental car. The brownie who wrote it out claimed I'd parked only eight feet from a hydrant. But I'd counted ten of my own feet to measure. (My hoofs are, uh, kind of large for a girl—but you know what they say about women with big feet. Big hearts.) I even took a Polaroid shot of my foot against a ruler to show that it was indeed eleven inches long. Though the judge was impressed with my visual aids, he "adjudicated" that I had to pay up in full. Apparently, the law requires you to park *fifteen* size eleven Doc Martens away from a hydrant in Gotham City. I promised to mail in my check—forgot to.

Feeling like an outlaw, I approached the front desk at the 18th Precinct. I told the sergeant behind it that I needed to speak to Jack Watson, former tennis star and alleged murderer. The cop's bushy gray eyebrows went up when I said murderer. She buzzed me through. She pointed across the room, but it was all a blur. I apologized and put on my glasses. That's when I noticed Detective Falcone sitting at a desk in the back of the room. She was alternating between drags of a cigarette, sips of coffee and bites of what appeared to be a Reuben sandwich with gobs of Russian dressing.

I licked my chops and walked over. She put her sandwich down when I got to her desk. She kept on smoking and drinking coffee. A string of her stringy hair dipped into the Styrofoam cup. She didn't seem to care. We made eye contact. The clarity in her mud-colored eyes made me feel uneasy for a moment, like she knew something about me even I didn't know. "Mallory," she said. "I've been expecting you." The seat of her chair wasn't visible with her hips spilling over it like that.

I had a sudden premonition: Was this dumpy, sloppy, saggy woman what I'd become in twenty years? Substituting the brown strings for my luscious red curls (they'll always stay that color—Mother

Nature, meet Miss Clairol), was Falcone the ghost of Wanda future? The thought sent a chill up my spine like a monkey up a rope swing. For women, being smart didn't cut it at fifty any more than it did at twenty-nine. Harsh, but it's the sad, unfair truth. I relied on my looks. If I lost them, I didn't think I'd be able to do this for a living.

"Jack Watson called me at my office," I said quickly to get my mind off my fears.

She nodded and smiled. "He's in the Brooklyn Detention Center on Atlantic Avenue. I sent over a pastrami on rye for him, but he wouldn't touch it."

"Too fatty," I said, and immediately felt embarrassed. "I meant the sandwich."

"I assumed so, Mallory. Because if you were talking about my body, I might get upset." Her eyes darted across my face. I didn't see a hint of emotion anywhere on hers.

I felt myself blush. This woman made me uncomfortable in an unfamiliar way. "Well, if he doesn't want it, I'll have it." I fiddled with a red tendril. "I like pastrami." When in doubt, eat.

Falcone watched me closely. Her stare made me feel worse. Finally, she said, "Pull up a chair, Mallory. Let's discuss your friend Jack Watson." I sat down. I checked with my hands to make sure my hips hadn't engulfed the entire seat of the chair like hers had. I had a solid half-inch of space on either side, thank God.

Falcone said, "Forget about the sandwich. I already gave it away. Should I order something for you?" She picked up the telephone on her desk. I noticed she had the phone numbers of a few local restaurants on a strip of tape stuck to the receiver.

Reconsidering, I shook my head. No food. Ever again. At least not when I was around her. "Let's just get down to business," I said. "I don't have all day." I could always get nicer from there.

Falcone frowned and leaned back in her chair. She took a long, slow drag on her cigarette and said, "I, on the other hand, have all the time in the world. This stack of paper isn't really piled on my desk." She patted the sloppy, high stack. "Let's just have a calm relaxed discussion about Jack Watson. He's been arrested. He was rude to the arresting officers. He's in for a while. I'm not really sure what I can do for you, Mallory."

"You can start by giving me one of those cigarettes." I regretted asking as soon as I did. She rummaged in her desk drawer and handed me one. I accepted. I fired my first cigarette of the day. It tasted gross. I hate menthol. I squashed it out. I didn't give her an explanation. "Next you can tell me exactly what Jack's in for," I said. "He was with me at the time of the crime." In theory, at least.

"Are you saying you're an accessory?"

"I am an expert at accessorizing."

"I can tell." She cocked her head at my outfit. Jeans, a tank top, no belt, no jewelry. I was completely accessory-less. "If you were present at the time of the crime, then I hope for your sake you tried to stop him."

"I knew exactly what he was doing, and I was fine with it. What's the big deal? Don't tell me jogging on the Promenade is a crime in New York now." (Not that it would affect me if it were.)

Falcone eyed me through her green, minty smoke. I heard once the menthol flavor comes from ground glass particles sprinkled on the tobacco. "You think Watson was arrested for the murder of Barney Cutler?"

Doy. "No, I figured you arrested him for his banana wedgie."

"Watson was arrested for attempting to break into the Western Athletic Club at five o'clock this morning. He made a hell of a racket, and he broke a window. We picked him up when we got a disturbing-the-peace call. And you're saying you were there?"

I had to shift in the chair. The money was digging into my abdomen. "Why are you handling this?" I asked. "Unless homicide in Brooklyn Heights has to keep busy with residential disturbances."

"When my prime suspect starts smashing windows at the murder site, you better believe I'm going to get involved."

She was pissed off now. Enough to scare me a little. "I want to talk to Jack," I said.

She slowly nodded and put out her cigarette. Before she answered, she lit another. I imagined those tiny glass particles tearing her throat. My lungs hurt just watching. She said, "His bail hearing will be tomorrow."

"I still want to talk to him today."

She picked up the telephone and turned her back to me. I watched smoke rise above her head. The air got thick with it. I followed its movements as it danced upward, brushing the ceiling above her desk. It seemed like a darker yellow than the rest of the paint job. For the first time, cigarettes seemed genuinely disgusting to me. I'd been a smoker for twelve years. I swallowed my small epiphany and tried to listen in on Falcone's conversation. Before I pricked up my ears, she was hanging up. "Okay, Mallory," she said. "Jack

64

has been screaming for you since he was brought in. You'd think he'd want a lawyer, wouldn't you? Any idea why he's so hot to talk to you?"

The money—I guess he thinks he can buy his freedom or something. "Just lucky I guess."

"Something tells me that the word *lucky* has nothing to do with you." Little did she know. Falcone stood. Her skirt waist dug into her belly. It looked painful. I owned two skirts myself that dug into my belly. But they were years old. With a couple weeks of intense dieting . . . I stopped the thought in midformation. The last thing I needed was more anxiety about my weight. I stood, too, happy to notice my jeans were loose around the gut. I still wore 501s, had yet to cross into the land of Easy Fit.

I followed Falcone through a maze of offices and cubicles toward the back of the building. "Two blocks that way," she said, pointing toward Atlantic Avenue. "They're waiting for you." I knew where the Detention Center was. I'd walked past it many times. Smack in the middle of Atlantic Avenue's Little Persia (where to go to find Arab grocers and Koran reading rooms), the center loomed largely between a curio shop and a spice store. Falcone turned to go, but first said, "I'm not amused by your client, Mallory. I think he killed Barney Cutler, and I'm going to make the charges stick. If I were you, I'd cut my losses. Today."

I smiled brightly and walked away from Falcone into the bright sunshine. Who the fuck does she think she is, I wondered. I don't respond meekly to threats. The two-block walk to the center was uneventful. I passed no tempting shops, and no one I imagined fucking.

The Detention Center was a squat gray building, from the outside resembling a giant Skinner box. I found the main entrance and told the guard at the front desk my name. He led me past a locked steel door. Another armed guard waited for me. She leaned against a locked door of bulletproof glass.

"I'm here to see Jack Watson."

The female guard asked the other, "Should I put them in a room?" A room with a two-way glass, no doubt.

The chubby guy guard glanced at me to see if I knew what she meant. Then he said, "Just let her into his cell." He left me alone with the female guard. She had a big, slightly cockeyed bun in her hair. She tilted her head funny. Around her hips, she wore a .45 pistol. I was impressed by its size. The weight on her hip made her walk funny, too.

She led me down a long row of jail cells. They had no beds—just toilets and benches. Most were vacant. I tried not to stare inside the cells as I passed, not wanting to inspire a jailbreak. Jack was at the end of the row. He sat on his wooden bench with his face in his tanned hands. When he heard the click of the door unlatching, he looked up. His cheeks were streaked with tears, his eyes red and puffy. The muscles in his jaw twitched.

"Here I am," I announced with a big smile. I walked into the cell. It was nice and cool.

Jack waited for the guard to leave before he said, "Wanda, thank God you're here."

"I guess you'll need your money back for bail, huh?" I asked.

"It's unlikely Ameleth is going to pay it after I beat up her club."

I shook my head. "What were you trying to do?"

"Get inside."

"And using your key would have been too easy?"

"I know this will sound nuts, but I forgot I had it."

He probably suppressed that information because he wanted to damage the club. His wife had an affair there, she blamed Jack for the murder. His life pretty much sucked and he needed to take out his aggression. "It makes some sense. Twisted, but legit."

"I wouldn't have done anything if Ameleth slept at home," he said.

"She didn't go home?"

"When I got there, the place was empty. I was upset, so I ran back to the club. I assumed she was staying there. So I tried to bust my way in."

"You'd do better to think of ways to bust yourself out. Of here, I mean."

4

Palm Jobs

Jack put his finger to his lips. "You think I should?"

Busting out of jail seemed like the kind of advice a client would want from a private dick like me. "Sure, why not? Pretend you're dying of claustrophobia."

"I know you're joking." He paused. "Even if I broke out, where would I go? Back to that empty shell of an apartment to stare at Ameleth's bodysuits in the closet?" Heartbreak and real estate. In New York, they go together like sham-a-lama-ding-dong.

"Get a room somewhere," I suggested. "In the meantime, let's talk suspects."

"Let's talk about the money first," he said. "You've got it?"

"Maybe."

"I'll need it tomorrow."

I sat down next to him on the bench. "So I guess this isn't the best time to tell you I'm a compulsive gambler," I said.

He seemed sufficiently terrified. I said, "Chill out,

Jack. I've still got the money." I patted his shoulder. "But it's mine."

He pondered this for a while. I watched. He really was a fine-looking man, for a sentimental type. Tiny blond hairs dusted his collarbones like tiny feathers. From where I was sitting, I could make out the outline of his cock. He said, "Yeah."

"Yeah, what?" I asked.

"Yeah, I thought you might say that."

I said, "Tell me about Ameleth. Any chance she'll drop the charges?"

"I don't know. She hates me—that's clear." Even his frown was boyishly charming. I felt that wave of protectiveness again. I almost considered returning his money, but got over that fast.

"How'd you sleep?" I asked.

"Very well, thank you," he answered like I really cared.

"What can you tell me about Janey besides how good she is in bed?" I asked.

Jack pondered this. "I don't know her very well. She's a good receptionist. She had a friendly relationship with Ameleth and Barney. I think Ameleth was angry at her for some reason." I raised my eyebrows to ask why he thought that. "Because Ameleth said to me a couple of nights ago, 'I'm pissed at Janey.'"

"Does Ameleth know about your affair?"

"No."

"Did Janey ever move in on Barney?"

"I don't know. I doubt it."

"What kind of security do you have at the club?" I asked. If I wanted to break in myself, I needed to know if it'd be a problem. Maybe there were video surveillance cameras I could check. That kind of thing.

"We'd got our security guard, Ergort, an ex-cop."

"The guy who stands out front?" I asked. "He's too young to be an ex-cop." I'd guessed he was around thirty. It's hard to tell with muscleheads.

Jack said, "He was kicked off the force. Something about a drug deal or an innocent bystander getting shot, I can't remember which." I made a mental note to ask Falcone about Ergort. Jack looked out the cell bars, busily wringing his hands. "Wanda, you've got to give the money back, so I can get out of here."

I said nothing.

"Wanda, listen to me," he pleaded, gripping my shoulders. He had strong hands. I felt feminine and overpowered. "I can't take another day behind bars. I insist you return the money. I demand it." I considered his plight. I decided to ignore it. What was he going to do, anyway? Fire me? From jail? He checked to see if the guard was within earshot. She was. His rant went on. "The walls, they're closing in." He started to jog around the cell in tiny circles. "Jesus, help me—I can't even work up a good sweat in this hellhole." He winked at me.

"Something in your eye, Jack?" I asked.

He seemed annoyed. "Nothing is in my eye. Just give me that money."

"If I give the money back, Jack, you're on your own."

"My God, Wanda. Are you some kind of sadist?"

Just sadistically cheap at times, perhaps. "I'll tell you what," I said. "I'll go talk to Ameleth and see if I can get her to drop the charges. If it gets too hairy, I'll just give you the money." So I lied.

His whole body sagged with relief. "Thank you," he breathed. "You've been indispensable during this whole nightmare."

"Save your sweat for when you get out, Jack." I turned toward the bars and called for the guard. She came and I went.

I went in search of Ameleth. I kicked myself pretty hard when I realized I hadn't the faintest idea where she and Jack lived. I found a working pay phone on the street and dialed 411. Information had none—Ameleth and Jack were unlisted. I asked a homeless guy by the subway entrance. He didn't know where to find their apartment, but he did tell me where I could shove a broom. I thanked him for all his help and tossed him a shiny red penny. He flipped me the bird.

I wandered the streets aimlessly—but educationally—in search of Ameleth's lair. My tour of the neighborhood included a quick sweep of Montague Street, the heart of the shopping district. Most of the restaurants on the street were serving *al fresco* summer luncheon. Each joint had terra-cotta pots of fresh flowers on the sidewalk out front and its own ethnic specialty: Italian, French, Irish, Polish, Mexican, Chinese, Japanese. This one block could satisfy the needs of the United Nations, if the delegates could live without Big Macs.

My favorite was a little Greek joint called Mr. Souvlaki. I went there often. They didn't deliver. It's been a while since I discovered a food. Stuffed grape leaves and spanekopeta had become an important part of my life. I ran inside and I broke a hundred spot for a chicken gyro, extra white sauce, hot sauce and napkins.

"Do you know where Ameleth Bergen lives?" I asked the gyro man named George Mouscatopolis. He shrugged. It was all English to him. I went outside with my lunch. I sat down at one of the sunny tables.

The sky was blue. The sidewalk had waves from the heat. A few people slowed down to admire my sandwich as they walked by.

I considered falling into the Gap when I finished eating. But I thought of Jack running in tiny circles in his cell. Was he for real? I wondered. I chucked my used napkins in the trash and headed toward the club. I doubted Ameleth would be there. Her lover had just died. She probably wanted to spend some time alone, mourning in a black Lycra bodysuit. But, then again, damage had to be controlled at the club. And if she wasn't there, I'd find Alex and get ammunition to tease him about his so-called bulging pectorals.

As I rounded the corner of Pierrepont Street, I didn't see the ex-cop steroid monster on guard in front of the club. Shit, I thought. Maybe the place *was* closed after all. As I got closer, I saw I was wrong. The club's iron-work doors were wide open. A board was put over the window Jack must have broken. And the steroid mountain was just inside, leaning on a mop (which, any second, would splinter under his weight). He was talking to Janey at the reception desk. She tolerated it. He was telling some story, his mouth twisted into a leer and his sausage-link fingers stumbling in the air. Could the behemoth be flirting? Apparently so. Janey was actually listening. I let myself imagine giant Ergort and Janey in bed together. I was repulsed, but puzzlingly transfixed at the same time.

I walked toward the odd couple. After a slippery step, my feet flew out from under me. My butt hit the tile with a crunch. Some kind of fluid seeped through my jeans. I looked down and saw a puddle on the floor. I touched it, and sniffed. Lemon-flavored. I'd slipped on a Gatorade spill—an unanticipated hazard to gym life.

The steroid junkie grabbed my arm, lifted me off the floor and shook me like a martini. Through the rattle in my ears, I heard him say, "You okay, lady? You okay? Listen up, lady, you sue us, I'll get fired, and then I'll track you down, you hear me? I'll track you down and twist your head off."

Janey said, "Ergort, let her down now." She hadn't moved from her position behind the reception desk. Ergort grunted and dropped me. My toes skimmed the floor. My butt hit next. I looked up at Ergort. He smirked and actually splashed some Gatorade on me with his sneaker.

Janey jogged toward me. She seemed genuinely concerned. "Wanda, are you okay?" To Ergort, she said, "Brilliant, you dummy. Now she *will* sue."

"Do you treat all your members this way?" I asked from the puddle.

"You're not a member," Janey reminded me politely. "But we do offer a special discount this week for women with coordination problems." She smiled wickedly.

"Then you'd better alert your mother," I said. "And tell Ameleth Bergen I'm looking for her." I struggled to a stand, carefully sidestepping the Gatorade slick. My spine felt splintered. Detecting was backbreaking work. "I want to talk to her right away. As soon as I've had my complimentary massage."

I heard the squish of rubber soles on the tiled floor. A couple of middle-aged women came into view in the mirrored walls. Ergort carefully escorted the women around the spill, and then busied himself with his mopping. Janey checked their club ID cards. I walked toward her desk once the women left. Janey put an ankle on the desktop and stretched herself flat out over her leg.

"These monitors," I said. "Do they record?" There were three minivideo monitors on her desk. I couldn't quite make out the pictures. My glasses might help with that.

"They just feed," she said as she placed a clipboard in front of them.

"Where are the cameras?" I asked.

"That's really none of your business," she responded. I was about to ask her if she saw anything on the day of the murder, but didn't think she'd give up anything for free.

I nodded politely. "The next available massage will be fine," I said. "As long as the next available slot opens in five minutes." I tried to glare intimidatingly.

Janey smiled. "I'll see what I can do," she said. She took a nice long gander at my soggy jeans as she dialed the desk phone. Ergort was nearly done mopping. His arm muscles shifted like sand in the wind under his skin. His legs ballooned with knots of sinew. The hair: tightly curled and brown, riding high over his round face. Not a bad looking science experiment, except for the zits all over his neck. He already had the belligerent attitude. Next would come the shriveled nads.

"Hey, Ergort," I said to him loudly. "I bet you've even got muscles in your brain."

"I've got muscles everywhere," he said proudly while pointing at his chest with his thumb.

Janey switched legs. Her head was resting on her left knee when she said, "Go to the second floor. Your massage therapist for today will greet you at the elevator."

I smiled inside. All that had been necessary was for

me to fall on my butt a couple times. I'd be all better soon. My relocated shoulder only bothered me when I made sarcastic remarks, which was hardly ever.

"Don't forget to tell Ameleth I'm here," I said to Janey. She ignored me, too busy chinning her shin. I walked down the mirrored corridor to the elevator banks. A car waited for me. I pushed the button. A computerized voice said, "Pool, spa, locker rooms, next stop." I looked around to make sure no one saw me start with surprise. Sure enough, a video camera whirred just over my head. I could picture Janey's perfect cheekbones lifting with mirth. I smiled at the camera and grabbed my breast. "Mirth this," I said.

The elevator said, "Spa," as the doors opened. A man stood directly outside. He had a big nose which hooked slightly to the left. His black eyes were dangerously close together. He had a goatee and long sideburns. He was slightly pudgy in the middle, but seemed to have strong arms and hands. He was dressed in white, from his smock all the way down to his orthopedic shoes. He smelled like potpourri.

I smiled at him. He smiled back. His teeth were as white as his pants. Have I mentioned that I loathe white pants on men? He said, "Freddie Smith, madam. I'll be giving you a full-body stress relieving treatment this morning." He was holding a white terry cloth bathrobe, presumably for me.

"I'm supposed to be getting a massage."

He laughed. "Ha, madam. A full-body stress relieving treatment *is* a massage. The fancy name goes with the price tag." I wondered how much a simple massage goes for at this club. "A hundred bucks, in case you're curious," he added.

A hundred bucks was a quarter of my share of the rent. That was a lot of peanuts to have my muscles de-stressed. I must have rolled my eyes because he said, "When we're done, madam, you'll think a hundred dollars is a bargain." That sounded promising. "This way, please." He pointed down another mirrored corridor. I could smell the chlorine from the pool and the disinfectant from the locker rooms.

"Is the steam room here co-ed?" I asked, thinking about Max and a certain fantasy I'd been having lately.

"No," he said succinctly. As I followed him, I couldn't help but notice that Freddie Smith had a bubbly butt. I watched it lift and settle with each step. The wood planks on the floor creaked slightly under his feet. He said, "We'll be using the Santa Fe room this morning. Would you prefer sage or jasmine?"

"I'd prefer a massage."

"Incense, madam."

"The name's Mallory."

"Pardon me, Mallory. I'll repeat the question: sage or jasmine?"

"What's the big difference?" I had to walk quickly to keep up.

Freddie said mechanically, "Sage reminds me more of a fresh spring day. A picnic, yes, with mozzarella and basil sandwiches on foccacio and a bottle of Italian red. Jasmine is more exotic. I think of a scented bath in a geisha house, being fed grapes off the vine and cooled with waving feathers."

"You got anything that smells like boiled hot dogs, flying dirt and carmel-coated pralines?" I asked. "Something that smells like summer in New York?"

"We have a Dumpster out back for that, Mallory."

"Sage it is," I said. I admired his comeback.

"If you enjoy the experience," Freddie said, "you

can purchase incense upstairs after the massage. Can I get you something to drink? Hot apple cider, or camomile tea?" His voice was soothing, but in a forced way.

I said, "Whichever one comes with a cheese Danish."

Freddie smiled patiently and said, "How does a sundae of frozen yogurt and hot carob sauce sound to you?"

Like no fun at all. "I'll take it."

"You can get one after our session at the restaurant on street level." He handed me the robe. "I believe it goes for five dollars."

"Cheap robe."

"The sundae."

I took the robe. "Pretty sad about Barney," I fished.

"Barney who?" Freddie snaked out of answering. "You can change in here." He ushered me into a meticulously clean bathroom with pickled-pine planks on the floor, a shower, a sink, and a few pegs to hang towels on. A basket of dried roses sat on the basin. A sign hung over the mirror said that all the Kiehl's bath products could be purchased upstairs. I wasn't surprised.

"What isn't for sale upstairs?" I asked.

Freddie twitched suddenly, which I found strange. I hoped he wouldn't flinch while massaging my ticklish spots. I'd had massages, but I'd never been kneaded by a man before (except Max, who needed my love daily). Freddie said, "Take off all your clothes, including your bra and panties." He didn't blush.

"I'm not wearing panties," I said loudly, and winked at him before kicking the door shut. This would be a new experience, I thought. I hungered for new experiences. I kiboshed for a moment of self-consciousness and then stripped. While I undressed, I imagined Alex huffing and puffing away with free weights, trying to impress chicks, his skinny arms shaking and struggling with each lift. I snorted to myself as I threw on the robe. It was thick and soft. I felt a wave of coziness. Embarrassed, I quickly squashed it. Cozy was for wimps, I thought to myself, not hard-boiled types like me. If I wanted cozy, I'd have pushed Max for a WBFPL (wood-burning fireplace). My legs were still speckled with stubble. I hoped Freddie cared as much as I did. He couldn't possibly care less.

I stuffed my clothes into a cubbyhole above the sink. I knew to do so because of the sign: "Cubbyhole for clothes." I felt a sudden panic like I was being watched. I quickly swept the room. No windows, no peepholes. Maybe I just felt awkward before getting rubbed by a strange man.

I shook it off and left the bathroom. Freddie waited for me outside. He led me into the Santa Fe room. I could smell the sage ten steps away. The room had a few Native American artifacts hanging on the walls: rugs, the skull of some long-dead desert animal. A cactus reached out in a few directions from one corner. In the center of the room loomed the massage table. Freddie patted it in the middle and said, "Lie down on your stomach. Put your face in the head cradle." I took the head cradle to be the bagel shaped padded growth at the top end of the table. I did as he asked, fitting my face in the cushioned bagel. I wondered who'd cradled their faces before me, and if they had any contagious skin diseases.

"Mallory," he said, clearing his throat. "You're

supposed to take the robe off before you get on the table."

I sat up, and shrugged the robe off my shoulders. Freddie watched as I did so. He didn't stare at my nekkidness. Ergo, he was gay or in need of glasses. I said, "This must be the best part of your job, Freddie."

"Some days," he said. I suddenly hated him.

I lay back down. Freddie put a towel over my butt. I felt less exposed, but I'll be damned if he was going to make me feel embarrassed or self-conscious. Piped-in music played softly—some moony new-age atmospheric ditty that was supposed to sound like rain and wind. I closed my eyes. Freddie's footsteps creaked on the wood-planked floor. "I'll be putting hot oil on your skin," he said. "You don't have any allergies, do you?"

"Only rude men," I said.

"Then we should be fine." He slicked some hot oil on my shoulder blades with meaty hands. His hand spread out over my back like a velvet iron. With each push and stroke, I relaxed more. His fingers dug into my shoulder like tiny shovels. He scooped and rubbed. The oil burned deliciously, but it smelled powerfully of Ben-Gay. So much for the sage incense.

"Your shoulder muscles are pretty tight," Freddie observed.

"From carrying the chip," I said. I waited for him to laugh. He didn't. Maybe he didn't hear me. I was talking to the floor after all. I loudly repeated, "From the chip."

"I hear you fine, Mallory," he said.

Humorless fellow, I decided. So light banter and meaningless small talk were out. I said, "When I mentioned Barney before, I meant the guy who was killed here last night. It was in all the papers." Freddie stopped massaging for long enough to turn up the music. Too loud, I thought. Must be my cue to shut up.

"It wasn't in the paper I read." His fingers came back at the base of my neck. The oil reminded me of junior varsity field hockey.

"I bet you read the *Times.*" If any paper didn't cover the murder, it'd be the *New York Times.*

"I read the *Mirror,* the *News, Newsday,* the *Times* and the *Post* every morning. And there wasn't anything in any newspaper about Barney's murder." Freddie's grip tightened around my neck.

"Easy, pal—I don't have any health insurance," I said, and tugged on one of his fingers. "Okay, I heard about the murder somewhere else—a friend of someone who works here's cousin." I let go of his finger. "Freddie, do that thing that feels like a soft-shelled crab walking up my back. Ooh. That's good."

He was churning me like butter. At the legs now. More junior varsity smell. "Barney was a great man," Freddie announced. "He taught me everything I know, about massage, and other things."

"What other things?" I asked.

"Janey said you were some kind of undercover cop."

"I'm a private investigator."

"I'm not interested in talking to any cops." I made a mental note to check Freddie Smith's police record.

"I just said I'm not a cop." That Janey was due a talking-to, I decided. I could take the inaccuracy. It was the disrespect I couldn't stand.

Freddie pressed his thumbs into my heel. It wasn't

exactly pleasurable. He said, "I don't care what you are. I'm not going to talk about Barney. You can roll over now," he said, handing me another towel for my breasts.

I turned over. "How long did you know him?"

"Long enough." He started with my arms, stroking and kneading. Then he turned his attention to each individual finger. He yanked on one, forcing the blood to the top, and then released his grip, letting the blood seep back down into my palm. It was divine.

Freddie cracked each of my toes. Each pop sent a shiver up my leg. Massages were good, I decided. I added them to my list of things I can no longer do without, like Greek food.

"So," I said, "what's a nervous guy like you doing in a place like this?"

"I'm giving you a massage."

"Full-body stress-relieving treatment," I corrected. "And I want you to trust me. I'm not a cop."

"Congratulations," he said.

I waited for him to say more. He didn't. "So," I started. "Who do you think killed Barney?"

Freddie dropped my arm suddenly and started massaging my throat. With his thumb and forefingers, he clamped his hand on either side of my windpipe. "In a second, I could cut off both your carotid arteries, stopping blood from reaching your brain. You'd pass out in seconds." He looked down the length of my body. He turned back and smiled.

"What, so you can knock me out and then rape and murder me? What are you, some kind of psychopath?" Softly, I asked, "Freddie, will you do that magic fingers thing on my temples?" Freddie frowned deeply. He seemed annoyed. His cheeks quivered slightly. "I'm scared, okay? I'm frightened to death." I gave him a scared bunny look. He seemed satisfied. He rubbed my temples.

"I don't know who killed Barney," he said. "And I don't like your asking questions about it. Just leave it alone. Let the cops handle it. No one around here needs some private detective—if that's what you really are—poking her big fat nose in Barney's death."

My nose was not fat. It was delicate, like a rose in first bud. "I think maybe you're the one in need of a massage, buddy," I said. "And your passion about this whole thing only makes me more curious. If I were you, and you really wanted me to stop asking questions, I'd answer a few." Some reverse psychology for the mix.

Freddie seemed to consider it. I said, "Did he have any enemies? Anyone want to take him out? And I don't mean on a date, mind you."

"Look, Barney was a friend to me, okay? He was a pal. A mentor. He was someone I respected. And I don't need some stranger talking about him like a slab of beef."

Actually, I thought of Barney more as a boiled lobster, but I got the point. "I'm sorry about your friend," I said. "And if you don't want to discuss why he died, I'll understand."

"Good," he grunted.

"Are you always this open about your feelings with complete strangers?" I asked. Completely naked strangers, for that matter.

Freddie stopped rubbing my temples. He ran his fingers through my red tendrils. "No."

I felt a chill. I didn't think if was from the scalp massage. Something smelled funny here, and I don't mean the sage, or the Ben-Gay. Call it a vibe. I'm psychic on occasion. I've learned to trust these feelings. "I also have a degree in social work," I lied. "A counseling session might be just what you need."

Freddie stopped abruptly and walked across the room. He lifted the robe off the hook and handed it to me. He mouthed, "Not here." Freddie wiped his hand with a towel while I slipped on the robe. He then turned the music down to a normal level. I swept the room for a video camera, but didn't find one. Freddie opened the door and led me to my clothes.

He said, "Feel free to take a shower. All the Kiehl's products are on sale upstairs."

"I noticed the sign." I couldn't help but notice. The sign practically covered the mirror. "When can I schedule you an appointment?" I asked.

"I'll call you," he whispered and walked away. I watched his bubbly butt bounce under his white slacks. I will most definitely ask Jack about Freddie Smith.

I took that shower. The flashbacks of junior high school locker rooms faded as I washed away the oil. The Kiehl's mango soap really did perk up my skin. I felt relaxed, loose as creamed spinach and ready for a nap. Right after I tracked down Ameleth Bergen, and maybe some frozen yogurt.

I couldn't shake that feeling of being watched, though. I quickly dressed—my jeans had since dried. I put on my glasses to carefully scan the walls as I buttoned my fly. I spent some time looking in the mirror. Could be a two-way, but I didn't think so. I heard the floorboards creak in the hallway. On instinct, I donkey kicked the bathroom door open.

Clunk went the wood against his skull. Fluffy white towels flew through the air. I grabbed the kid by his shirt and threw him in the shower. I turned on the water. Then I inspected the door. Sure enough, there was a hole drilled into the wood right below one of the towel hooks—right at tit level. The kid was sputtering in the shower, water spilling unforgivingly into his mouth.

I said, "Name."

"What difference does it make?" he asked. "I'm dead."

"I'm not going to report you, asshole." I turned off the water. If this kid peeped a lot, maybe he saw something yesterday evening.

"Right," he mocked. "Since when does a zitty perverted towel boy get a break?"

I threw one of his precious towels at him. "Get up." He got up. Must be six feet, if he was five inches. About sixteen. "You know a man was killed here last night?"

"Yeah, so what?" he asked. "Barney Cutler was a dick."

"Why do you say that?"

"He never let me watch."

"Watch what?" I asked. "Women in the bathroom?"

"Whatever. Look—can I go? If I get caught in here, I'm dead."

I nodded reluctantly. He ran out, all awkward limbs and dripping clothes. I wondered what Barney was trying to keep private. I made a mental note to track down the peeping towel boy again. Maybe I'll bring some candy or baseball cards. Maybe a copy of *Penthouse*. I wasn't above bribery. In fact, the only thing I was above, on a regular basis, was Max.

I left the bathroom. I headed for the elevator banks. Imagine my surprise: Ameleth Bergen sat on the couch right next to the elevators, enjoying what I took to be a cup of hot cider. Her hair was calmer than it'd been the night before—probably because we weren't in a room full of steam. Our eyes met. With my four eyes and her two, they could have had a party. Hers were flinty gray with big flecks of gold. Except for the scowl on her face, she was a decent looking woman. I smiled as I approached. She stood. She must have bought her all-black bodysuit (told you) in the junior department. With a good six inches on her and at least forty pounds, I could win in a cat fight. Her waist couldn't have been more than twenty inches around.

"Ergort said you were looking for me," she said.

"You heard right," I said.

"You found me," she said. "What do you want?"

"I want to talk about Barney's murder."

"I thought you wanted to talk to me about dropping the charges on Jack."

"Whatever gave you that idea?" I asked.

Ameleth arranged her mini arms akimbo. She stood there like a statue for a minute, staring at me accusingly. I almost broke, but she said, "Come with me." She pushed the elevator call button and the door opened immediately. We stepped inside. "We'll go to my office," she said, fitting her key in the slot Jack used the night before. I found that strange. Surely the room was sealed. The elevator whisked us heavenward.

"Returning to the scene of the crime," I said.

"Maybe we'll find the killer there," she said. "But I doubt it, considering that the killer is currently in jail."

"I suppose couples counseling is out of the question." I almost offered my social services again.

She glared at me with her flints. "Jack Watson can rot in jail for all I care."

The elevator doors whooshed open. We stepped into the suite. The tomato stains were all over the carpet. In fact, everything looked pretty much the same as last night, minus the cops. Ameleth didn't stop at the bar for a celery cocktail. Nor did she hop on the treadmill. She stormed straight into the back room. I followed. Barney's clothes were gone. Ameleth's clean, clear desk was now strewn with papers. She grabbed a handful and shook them at me. "Bills. Thousands of dollars worth. Like I need to pay for a broken window, too? With Barney gone, the club is my entire life. If I go bankrupt, I might as well die."

"Don't you have a bank account? Savings?" I wondered if she cared about the three grand Jack took from her safe.

Ameleth dropped the handful of papers. "I don't know where Jack found you, or who the hell you are. But it's none of your goddamn business how I run the club. Jack said this morning that you had three thousand dollars of my money."

"You spoke to Jack?" I asked, confused.

"I spoke to the detective, actually. She told me Jack said he had three thousand dollars to pay off his bail. He just had to get it back from you. Of course, I checked my office safe. If you don't get the money back to me by the end of the day, I'm going to have to send a friend of mine over to see you."

I was shaking in my sneakers. "Tax cheaters never prosper," I said with a tsk. "And please do send someone over. I'm new to the neighborhood and I've always found it so hard to make friends."

"Look, Mallory—whoever the fuck you are—something else is missing. I have to assume Jack took it. I want it back."

"And what would that be?"

"I think you know what's missing, Mallory."

I leaned my fingertips on the edge of her desk. Did she mean the knife? I played dumb. "I don't have a clue what it is you're looking for, lady, but if you'd be interested in finding it, then you're talking to the right chick."

She frowned and sank into her chair. It seemed too big for her. I feared she might skip off and hurt herself. She didn't say anything. I said, "Consider hearing me out as a temporary alternative to having me beat up." She nodded. "First of all, I need to know what we're talking about."

She paused to think before she said, "The club membership roster."

"Bullshit."

"Are you calling me a liar?"

"Yes."

"I ought to have you trounced."

"Let's get one thing straight here, Ameleth. I'm not an idiot. Unless your club roster documents that heads of state have sexually harassed a Soloflex machine, it ain't worth dick."

She squinted at me, the muscles in her arms flexing and unflexing automatically. "You expect me to hire you."

"That hadn't occurred to me, but now that you mention it, I'd be delighted."

She wasn't convinced. "Who do you think took it?" she asked.

I had no idea who—or what, even. "Whoever killed Barney," I said. It was the logical guess. The person showed up, took It (whatever It was), and killed Barney who might have caught him or her in the act of stealing It. I wondered why the thief left behind the three grand.

"Let me just ask you this one question. Why did you marry Jack if you hate him so much?"

She got all pensive for a second. "I didn't hate him when I married him," she said plainly. "I won't pay you a penny until you recover the stuff. Then you can have five hundred."

So now, at least, I knew I'd be looking for "stuff." That didn't sound like a knife. I said, "Five thousand."

"Forget it."

"Nonnegotiable."

She mulled and then nodded, resigned. "Five thousand, but only if you get it today. Tomorrow, it'll be four. The day after, three."

Sounded suspenseful. "Deal," I said, "if you drop the charges on Jack."

"I'll think about it."

Good enough for me. Jack wouldn't get into any trouble in the slammer. And he'd stay out of the way. "Now that we're partners," I prompted, "let me ask you this: As a cheater, do you feel guilt or just the passion of something new?"

"That's none of your fucking business." She seemed pissed. So much for female bonding.

"Tell me about Freddie Smith," I asked. "He and Barney must have been close."

Ameleth stared at me strangely. "Who's Freddie Smith?"

"He's on your staff. A massage therapist."

"I don't have a massage therapist named Freddie Smith on staff."

5

One Lump
or Two

"Then who gave me a massage five minutes ago?" I asked.

Ameleth said, "Janey said she sent you downstairs to see Olga."

"Does Olga have a hooked nose and hairy arms?"

"She does actually." I decided to drop it. The murder must have affected her brain. Ameleth stared at me ponderously. She seemed to think we knew each other in a former life. "I'm hungry," she announced. "Let's get some food. And I want to show you something."

Never one to argue with that proposition, I followed her. We walked through the exercise room of her suite, and down the elevator to the restaurant level. I know that's where we were going because the elevator told me. She was steely silent the whole ride.

"Lobby level. Slimmy Shack restaurant, please try our delicious frozen yogurt sundaes, only fifty calories and two grams of unsaturated fat," said the elevator as the door opened. We got off.

She turned down a short corridor. She stared straight ahead. "You must wonder how *I* married a useless sentimental like Jack," she said. "And how I destroyed that by having an affair with Barney, who has been murdered in my own club, which is going bankrupt." She stopped in front of a pair of glass doors.

She pushed open the doors. The Slimmy Shack restaurant reminded me of Long Island diners, but painted yellow and pink. The colors alone reminded me of junk food. A zigzaggy counter slinked across the room. A dozen or so women in wallpaper matching workout togs sat around the counter. Not a smoker among them. They sat by themselves or in quiet pairs. I had the strange feeling I was in a church. Hanging from the ceiling, plants grew with long arms.

"Feel that oxygen," Ameleth said, taking a deep breath. We walked past a massive philodendron, and she kissed one of the leaves. "With Barney dead and the club in near ruin, these plants are all I've got."

I studied this tightly sinewed creature. Even on the verge of bankruptcy, she was richer than I'll ever be. But she had bigger problems than I'd ever want. And I could carry her home in my overnight bag if I tried. We took a seat at the counter. The stools were just like the ones in her suite, except these had cushions. The counterman—another well-oiled example of pumped human flesh—doted over Ameleth like a man due for a raise. She said, "Two sundaes, Larry, and a carrot juice garlic Power Drink for me."

Larry turned to me. I said, "Diet Coke. Extra diet." He walked off to prepare our gruel. I stared at the beet juice churning machine for a few seconds. Then I leaned over to Ameleth and whispered in her ear, "What did you mean before when you said 'stuff'?"

"He is attractive." She nodded. "I hire only the firmest and fittest for my club."

A mental image of Freddie Smith flashed before my eyes. "Look, Ameleth. It's going to be near impossible to find the *stuff* if you don't tell me what it is. Perhaps you have a photograph of It to show me?"

She shook her head to herself, deciding. Finally, she said, "I'm stuck." She turned toward me. Her flinty gray eyes carving holes into my green ones. "If I tell you the truth, then you'll want in."

"I hate being in," I said. "I'd never want in. I always want out. Even as a child. The farther out the better. And I don't mean belly buttons."

She glanced at my gut. "You have to swear. If you go back on your word, I'll send someone to your apartment."

"Will he do windows?" I laughed. She didn't. I put on my serious mask. "But seriously, folks. I'm on the payroll."

Our food arrived. The sundae couldn't have looked more real. I tasted. The carob sauce and wet nuts (my favorite) were lip-smacking. Just like the goo back home. Not a fan of frozen yogurt, I was surprised by how full of fat it tasted. It even chilled my brain slightly. Ameleth wasn't having the same revelatory experience. She wasn't a virgin. After removing a clean-licked spoon from her mouth, she said, "Tastes pretty good. Like the real thing." I nodded. "That's because it is the real thing. There are about fifty million calories in that spoonful, and about ten million grams of saturated-as-hell fat."

I think she expected me to drop my spoon in horror. I didn't. "Let me guess," I guessed. "You dish out real ice cream so these poor suckers have to work out twice as hard to lose weight. More business for you."

Ameleth ate in silence for a minute. Finally, she said, "Look around, Wanda."

I did. "I'm really a blues and reds kind of decorator."

"The women, Wanda."

We were surrounded by them, some thin, scarfing down these sundaes like life's blood. "Their goal is to deny themselves every pleasure in life," Ameleth said quietly. "Can't eat if it's fattening. Can't exercise if it's not cardiovascular. But not one of these women will ever be satisfied with how she looks. She'll always be five pounds heavy and five hundred crunches flabby. By serving them real ice cream and calling it low-fat, I'm giving them a taste of sin, without the guilt. And they need some fat in their diets to lube everything up anyway."

"Good thing they have someone like you to decide what's best," I said. She nodded as if I meant it. "And what about the stuff in the safe?"

"It wasn't really in the safe. It was in the bar refrigerator in my suite. Two samples—the results of sixty thousand dollars' worth of research. One was a new anabolic steroid which develops muscle tone without exercising at all. The other a chromium compound tablet that burns fat so powerfully that it doesn't matter what you eat. Now they're gone."

I contemplated what I'd just heard while munching a maraschino cherry. "Can you describe the samples?"

"You mean how much beta carotene and niacinamide in the chromium? Or how much diabasic calcium phosphate in the steroids? I guess the steroid looked like testosterone. And the chromium looked like ascorbic acid and riboflavin."

I blinked. "That should help. Thanks." I wondered how a police sketch artist would handle that description. "Who knew, besides Barney?"

"Only Barney. And my chemist. He designed the stuff in his private lab."

I said, "I can see why you'd think I'd want in."

"No one's getting anything if the samples can't be found. Barney bought the chemist's notebooks when we paid him for the samples. Barney took the notebooks, and I'm not sure what he did with them. This whole money/drugs transfer only happened yesterday afternoon. I was a wreck even then. Now I'm a total wreck." Ameleth wiped her mouth carefully, and then sucked down her carrot-garlic concoction in one big gulp. "I love that garlic rush." She relished it for a moment, eyes closed. Then she said, "And I'm not going to tell you who my chemist is. The last thing I need right now is to deal with you asking him questions. He's not a well man. He may be insane."

"How can you tell?" I asked.

"I'm not falling for that one," she said.

I could smell the garlic rush from my stool. I said, "Take the story from the transfer to right now."

Across the room, a waiter in a white button-down and loose black shorts walked across the room with an ice cream mountain on a tray. He brought it to a woman who must have been fifty pounds overweight. Ameleth said, "I don't really have much to lose. Okay, yesterday morning, I told Jack I was going to the Fitness Convention at the Jacob Javits Center. I'd be gone all day. He could take the day off himself. Jack, of course, offered to go with me to the convention. Poor idiot, he doesn't even know when I'm trying to get rid of him. I sent him on some work errands—see how all of the new sneakers rate on a five-mile run, that kind of thing. And, wanting to please me like a jerk, he left me alone to get ready for the drop.

"The chemist showed up at the suite in the club at noon," she said. "I've never met the guy. Barney thought it was best if I never laid eyes on him, so he sent me on an important errand while he paid him. The chemist had been working on these formulas for years. We bought him a lab to work in and an offer of sixty thousand dollars in exchange for half the royalties. For our share, we'd get FDA approval, a marketer and a distributor—the grunt work. But Barney had a plan. He was going to buy the notebooks and the samples from the chemist at the club. Meanwhile, I was on my important errand locking up the lab we bought for him. We'd have it all, you get it? In the time I'd take him to reconstruct his formulas, we'd be on the market."

I slurped my Diet Coke. "Where is this lab?" I asked.

"Forget it. I'm not falling for it," she said. "I got back to the club to meet Barney with the samples. He was in the suite, just like we'd planned. The chemist was gone. The samples were in the fridge. The notebooks were safely hidden, he told me. We chased each other on the treadmill for fun, and then took a nice Jacuzzi and made love in the bubbles. I left soon after because I thought Jack might show up to tell me about his jogging mission. I didn't want him to catch me with Barney."

I rudely interrupted. "I thought that was what you wanted."

She ignored me. "I took the elevator down," she said. "I went back to the apartment—"

"Which is where?" I asked.

"That won't lead you to the chemist."

"I was looking earlier today. I'm curious."

"I'll write you a card when you find the samples. As I said, I went back to the apartment and changed into dry clothes. I did some stretching exercises to loosen up. I napped. At nine o'clock, the phone rings. A cop tells me there's been a murder at the club. I race over there, and find Barney murdered. I look in the fridge in the juice bar—empty. I check the safe in the back: money gone."

"I still don't get why you assume Jack killed Barney."

"I know he did it," she said firmly. "It's as simple as that. And then to get word that he tried to demolish the club? I've had enough emotional wrenching for one day. With Barney gone, the samples stolen and my garlic rush over, I need some time to think about what else to live for."

On that happy note, Ameleth wiped a tear from her gray eyes, and left me to my sundae, and the remains of hers. It was a pleasure to watch her go—she had a nice butt and she was a real downer. Ameleth hadn't mentioned where she slept the night before. I wondered if the samples were in pill form, or a liquid. I tried to think of who I could ask.

I looked around. There was a new lineup of women in Lycra and strategically ripped T-shirts. Some were fit; some were fit to be tied (or lassoed, as the case may be). Losing weight takes effort and time—two things New Yorkers have little to spare (the third being loose change). I watched the ice cream mountain eater shovel the last spoonfuls of faux yogurt into her now sticky mouth. She wore a pair of black leggings and a loose parachute material sweatshirt. Her curly brown hair was tied up in a high ponytail. The ring on her left hand dug into her plump index finger. I wondered how much weight she'd gained since her wedding day. Her eyes jogged around the room, inspecting other women's butts and abs. Her jealousy was so fierce I could taste it.

I fantasized about going over to her table and saying, "A perfect body isn't going to solve your problems or make your husband love you." I didn't think she'd appreciate it.

But that's not the reason I didn't go over. Another woman, one of the wait staff in the restaurant (I could tell by her little white change apron), approached the fat woman's table with the check. She whistled an old TV tune while she walked. Chubster gave the waitress a fifty-dollar bill (I was wearing my glasses). I thought that was a lot for a scoop of ice cream. The waitress glanced quickly around the room, reached into her change apron and deposited a clear-plastic Baggie and two single-dollar bills on the counter. Chubster scooped the bag into her fist. She offered the waitress a wan smile, and then split the shop like a furtive banana.

I couldn't quite make out what was inside the Baggie. If only I'd worn my magnifying glasses instead. If I had to guess, I'd say there were drugs in there. Maybe the missing samples of the missing chromium compound? The waitress glanced around the joint again, this time noticing my stare. She frowned, making lines on her face. She was about thirty, skinny in the way that makes you look older. Her hair was straight and dark, her neck long and graceful. She seemed to have no hair on her arms. Her legs were equally bald. I smiled when we made eye contact and called her over with a head bob. She scowled slightly, did a bad job of pretending she didn't notice, and disappeared behind the door to the kitchen, whistling the TV show theme music nervously.

I left a quarter on the table for my waiter and followed the Baggie lady. Just as I swung the kitchen door open, I saw her hairless limbs fly through another door in the back. I raced through the room, remarking as I dashed by how clean the kitchen was and how shiny the silver countertops and stove were. Slamming hard into the back door with open hands, I bounced off with enough force to send me reeling into a freezer behind me. My head hit the handle. I felt myself float toward unconsciousness.

Remembering what to do from the time I passed out while having drunken sex in a too-hot shower, I counted my breaths, lowered my head and tried to relax. The waiter who'd served me—Larry, was it?— rushed over. He said, "Are you all right?"

I said, "Water."

"Sink's over there," he said and pointed. "For that quarter tip, you can get it yourself." I should have stiffed him.

I took a woozy walk to the sink and helped myself to a cold drink. I tried the door again. Push as I might, I couldn't get it open. The waiter watched my efforts closely. Finally, after I'd broken a sweat, he said, "Try pull."

The bastard. Pull worked. The door opened into an alley. A few Dumpsters were lined up against a brick wall, overflowing with empty Haagen Dazs ten-gallon containers and cardboard boxes with tomato and lettuce stains. I said to the waiter, "Don't you recycle?"

Arms folded across his chest, he said, "I bet you want me to tell you her name."

"Whose name?" I asked. The bump on the back of my head was now Ping-Pong–ball size.

The waiter smiled. He said, "Janey told everyone that you're an undercover cop."

I grumbled inside. I've spent my whole detective career dukeing it out with the fuzz, and now to be called one. It cut. Deeply. "Let's start with you. Name. Age. Address." I waited patiently.

His shiny brow furrowed. "Aren't you going to write this down?"

"I have a photographic memory."

"Oh," he said, nodding. Another dunce. "Larry Black, just twenty-four but mature for my age. I live in the Bossert Hotel on Montague Street."

The Bossert was a massive two-square block apartment building populated exclusively by Jehovah's Witnesses. Brooklyn Heights was the Jehovah headquarters for North America, has been for decades. In fact, the Jehovahs owned one-third of the Brooklyn Heights real estate, including some of the oldest and most beautiful examples of prewar Gothic architecture in the city. *The Watchtower,* their newsletter and national plea for converts, was published in plants on the dock of the East River and stored in warehouses under the Brooklyn Bridge. Midnight blue vans transport the flock from the Bossert and other Jehovah buildings to the printing plants every morning and then home every night. At noon on weekdays, streams of them walk up from the docks into the heart of the Heights for lunch, and at exactly one o'clock, they stream right back down in one big trickle. I've heard rumors that they eat only in cafeterias in the Bossert basement. They grow their own vegetables, sew their own clothes. Max calls them the "haircut people," because they all have the same do, probably styled with the same bowl. Even the women.

"Jehovah?" I asked this Larry Black. He had long-ish hair, tucked neatly behind his ears.

"You got a problem with that?" he asked.

I said, "Only if you do." I would. The religion is baffling to an atheist like me. Only 144,000 of them (1,200 times 1,200—they use those numbers because of the twelve days of Christmas, the twelve apostles and the twelve *Halloween* movies) will go to heaven after the apocalypse. God chooses who gets to go based on how good a Jehovah you are, but the way to be a good Jehovah is to get converts. So the way to heaven is by creating competition for yourself. I prefer to demolish competition. It's the American way. "How come you don't work at the plant?" I asked.

Larry shuffled his cross-trainers. "If you must know, I've decided to devote my life to physical fitness. It's a very rewarding pursuit. You should try it."

The poor bastard was still looking for converts. "I've already decided to devote my life to fighting crime. Who was that girl and where can I find her?"

"It's my duty to help the police, but I don't want to squeal." He squirmed between the horns of his dilemma. "I mean, what kind of friend would I be if I told you her name? I could go to hell for that, drown in a field of blood, devoured by vultures of fire, choked by chains of hot lava." His conviction heated as he spoke.

"I didn't know squealing was one of the seven deadly sins."

"Oh, yeah," he said, nodding. "It falls under the adultery category."

I considered this. This whole discussion fell under

the bullshit category to me, but I've learned over my years of gumshoeing to give zealots their eccentricities. "Does the phrase police brutality mean anything to you?" I asked.

"For Pete's sake, lady." Larry blanched. He seemed nervous, but tried to hide it. "If you're going to threaten violence, you might as well hit me now. I'm prepared to martyr myself."

I thought of Jack in his jail cell, lonely and desperate. I wondered if Max would put himself on the line for me. I knew Alex would—he had many times in capers past. Larry put his hands behind his back and closed his eyes like he was ready for a sock on the jaw. Never one to disappoint, I removed Mama, my pearl-handled .22, from my purse. The safety was on. I aimed the barrel at Larry's chest. "Let's see how brave you are now, sucker." I have little tolerance for this kind of crap.

Larry's eyes fluttered open. He backed up against the freezer when he saw the gun. I said, "Your friend may be in big trouble, Larry. And here's another secret—I'm not a cop. I'm a private detective working for Jack Watson. I like him. I don't really know why. I've never been attracted to blonds, but he's paying me. I want to know that woman's name, and where she might be right now. And if you don't tell me, I'll shoot you." So I lied. I half expected Larry to know that.

He didn't. He started to stammer. His eyes were wild. Then he passed out. Fainted clean away, leaving me holding the gun in my hand like a limp dick. Before I could put it back in my purse, I heard a scream behind me. I turned to see who was there.

She was just a blur of dark hair and naked nails, coming at me like a whirling dervish from hell. I ducked. She rammed me square in the gut with her shoulder, knocking the wind out of me. I collapsed to the floor like a deflated balloon. I struggled to catch my breath, but my lungs billowed uselessly in my chest. A hot pain gripped my sternum. I wasn't sure, but I think she broke a rib. Despite my agony, I didn't drop the gun. I pointed it at her feebly. She was on the floor next to Larry, kissing his forehead and smoothing down his hair. My search for the Baggie lady was now over. If I ever needed to fill slots on a roller derby team, I'd give her a call.

I said, "Gasp, sputter, groan."

She said, "You killed him."

Maybe scared him to death. She was the second woman in the last twenty-four hours who'd rushed me to protect a man. I said, "Choke, cough, wheeze." I sat up and began to feel a bit less like a pancake. I shook my head to clear it. My neck was stiff—so much for my complete body stress-reduction therapy. I attempted a deep breath and a white hot flash exploded behind my eyes. I stuck with small breaths, like baby sips from a water fountain.

Meanwhile, Larry regained consciousness. He said, "Molly, thank heavens it's you. An insane woman drew a gun on me and threatened to kill me if I didn't tell her your name." He screamed suddenly. "Oh my goodness! She's right there."

I waved lamely. "I need tequila," I managed to say. I slipped the gun back in my purse. Molly glared at me suspiciously and went back to caring for Larry. He watched me lolling in pain. Sympathy seeped into his eyes.

He said, "She looks bad."

Molly checked me out. "But are you okay?" she asked Larry.

"Maybe we should take her to a hospital," he said.

I shook my head, sending stabs of pain into my cranium. Molly sighed. She said, "Larry, you're just too nice a guy." She stood up and opened the freezer door. Her body was one of the most athletic I'd seen at the club, with long limbs and muscle lines. She looked like a marathoner, with tight skin and a gaunt face. When she bent at the waist to look in the freezer, her calf muscles blew up under her skin like a gum bubble. She flung her long, straight brown hair aside, and reached behind a few pounds of frozen tofu. She dug out a large plastic Ziploc Baggie. Inside were a few hundred different colored pills and tablets. She yanked the bag open and dug around for a big white doorknob-size tablet. "Here," she said. I put the pill in my mouth and downed it with saliva. "You just took fifty milligrams of Valium. You should feel better in about twenty minutes."

I felt better immediately. The sound of the word *Valium* was soothing in itself. I smiled at Molly, dispenser of sunshine and light. I said, "Give me that bag." It hurt to talk. Max will love this.

She said, "No way."

"I just want to look at it," I squeaked out. Maybe the chromium compound pills and the steroids were in that bag. Not that I would know them if I saw them.

"The hell," said Molly the Marauder. "Jesus Christ."

Larry said, "Molly, please."

"For Christ's sake, Larry. I just saved your life and you want me to watch my language? God, are you an ingrate."

"You're doing it again," he scolded. We all turned toward the rapping on the kitchen door.

A muffled voice said, "Hello? Is anyone in there?"

A woman. I could hear the ice cream lust dripping off her tongue like syrup.

Molly said, "Larry, go take care of the customers. I'll deal with her." Larry exited the kitchen. Molly shoved the bag back into the freezer and helped me to my feet. I had one arm over her shoulder, and one around my rib cage. "I'm sorry I hit you so hard. It looked like you shot Larry."

My knees nearly buckled. Molly led me outside, past the Dumpsters, and into the sunny afternoon on Pierrepont Street. A few kids skateboarded by. It felt like a band of carpenters had gone to work in my chest, constructing a house of pain. And I don't mean the ones who sing "On Top of the World." I wanted that bag. I could give it to Ameleth to search for her samples. I said, "A thousand bucks for the bag. I won't tell Ameleth anything. Everybody's happy." Molly eased me down on a brownstone stoop right in front of the club entrance. I felt woozy. She sat next to me. "You don't happen to be a smoker?" I asked.

"I'm not selling my stash. If you want to tell Ameleth about it and get me fired, that's up to you."

I said, "I'm not trying to get you fired." I flashed to the towel boy. "Everyone thinks I'm out to get them fired. I just want to examine the stash." The Valium was beginning to kick in. I began to relax.

Molly looked at me strangely and said, "Look, if Ameleth finds out I'm selling at the club, she'll fire me. I need this job. I've got regular customers. I'm not pushing. Just moving my painkillers and speed. No one gets hurt. And no one knows—except me, Larry, and now you."

I was confused in my haze. "And your supplier, don't forget."

"And my supplier."

"Who is?" I asked.

"No one you know."

"I know a lot of people."

"Not this kind of person."

"I knew a lot of sleazy people."

"He's not a sleaze," Molly said defensively. "I met him at the club. He gets his cut, but most of the money goes to me and Larry." She smiled sweetly, her taut face wrinkling. "We're in business together."

"The business of love?" I asked drunkenly.

She shook her head. "I wish. He's willing to sell drugs—he rationalizes that they help people in their quest for physical fitness—but sex before marriage? Forget it." Damn Jehovahs. She didn't say it, but I could hear her think it. "I've got to get him out of Brooklyn Heights. He's living in that Bossert Hotel surrounded by all those weirdos. I've been saving for years. Just a few more weeks of this, and we'll have enough money to get out of this town."

"And move to Hawaii where you plan to raise island children and get as far away from Brooklyn Heights as you can and still be in America."

Molly's eyes narrowed. "How the hell did you know that?"

"When you walked past me in the restaurant, you were whistling the theme song to 'Hawaii Five-O.' It was kind of hard not to notice." I did a head bob. Even drugged, I was born to sleuth.

"Ever been?" she asked. I shook my head no. "Me neither," she said excitedly. "But I've got a cousin in Nebraska who went there on her honeymoon, and she said it was paradise. That's where I'm from— Nebraska. We've got tons of Jehovahs out there." I'd heard that Jehovahs were Nebraska's largest export crop next to corn.

"Ameleth doesn't know you're selling drugs, and you'd like to keep it that way." She nodded. "So," I said. "What's in it for me?" Her face scrunched up like she didn't understand. "And don't think I've forgiven you for breaking my ribs either."

"I hate you, and I refuse to pay."

If I wasn't pain-free from the Valium, my feelings would have been hurt. "I didn't say I wanted money."

"Forget sex—I'll never do that again."

I didn't know if she meant never having sex with a woman, never having sex at all, or never again having sex for a bribe. "Look, I don't want your savings or your body." My eyelids were beginning to flutter. Shit, I needed a bed, and fast. "I'll be in touch." I stood up to leave, but sank back down on the stoop. I repeated this exercise (in futility), and even broke a sweat. Jack would be proud.

Molly watched my attempts at standing. She said, "If you aim your gun at Larry again, I'll kill you." Then she loped like a gazelle down the street and back into the club. I wondered if Ergort watched the whole exchange from his post. I should have cared, but I couldn't find the energy. In fact, I couldn't quite find the energy to keep my eyes open.

"I thought this might happen to you someday," said the voice. I heard a slap sound and my cheek tingled. "Though I must say you look beautiful by stoop light."

"Alex?" I asked. My brain crawled its way to consciousness. I heard another slap. "Ouch, you bastard." I cradled my cheek with my hand. It felt hot. I opened my eyes. Alex was standing over me, shaking me not too gently. He was wearing sweatpants and a white T-shirt. He looked cute, as usual, and sported a devilish smile. "I'm in agony," I whined, holding my ribs.

"I barely touched you," Alex responded. "And, despite how flattered I am that you've been waiting for me prostrate on the stoop, I must admit that I'd have thought you'd net more than a buck twenty-five." He pointed to a pile of change at my feet. "You'd think the people around here would be more generous with the local riffraff."

"My purse," I said, panicky. Someone had stolen my purse with the three grand and the gun inside. "Fuck!" I screamed.

"Calm yourself down, Wanda," Alex said and handed me my bag. I exhaled loudly. The tip of my broken rib stabbed my lung and I thought I might die from the pain. "I hope your day was as eventful as mine," Alex bragged.

"Can't you see I'm hurting?" I rummaged in my bag. The money and the gun were still there. I scooped up the change at my feet and chucked it in my purse. Good for one subway token. "What time is it?"

"Time for you to go home, shower, and meet me and my brand spanking new lady love at Teresa's in one hour. Bring Max. We'll double."

It was getting dark. Twilight in June meant 8 P.M. Max must be home from the bank. "Damn," I muttered.

"Now, Wanda. We've discussed this a million times," Alex said. "You know I'll never get over you completely, but you've got to give me a chance to find happiness with another woman."

"Everytime you get a new girlfriend, I get beat up," I said. "And don't flatter yourself—that's not why I'm upset." It was too late to call Jack at the Detention Center. I made a mental note to never take that much

Valium again. At least not in the middle of an investigation. "Just shut up and help me home." Max would take care of me. I let a small sob seep out of my lips. Alex was on the Planet of Love—too far away to hear my whine of misery. He lifted me to my feet. The slightest movement killed.

"Is there something wrong?" he finally asked. His eyebrows made accent marks of concern. I felt I might cry on his shoulder, but I was too manly.

I shrugged off his help. I could stand on my own two feet. "I'm fine."

"Cool!" he exclaimed. "I'll see you in an hour. Don't be late." He giggled like an idiot, waved goodbye, and jogged into the Brooklyn night.

I limped the four blocks home. Mr. Burpe, my ancient Irish landlord, was sitting in his regular post on the stoop. He lived in the apartment under ours. He sat at his post all day long, smoking Pall Malls. His wife, Mrs. Burpe, never left the house, except to scream at her husband for leaving her alone inside all day. I'd only seen her a couple times. A frightening sight with her thinning shock of white hair and balloonish orange housecoat, she avoids contact with humans—not that I'd seek out her company. But it was impossible to avoid Mr. Burpe. As I struggled up the stoop, he said, "You made a lot of noise up there last night. I told you about that noise. Mrs. Burpe needs her sleep or she's cranky the whole next day."

As demonstration, we heard her shrill voice come barreling out the open window of her apartment. "Is that her? You tell her to shut up or we'll call the police." I saw a shadowy form move inside their apartment window. I shivered from fear. She had wrinkles like other people have skin.

"I'm sorry about the noise," I said, "but if I don't

get upstairs in the next five seconds, I might throw up."

Mr. Burpe cleared the way, and I forced myself up the stairs. Otis dashed between my legs as I opened the apartment door. I had to twist slightly to avoid falling down. Oh, the pain of it all. Max sat on the floor, unpacking his boxes. We'd agreed to let each other take care of our own stuff. He was more than halfway done. I hadn't started. I could tell he was hoping I'd fall so behind he'd be justified in yelling at me about it. He looked up at me standing in the doorway. "Your fucking cat pissed on my sweater box," he said.

"Max," I said. "I love you." Then I started to cry. I'd taken a beating investigating this case. Despite my padding, I was pretty banged up and I needed someone to be nice to me. "Even parts of the massage hurt," I muttered.

His expression changed from annoyance to confusion. He gracefully bounded toward me. He put his arm around my shoulder. His skin was warm and dry. I'd sweated like a beer bottle all the way home. "You've got twigs in your hair," he said, kissing my face. He hugged me closer. I yelped. "What happened to you?" he asked. I told him about my hell day. The stiffness in my neck from sleeping on a stoop was getting worse. Max led me into the bedroom and slowly peeled me naked. I'd been naked twice today. My personal record was ten times. The night was young.

Max had me stand next to the bed. He sat on the edge of the mattress and gingerly felt up my rib cage. "Right here?" he asked, gently prodding the epicenter of my agony. I looked down between my jugs. A huge black splotch was painted across my middle. I nodded my head, tears gushing down my cheeks. He kissed the splotch. His lips were warm and soft. I felt protected. He said, "You've definitely got a bad bruise, but your rib isn't broken. You'll be sore for a few days."

Like he knew. "A bruise wouldn't make me feel like I'd been stomped on by the hooves of a million horses," I insisted.

"No offense, Wanda, but you've got the pain threshold of a gnat."

"You're saying I'm a wimp?" I asked, insulted. So much for feeling protected and secure. I turned around and tried to storm off into the sunset.

He grabbed me around the legs and eased me down on top of him. We rolled onto the bed. "I'm in no mood," I barked.

"That's unlike you," he said, nuzzling my neck.

"The next thing I know, you'll be telling me to quit detecting because it's too dangerous."

"Making you quit smoking was enough," he said. "But if you think it's too dangerous, then I'd support your decision."

"So you're saying I should quit?" I demanded.

Max rolled away and sighed. I hated his sighs. "Come on," he said, lifting me like Tarzan. He grunted. "Good thing I've been working out." I opened my mouth to bitch and he muzzled me with his tongue. "I'm just kidding," he said as he carried me into the bathroom. "You're light as a hundred-thirty-pound feather."

Max deposited my bruised and broken body in the bathtub. He knelt on the side and turned on the water. "Just relax," he said while lathering me. I leaned back against the cool porcelain. He rubbed a warm wet sponge over my legs and belly. The water level rose to my breasts. They bobbed like apples (C-cup apples, that is). I'd never been bathed before, by him or any other guy. I didn't mind.

"Dunk," he said. I eased down into the water, soaking my hair. Max rubbed shampoo into my scalp. My neck loosened with every stroke. He rinsed me off and wrapped me in a towel. I walked by myself to the bedroom and stretched out on the bed. Max followed me, his arm and chest dripping with soapsuds.

He lay down next to me. My agony had subsided to intense discomfort. I said, "Strip."

"I thought you were in no mood," he said, smiling. He pulled off his shirt. His chest was freckled and nearly hairless.

"I'm all wet."

"You just got out of the bath," he said.

"Lie down." He did. I climbed on top of him. We had careful sex, nothing too outrageous. I was thinking that I just might be in too much pain to enjoy this, then I came.

Max said, "There you go," and kissed my shoulder. By the time we finished, the night was black. We were already late to meet Alex and his new crush. "I'm hungry," Max announced.

"Conveniently, we've got dinner plans," I said. I rolled off him and started to get dressed. Max seemed baffled. "At Teresa's, with Alex." When he heard the name of the joint, he smiled and stepped into his jeans. Teresa's was the local Polish restaurant, specializing in pierogi—dumplings stuffed with potatoes, cheese, sauerkraut or meat. I have no idea what kind of meat. It's grayish and beefy looking, but tastes so good I don't ask.

We hit the pavement minutes later. I took a few

aspirin before we left. We made it to the restaurant by 9:30 P.M. Alex wasn't there yet.

We ordered anyway. Max got stuffed peppers and kasha. I got a bowl of borscht and an order of pierogi, extra fried onions, extra sour cream. Our food was just arriving when Alex walked in with his date. He made a beeline for our table.

I dropped my fork. Alex said, "Wanda, Max, I'd like you to meet Leeza Robbins."

6

Love Hurts

I've never really gone for any one type of guy. Uptight Wasps, short Jewish intellectuals, brooding tortured romantics—I've screwed them all. I think the reason why I fell so in love with Alex was because he threw me off balance by not fitting into any type. He drew on multiple facets (and possibly personalities). Max also had a quality I'd rarely seen in a man before: limitless patience—along with uncommon good looks. The only thing Max and Alex seemed to have in common was my attraction to them, and theirs to me.

When I saw Leeza walk up to our table, I realized that Max and Alex shared something else. Namely, their attraction to Leeza. She seemed as shocked as I was, staring numbly at Max with her mouth open. Max kicked me under the table. I kicked him back harder. He flashed me a warning smile and whispered, "Easy, Wanda."

"I can tell by your expressions that you're as struck by Leeza's beauty as I was when I first laid eyes on her this afternoon," Alex shared. "She's radiant. A shining light, beaming across the aerobics room and into my heart." It was hard for me to recall Alex ever waxing so poetically over my radiant beauty. I did get a few, "Ain't she cute?" to strangers on the street. I stared at him. Then her. I wasn't quite sure where to vent my spleen short of a hospital.

I knocked my chair back as I stood. "These are my men, Leeza," I announced loudly. So much for not making a scene. Max and Alex acted surprised to learn this. "And keep your grubby hands off them," I added.

Alex asked, "Why on earth would Leeza put her delicate, flowerlike hands on Max?" He said *Max* like a curse.

"Are you saying that Max isn't good enough for the flower's attention?" I asked.

Alex glared at me. "Well, maybe *I* am."

I retorted, "Once again, you know not from whence you talk out your asshole."

"The hell," he answered.

Alex and I began to circle each other like rams. Max sat patiently and watched. Seconds before we came to blows, Leeza squeaked, "Remember how I said I came to New York to see an old boyfriend? Well, heh, Max is the guy."

Alex froze midcircle. "About fucking time," I complained and drew up my chair to sit down, the legs screeching across the floor.

Max kicked me under the table again. I turned toward him. He whispered, "If you still want Alex, you can have him." He then folded his arms across his chest and looked away.

He'd totally missed the point. I'd been defending *his* vanity. I said to Leeza, "Don't worry—Alex has really cut down on his compulsive handwashing."

Leeza brushed hair off Alex's glowing red face. A strand of her bouncing blond hair spilled across her collarbone. She said, "Max and I dated for a while when I lived in Washington." She bit her pink lip. "It was years ago, Alex."

Alex considered this. "I don't think I'll be able to accept this tonight, but in time, I should recover from the shock and even find the humor in it."

"You'll be way ahead of me," I said. I already saw the humor in it, but I still might not recover. The fact that I'd slept with both of the most important men in my life (at different times, that is) wasn't always convenient. And if Leeza played her cards, oh, just about any old way later that night, she'd add Alex's notch to her hosebag. It was like having secondhand sex with Leeza. If Max and Alex did it, then the circle would be complete. I decided not to suggest it.

"The waitress should be here any second," Max said, obviously uncomfortable. He caught my eye. "Female waiter. Just waiter, Christ."

"Maybe we shouldn't have dinner together," I suggested. I went the spiteful and immature route.

"If you've got a problem with me, Wanda, then say so," Leeza challenged. Max waved his arm to beckon the Ukranian teenager.

I laughed. "I've got a problem with your kissing my boyfriend on the Promenade, with your dislocating my shoulder, with your blowing my best friend—and ex-lover—in the aerobics studio. And I also hate women with perfect bodies as a rule."

Alex was aghast. "She was not in the aerobics studio."

"Can you please try to get along? Wanda? Leeza?" Max asked the ceiling. That's where he was looking, anyway.

"Take your lesbian fantasy and shove it." That was me.

"God, you're being entirely unreasonable," protested Max.

"She can't help it," said Alex.

"She can learn to," countered Max.

"If someone doesn't start paying attention to me now, I'm leaving." That was Leeza. Alex immediately turned toward her and started stroking her arm. She stared at me the whole time with a slow smile on her face. She sure knew how to be a bitch. I like that in a woman, if I didn't hate her already.

Max finally flagged down the waiter and she gave Leeza and Alex menus. They read. I watched them examine the food choices and wondered how either of them would eat. For the hell of it, I kicked Max under the table. He looked up angrily, then smiled when he saw me kiss the air at him.

Alex and Leeza ordered a chicken cutlet platter with mashed potatoes and a green salad respectively. Max popped the last bite of his stuffed peppers into his mouth. I watched. He had a nice chew.

I said, "I'd like to say that Alex and I have no lingering romantic feelings for each other, and that he was a wonderful boyfriend, except for the fear of commitment problem. Not that you'd care."

Leeza smiled. "You'll have to excuse me if I seem tired. I didn't get much sleep last night." She turned to Max. "You didn't get much sleep either. You must be exhausted." She gave him a secret smile. I was now certain nothing happened between them.

"I am exhausted," Max said, clearly irritated by her.

"Wanda." Leeza turned toward me, her long neck

in a graceful stretch. "Alex tells me you're making progress investigating the murder at the club."

I glared at Alex. "Another thing about Alex. He's a pathological liar. But don't you worry. He only lies about important things."

Leeza bowed her blond head. She seemed perplexed and upset. Alex watched her in apparent amazement. He said, "Your hair is like a sunshine waterfall." I gagged inside.

Leeza seemed appropriately embarrassed, especially in front of a hostile stranger and her ex-boyfriend. All the bitchy spunk she could muster couldn't hide her loneliness. She must hate the fact that I would be hanging around her new job. And her new boyfriend. Tough, I reminded myself. Murder is intrusive business.

"So tell us about your day as an aerobics instructor, Leeza," I spurred. "I'm fascinated by jumping up and down." I realized after I said it that I'd sure lobbed an easy one out there.

Alex didn't take the bait. "I'm sure Leeza had a physically challenging day—which isn't intellectual, but neither is visiting a client in jail."

Max defended me. "For your information, Alex, Wanda had a physical day, if you know what I mean."

Alex responded, "So did Leeza, if you know what I mean." They squared off in their chairs, eyes locked. We all knew what both of them meant. I hadn't seen Max and Alex spar like this in quite a while. I wondered if it was for Leeza's benefit or mine. Their food arrived. I ordered tea.

I didn't want the night to be a complete ruin. I said, "Despite what you may have heard, Leeza, I am capable of overlooking people's faults to benefit a common good. The idea of you working on this case is growing on me"—like a fungus—"and I'm still at the information gathering stage at this point. Did you meet a guy named Freddie Smith at the club today?" I asked Alex, too. Leeza joined him in shaking her head. "About thirty-five. Mediterranean skin. Chubby. Goatee with sideburns. Bubbly butt. Meaty hands, soft skin." Max raised his eyebrows at that.

Leeza paused between munches on lettuce. She searched my eyes. I tried to hide my true feelings, but my emotions are as opaque as lead. She seemed to make some mental decision—to be nice and try to have a pleasant dinner, I supposed. She had manners which I hate. She said, "Freddie Smith? No bells. But I did meet a lot of people. Including the head aerobics instructor—Janey Johnson. She gave me a tour of the place when I got in after my morning at the convention. That's when I met Alex. During my tour of the weight room."

"And you were impressed with his bulging muscles?" I asked.

"Leeza, tell Wanda what Janey told you," Alex said with a drop of the mashed potatoes on his chin. I pointed. He brushed.

I held up my hand. "I want to hear about the bulging muscles."

Leeza laughed prettily at Alex's expense. "I was taking the tour," Leeza continued. "Just as Janey and I were walking past Alex on the bench press, he started to call out for help. He'd put too much weight on the bar. I spotted him, and one look at his struggling, twitching face was enough."

"And how much weight was that?" asked Max. He could bench press three hundred.

"Forget it," Alex protested. "Tell Wanda about the old man."

"One hundred twenty pounds, was it?" Leeza asked. She then kissed him on the cheek, which had turned maroon. "Strong muscles don't mean you have a big heart."

"How much was this old man lifting?"

Leeza flung an errant strand of her blond hair over her shoulder. The movement sent a whiff of her scent up my nostrils: Obsession. "He wasn't from the weight room. I met him later in the day. After the tour, Janey just mentioned to me that a nice gray-haired old man—must have been around seventy-five—would probably proposition me. He might even offer me money. She said he hits on all the new aerobics instructors."

I let Leeza take a bite of radish. "And you thought it'd be a challenge to fight him off?" I asked, not getting the point. Alex finished eating. He dipped his napkin in his water glass and cleaned his hands and mouth with it, a habit that always annoyed me.

Leeza said, "He came to my first class of the afternoon. He's in pretty good shape for a man his age—he couldn't jump much, but he tried hard. After the warm-up, he walked over to me and whispered, 'Meet you in the laundry room after class.' Then he poked me in the ribs and winked."

"The laundry room?" That was Max.

"On the spa level, behind the locker rooms," said Alex.

Leeza confessed, "I thought nothing of it because Janey said to ignore him."

"But I took it seriously because I'm a trained detective," crowed Alex. Leeza beamed at him. My gut lurched. "I staked it out for a couple hours after Leeza told me this story."

"You learn anything?" I asked dismissively.

"Yeah? What did you learn today, Wanda? How to pass out on a stoop?" Alex asked.

"Your hostility is a mask for your insecurity," I shared. "And, for your information, I learned how to pass out on a stoop years ago."

"As I was saying before I was so rudely interrupted," Alex said, "I followed this septuagenarian gentleman to the locker rooms after the class. We showered in adjacent stalls. Had a sauna at the same time. Dressed next to each other in the locker room."

"And he kept telling you to stop following him," I mocked.

"I was establishing a relationship," Alex defended himself. "And we talked. About the weather. About the price of real estate—and I must say that you guys have gotten yourselves quite a deal for Brooklyn Heights." I smiled smugly. Indeed we had. Our floor-through one-bedroom, with a tiny office alcove, costs only nine hundred a month. I realize that in Podunk, people pay as little as three hundred a month for a whole house, but we're talking New York City here.

Alex continued, "His name is Eric Van Owen. He's seventy-nine, but looks not a day over seventy-eight. A very forthcoming man. After five minutes in the sauna he told me about his unflagging sex drive and how this club is really the place to come for men who are looking for a certain kind of workout. I took that to mean exercise of a sexual kind. I knew this from all this incessant winking and poking."

"He's got a mean poke," Leeza said, nodding.

"If I wasn't so tough and rugged, I'd probably have a bruise," Alex said puzzlingly.

I made a puke sound. That got everyone's attention,

including our waiter who was busy getting rid of the plates. "Heimlich maneuver," she screamed with a heavy Ukrainian accent.

She tried to grab me around the middle. I said, "If you lay so much as one finger on my battered ribs, I'm going to suck your brains out through your nose with this straw." I held the straw up so she could see it. Her face turned as white as the Ukrainian winter and then she bolted, leaving some dishes and the check in her wake.

No one was quick to pick up the bill. I prompted Alex, "Just stick to what Van Owen said. Spare us the insight about your skin."

Alex nodded. He knew better than to argue after I've almost been touched by a stranger. "Van Owen said that the aerobics instructors were all very friendly at the club. I told him it was my first day and that I had found the one instructor I'd met—Leeza—to be a very kind and understanding woman indeed. The kind of woman I'd like to be my girlfriend." Afraid to make the puke sound again—I rolled my eyes as loudly as I could.

"After I said the girlfriend comment," Alex continued, "Van Owen laughed. He said he didn't think a nice boy like me would want any of the club's instructors as a girlfriend. He said they weren't exactly the type you could take home to mother. He went on to say that his mother had been dead for years, and that after three failed marriages, he's not interested in taking anyone home at all. He was interested in feeling young, staying in good health and in good shape. He poked me again in the ribs when he said that."

"This Eric Van Owen is basically saying that he regularly hits on the club's aerobics instructors to some success," I said. "That's what Janey said he'd try to do to Leeza. So what's the big shock here?"

Leeza jumped in. "I kept telling Alex I didn't think there was much to it. But if anything bothered me, it was the way he assumed I'd show up in this laundry room."

"Where Van Owen waited for an hour before he left, grumbling." That was Alex. "At first, I thought that he was just a little off his rocker to assume Leeza would actually show. I found it even more curious that this sixteen-year-old towel boy was also staking out the laundry room—I saw him hiding in the linen closet."

"Did he have an acne problem?" I asked, assuming that the kid who peeped on me was also peeping on Van Owen, or the promise of an impending date with an aerobics instructor.

"Not sure. I couldn't see him that well. The whole thing was like waiting for a shoe to drop. And then it occurred to me: Maybe Van Owen thought it was part of Leeza's job to meet him in the laundry room. He acted like he had it coming to him, for more reasons than his dashing good looks and sparkling personality."

"Like what?" asked Max. "He got no encouragement from Leeza. I've never seen anything suspicious in the laundry room."

"You hang out there, too?" I asked him. "This laundry room gets a lot of traffic." I turned to Alex. "What next? The line formed at the water fountain, waiting for a bevy of sweaty aerobics instructors to come along and offer blow-jobs as part of the cross-training circuit?"

"Is that so impossible to believe?" asked Alex.

"Completely," Max protested.

I considered this. Janey Johnson seemed like a

crafty wench. "I'll ask Ameleth Bergen about it tomorrow."

I didn't want to fill Alex in on all my activities—partially because other people were around (namely, Leeza) and partially because I was pissed off he was being such an ass. I thought about Jack. He was probably bouncing off the Detention Center walls by now. And Ameleth—hardly the grieving wife—had a ruthlessness about her. I liked that in a woman, too. "Yes, Ameleth and I are as tight as I am." Which is to say, pretty tight.

"Good," said Alex. "Here's the plan. I want you to get access, through Ameleth, of the membership billing computer files. I'll go through them and see what I can see." Alex was something of a computer geek. He wished he was more of one. The city was loaded (no pun intended) with wannabe geeks. I feared for the future of dating.

"And what might a computer break-in turn up?" I asked.

"I really don't know," Alex said snippily. "But perhaps we'll find out that Eric Van Owen is paying more dues than he should be, for services that aren't included on the brochure."

Max said, "Sex with aerobics instructors *is* in the brochure." He smiled.

I laughed—he was so cute when he was trying to be funny. To Alex, I said, "Better yet, why don't we ask Leeza here to keep a date with Van Owen in the laundry room and find out what will happen? He's an old geezer for Christ's sake. Surely," I turned to Leeza, "you could handle him."

"I think that's a dangerous position to put Leeza in," countered Alex.

"Then why don't you dress up in Lycra, and go meet Van Owen in the laundry room," I suggested.

"He already knows me," countered Alex.

"You're a slut," I said.

"And you—a whore," he said. We laughed. Max and Leeza looked at each other in bewilderment. I stopped laughing.

"I'll get you inside Ameleth's office," I said. "She's got a computer on her desk. A PowerBook. I'll keep her away and you can hack until your fingers fall off." Jack still had his key to the suite. I'd have to get it from Falcone. That should be a challenge.

"I *want* to rendezvous with Van Owen," whined Leeza. "I want to help." Her eyebrows tilted upward. It was obvious Leeza needed something to do. She wanted to make some kind of connection, to feel like a part of a team. The Western Athletic Club softball game must have filled up already. Her loneliness made me feel sorry for her.

But not that sorry. I said, "Forget it. You're like a tall glass of milk, Leeza. We need a shot of tequila."

"I'm begging, Wanda." Her blue eyes were really something by diner light. Okay, I decided.

"You want in, you're in. But one man's dead. Someone out there would probably kill again to keep from getting caught. We don't know who it is. For all we know, it's Van Owen himself."

She seemed to consider my warning, but said, "I'm fine with danger."

Max shook his head. "I'd rather you didn't, Leeza."

"You're the one who suggested it last night," I reminded him.

"That's because I knew you'd never go for it."

"It's unsafe for her, but just fine for me?" I asked.

"Wanda, it's totally different," Max protested.

"If Leeza got stabbed, it'd be worse than if I got stabbed?" I asked.

"In a way, yes." Max took a sip of water. I couldn't believe what I was hearing. "I'm not responsible for getting you involved in this business. But if Leeza got hurt, it'd be because of me."

"You're still in love with her, aren't you?"

Leeza and Alex's chairs scraped on the floor as they pulled away from the table. "We'll be going now," said Alex. He threw a ten on the table (not nearly enough to cover them, cheap bastard) and they left. I guess they were going to his place in the East Village. I turned back to Max. He was removing a twenty from his wallet.

"Wanda," he said as he dropped the money on the table. "I'm not in love with Leeza. One of the reasons why is because she could never handle what you're asking of her. She's not a strong person. And she'll get hurt. That isn't fair, and I don't think you should be so eager to put her in that position. It seems to me that you wouldn't mind if Leeza got hurt because that would probably get her out of my life and out of Alex's life, too. And that scares me about you." He had a point there. I didn't have a snappy comeback for an astute, negative observation of my character.

"Let's just go," he said and we split like a divorce.

I wasn't sure if I should be pissed off. On the one hand, I appreciated Max's respect for my abilities. On the other hand, how dare he act so nonchalantly about the possibility of my getting killed? Detecting was a dangerous business. I was, therefore, a dangerous woman. And did he care? Only when it came time to whip out a set of handcuffs for recreational purposes. On the other hand, if I got shot, he'd be alone. The specter of that should be so painful that Max might as well move to the Bottomless Pit of Denial. Santina, my surrogate mother over in Park Slope, told me that I should take it as a given that Max would prefer I wasn't a shamus. She said that he hasn't told me to quit out of respect. But I think that if he truly loved me, he'd tell me what he really wanted.

On the four-block walk home, I wondered if I should act apologetic or depressed. I went with accusatory. "The least you could do is wait up nights, frantic, sweating. Praying that I'll come home alive, or at least in big enough pieces."

Half of me hoped he'd say, "Big enough for what?" But instead he said nothing. Mr. Burpe wasn't on the stoop that late. I said, "Burpe managed to crawl back into his cave." An attempt at conversation, small-talky though it may have been.

He fit the key into our front door. "I do wait up nights, Wanda," he said. "I waited up last night."

"But not alone." I smirked. "You had company."

Max pushed the front door open and we walked up the stairs. "You're really beginning to irritate me," he said. The clunking of our shoes echoed in the hall. Otherwise, the building seemed quieter than usual. The octogenarian upstairs usually rattled around until midnight. I felt a prickle on the back of my neck. Something wasn't right here. And I didn't mean my relationship.

"Did you realize that you were talking down to me throughout dinner?" Max asked. "I don't need that. Especially around Alex." He unlocked our apartment door and pushed it open with a meaty fist.

Syd, Max's bathtub-dwelling tabby, raced past us into the hall. She's never even poked her nose outside the bathroom before. She cowered in the hallway, completely terrorized. Someone was inside. I felt a presence as cleanly as a shower. I reached into my purse for Mama. With the other hand, I pushed Max against the wall outside. I whispered for him to keep quiet. Then loudly, I said, "Shit, honey. I forgot to get tampons." They were the only things I could think of that someone in need could not live without for one minute. "Walk to the store with me," I said.

Recognition clicked behind his pretty green eyes. "Sure," he said, a little too loudly. "Let's go to the store."

"Leave Syd in the hall," I said, and pointed for Max to walk down the stairs. I followed him. We made a loud show by thumping our feet on the steps. We opened the front door and slammed it shut.

Once outside, I whispered to Max to walk to the corner deli and wait for me there.

Max whispered back, "The hell I will. I'm going right back up there and taking care of this. You, honey, are walking to the pay phone on the corner and calling the cops."

A voice out the stoop level window called, "I'm calling the cops if you don't shut up!" It was the croak of Mrs. Burpe. I flipped her the bird.

I whispered back, "I'm the one with the gun here, buddy. I'm the trained professional. My cat might be decapitated in there, for all we know. You will walk to the corner and let me handle this." I started toward the door, gun in hand.

A voice from the second floor window (ours) said, "I've heard softer whispers at the Grand Canyon."

We looked up. Leaning out our bedroom window was the man I knew as Freddie Smith. He'd seen me naked. "I'm sorry if I scared you," he called down.

"You told me to call you. The old lady who lives above you let me in." To Max, Freddie said, "I'm not a crazed rapist or anything. I just need to talk to Wanda."

"Then talk inside!" croaked the stoop window.

We went inside. Max grumbled all the way. He reminded me that he needed some sleep to succeed in the rough and tumble world of big banking. He said it with enough irony to be charming, but his annoyance was clear. If he didn't like the consequences of my work, he could just go to the next corporate Christmas party alone. I made a mental note to tell him this come December.

We found Syd hiding behind a radiator in the hallway. We left her there. Freddie greeted us as we entered our apartment. After making introductions and shaking hands, I said to Freddie, "Thanks for calling first." He shrugged. How rude.

"Maybe if I got a tip for the massage, I'd extend courtesies to you."

"How'd you get the address?"

"Brooklyn information."

I scowled menacingly. "Look, pal, I can melt steel just by thinking hard."

"No need to," Freddie said. "Everything in this apartment—including steel—has already melted. Haven't you people heard of air-conditioning?"

"Haven't you heard of chlorofluorocarbons?" I asked.

"Not really."

"I feel personally violated when anyone breaks into my place," I said testily. "If you don't have the juiciest hunk of dish this side of McDonald's, I'm going to have to hurt you."

"Can I have some water, please?" he asked. A bead of sweat rolled under his goatee. "You wanted to talk about Barney Cutler's death," he said. "And, after I get something to drink, that's what I'll do."

I looked at Max. He shrugged. I fetched Freddie a glass of water. Neither the glass nor the water sparkled. He took a drink. Then the three of us sat down in a row on my couch. It was a tight squeeze, and there was nowhere else to sit. Freddie looked around for a place to put his glass. Failing to find a coffee table, he settled on the floor. I checked the time: half past a cow's ass. I had to be up before nine to go see Jack in the slammer.

I said to Freddie, "How long do you think you're going to need?" He seemed puzzled. "I mean, are we going to be talking all night about this, or will it only be an hour or so?"

Freddie turned up his round nose. "I'm not saying anything at all with him in the room." He meant Max.

"I'm not leaving you in here alone with my girlfriend." I still love to hear Max call me his girlfriend. Other boyfriends, in my past, have introduced me by saying, "This is my . . . this is Wanda," which wasn't exactly reassuring.

"Max, boyfriend, darling. Go stand in the hall."

"I will not," he responded.

I leaned over to him and whispered my usual bribe: a blow-job for the entire episode of next week's "Seinfeld." Max muttered under his breath. He stood and fanned out his chest by drawing his arms back. He bore into Freddie's eyes with his own. "I'll be right outside," he said. "And if I hear so much as a hair grow, I'm going to kick your fat ass down those stairs." And Max could damn well do it, he didn't bother to say. He slowly walked to the door and closed it behind him. He probably had his ear pressed against the dead bolt.

"You know that spot you worked on earlier? On my back. Under my shoulder blade. It still hurts."

I pointed over my shoulder at the spot. Freddie rolled his brown eyes, and began rubbing. "I want you to know that the only reason I threatened you today was to scare you," he said. "I wanted to see if you'd talk under pressure."

"The only thing I do under pressure is cook." His fingers were divine. "And despite the fact that your fingers are like the golden rods of Olympus, I know that you're not a massage therapist. At least not in any official capacity at the Western Athletic Club."

"Janey is a friend," he said cryptically. "And I am a real massage therapist." He untwisted my muscle knot like a sailor. "The big lie I told you was that Barney and I were buddies."

My spine crackled under his palms. I said, "Ooh, that's good." I might have been too vocal in my praise. The apartment door slammed open. Max's impressive body loomed in the door frame.

"What's this?" he asked, seeing Freddie's hands at my back.

"An open exchange of information and ideas," I said. "And a little back rub on the side."

"Take your hands off her," Max demanded of Freddie.

Max hated to give me back rubs. The way he gets out of this boyfriendly duty is to squeeze my shoulder muscles too hard. I tell him to lighten up, and then he stops, claiming to be unable to please me. I said, "Either Freddie or you, honey."

"I think I hear Syd calling me," Max said and disappeared into the hall again.

Freddie stopped rubbing. "I don't feel comfortable with this," he said, staring at the closed door. "Maybe I should go."

"I know why you came up here. Besides the fact that I sort of invited you," I said. "Freddie Smith isn't your real name."

"I'm amazed," he said like he wasn't.

"Well?" I asked.

"Kruger," he said. "Freddie Kruger."

"I can see why you lied."

"Oh, I don't usually lie. But I didn't want you to know my name, depending on what you already knew about me in connection to Barney. And Smith was the first thing I thought of."

"Not Jones?" I asked.

"Okay, so it's not the most inventive. I'm a massage therapist, not an advertising copywriter."

I forced a smile. "I wouldn't have believed Kruger either."

"Few do. I'm president of a support group for people with negatively associated names. Vice President Daumer and Secretary Harding have it worse than I do."

"I'm sure." I checked my watch: late. "Look, Freddie, let's cut to the chase here. I know you're the scientist Barney and Ameleth commissioned to work on the chromium compound for losing weight."

Freddie looked perplexed. He said, "The what?"

"Like you don't know. Ameleth as much as told me it was you." Actually, Ameleth told me nothing of the sort, but I hadn't bluffed someone for information in hours.

Freddie shook his head. "Ameleth Bergen and I don't even know each other. I doubt she's ever laid eyes on me. Barney was the one I knew. He hardly even talked about Ameleth. And when he did, it wasn't terribly flattering."

I searched his eyes for a lie. He had to be the one. Why else would he be trying to figure out what I knew? "What is it you're so busy trying to protect?"

He thought for a moment. "What the hell is a chromium compound? Is it some kind of militant fat farm? Is this something one might consider to be a healthy investment?"

"Forget that," I said, almost convinced he had nothing to do with it. "Tell me all about you and Barney. And after we talk about that, I'd like you to step into my kitchen." Provided that I can unearth a sharp knife in this mess, I would ask him to demonstrate how quickly he could slice bread. I hoped Max wasn't bored out in the hall. I added quickly, "And I think Max should come inside now."

"No!" Freddie said. "I've seen him at the club. For all I know, he's a member."

"Of course he's a member."

"I mean a member of the club within the club," said Fred. I was confused. I hate it when that happens.

"Ah, yes," I said. "That club." I nodded knowingly.

"For the record, the whole thing was Barney's idea. He only recruited me to train the girls."

"And you trained them well, I hear."

"The art of sensual massage is my calling in life, Wanda," Freddie bragged.

"And that, of course, included a demonstration of how to kill someone by pressing their carotid arteries," I said.

"Well, that, too. But only in case a client gets out of hand. Sometimes hookers find themselves in the darnedest situations."

Did he say hookers? "You don't have to tell me."

"You were a hooker?"

"Once, long ago," I lied.

Max burst inside. "What?" he demanded. "Did I just hear you say you were a prostitute? I've gotten used to this detective crap, and I'm okay with the fact that you've slept with more guys that all of us can count on our fingers and toes, but I'm not sure I can spend eternity with a woman who used to have sex for money. I'm sorry, Wanda." Max sank down onto the couch, completely dejected.

I turned to Fred. "Would you excuse us for a moment?"

"Go in the hall?" he asked.

"If you don't mind."

Fred went in the hall. I punched Max on the shoulder and whispered, "What kind of moron are you? No, don't tell me. You're the moronic kind."

"Don't you turn this around," he said.

"I was trying to relate so he'd talk more. Jesus, you can be such an idiot. Do you really think I'd have sex for money? For jewels, a castle in France, my own talk show—maybe. But for money? Am I so crass? If you really think I could have, maybe you shouldn't marry me."

"Who said anything about getting married?" he asked.

"You did, asshole."

"I said spending eternity together—a completely different thing."

"So you'd join me in a suicide pact, but not in marriage?"

"You're losing it, Wanda. This time, you're really gone."

The fight continued. Freddie's knock was barely audible. Finally, he just walked back into the apartment and sat down on the couch. Max and I shut up. Freddie said, "You don't have to pretend you were a hooker. I want to clear my conscience of the whole sordid business."

"Then talk," barked Max. "Keep your paws off my girlfriend. And talk fast so you can get the fuck out of here."

Freddie nodded. His droopy chin sank. "Barney and Janey were running an aerobics instructor prostitution ring in the club." He cut to the bone. Alex was right. It'd hurt to tell him. "Barney was in charge of getting the clients. He'd mainly scope out the guys who came into his Cut Me store to buy protein supplements to make them more manly looking. He preyed on their insecurities, but it was good business. Janey was in charge of the girls. She'd teach them aerobics so they'd blend in and she'd schedule sessions in the laundry room—and sometimes Ameleth's office when she was out of town—with the members. The girls would give the guys a sensual massage—that's where my training comes in—and then whatever the client wanted. Janey kept tabs for each guy. They paid up in cash at the end of the month. This has been going on for about six months. Ameleth has no idea.

"I got a flat fee per girl for teaching massage," he said. "Janey and Barney were making seventy percent, the girls got thirty. Everyone was getting rich, but then Barney got killed. The only reason I was in the club at all today was to scope out the new instructor—Leeza Robbins. I think that's her name. Janey was going to see if she was game, and if so, I'd train her immediately. Janey is very committed to keeping the business going, and growing. Of course, she'll make twice as much money now with Barney gone."

Freddie found his glass of water on the floor. He sipped and smacked his lips. He continued: "And then you showed up. Janey wanted me to find out if you had any idea about the ring, so she set up the massage with the two of us. And let me tell you, Janey was pissed because nothing came of it. She doesn't know I'm here, by the way. I want out. I'm having a bout of conscience. Barney might have gotten killed over this. This Leeza seems like a nice girl, and I don't think Janey should pressure her into getting involved. Plus, well, let's just say that I don't know where Janey was at the time of the murder. The whole thing is getting too nasty for me. When we started, it just seemed like a lot of harmless fun."

The phone rang. Max went to get it. He said, "Hello?" Then he held the phone out. "It's for you."

I put the receiver to my ear. "Mallory," I barked.

"Falcone," said the phone.

"Detective," I cooed.

"Watson's escaped. I thought you might know where he is."

7

The Swamps
of Jersey

I took the cordless phone into the bedroom. Falcone said, "He's running, Mallory. I have to assume he's running to you."

I checked the closets. No Jack. Just a few suits. I also saw a piece of paper taped to my side of the hanger rod. It read: "Fill me." Max's little jibe to get me to unpack. "He's not here, Falcone," I said. "If you want to send someone over to make sure, go ahead." I checked under the bed. I found nothing but a dried hair ball.

Falcone said, "A cruiser should be arriving at your place in any second."

"Thanks for the warning," I said, "not that I need it." Max came into the bedroom and raised his eyebrows at me. I waved him back into the living room. He didn't move. I looked out the window. Sure enough, I could make out some flashing blue lights up the block. No siren. I mouthed to Max, "Get rid of Freddie."

Max whispered back, "Get Syd a teddie?" I rolled my eyes. I pointed into the living room. Max got it and left the bedroom.

"Mallory?" the phone asked. "What's going on over there?"

"Nothing," I said. "I had a cramp."

"Feel better?" she asked.

"Not really." Why had Jack done it? Running was like an admission of guilt. But guilty of what? Disturbing the peace? Big patootie. "How'd he do it?" I asked Falcone. The cruiser was on my block now, slowly swimming toward my building like a shark.

"He claimed to be having a claustrophobic seizure, and flung himself on the cell floor, twitching," she said.

A claustrophobic seizure? "I guess he needed his medication bad," I tried.

"Medication for a condition that doesn't exist," she retorted. "Jack did a fine job of scaring the guard to death. He threw himself into the bars. Bloodied his nose. Officer Martinez got backup, but when the guards entered the cell to restrain him, Watson karate kicked each of them in the solar plexus and then sprinted out of the Detention Center. He's fast, the guards tell me."

Assaulting police officers. Escaping jail. Jack was in bigger trouble than he could possibly imagine. I can see the *Daily Mirror* headlines now: Double Fault for Former Tennis Star. I hoped he was all right.

The buzzer *fzzzz*ed. "You'll have to excuse me," I said politely. "Some unexpected guests have arrived."

"They'll shoot first, Mallory."

"Just as long as they ask questions later," I said. "My landlord isn't going to like this."

"Too bad," she grunted. "For the last time, Mallory, stay out of this. Leave Ameleth Bergen alone. Her business doesn't concern you." Then she hung up.

I looked at the dead receiver. Had we been talking about Ameleth? I sulked back into the living room. Max sat on the couch, nervously stroking Otis. I cocked an eyebrow. He said, "Freddie's gone. What the fuck is going on here?"

"You didn't hear the buzzer?" I complained as I opened the door to let the cops in. Syd ran inside. I nearly tripped.

"First day with the new legs?" Max asked by rote. "And who the hell is buzzing us at twelve-thirty on a school night?"

"The Avon lady," I said. "Or your mother." The buzzer sounded again. "In a second," I yelled and ran downstairs.

There were two of them: uniform dunderheads with greasy hair and big necks. Freddie was nowhere in sight, so I figured he'd made it around the corner. I said, "I've just warmed the toddies. Come on in." They sneered.

Max and I stood in the kitchen while the cops combed our apartment. I didn't mind. A sweeping would have been better. The one with the hairy nostrils even checked the fridge.

I asked, "You ever hear of an ex-cop named Ergort?" This inspired squeaks of laughter.

He yelled to his comrade in the bedroom, "Hey, Frankie. This broad wants to know if we know an ex-cop named Ergort."

The cop called Frankie swaggered into the kitchen. He checked the fridge, too. He tittered with his buddy and then said, "Yeah, I know him. Scrawny wuss. Got beat up by a female perp and quit. Toothpick jerk-off."

I said, "The guy I know has boils bigger than you."

"Must not be the same asshole," Hairy said. He helped himself to a beer. "You got any Brooklyn Lager?"

"I keep cases of it down at the corner store," I said. They each guzzled a Rolling Rock. "So the Ergort you know was a real wimp?" I asked again. I found it hard to believe that there could be two ex-cops from Brooklyn named Ergort.

"You got any pretzels?" Frankie asked. I shook my head. He then thumped Hairy in the chest and said, "Nothing here." He turned to me. "We're not going far, so if Watson comes over here, he's dead." Then they left without thanking us for our hospitality. Well, they simply will not be invited again.

Max locked the door behind them. He seemed distracted. "Let's go to bed," he said. We counted two cats and then went back into the bedroom. Knowing that the cops had picked through our stuff made me slightly queasy. Or maybe I really was getting cramps. While we were undressing, Max said, "Break-ins. Visits from the police in the middle of the night. Is this what it's always going to be like?"

"I saw your cute sign in the closet."

"I hung it up there two days ago, Wanda." We slid under the covers. Max's skin was soft and warm, as usual. We spooned.

Max rolled away from me and onto his back. "So Watson busted out of jail and the cops came over here to look for him."

"I honestly have no clue where he is." Max sighed and put his hands behind his head. He didn't look sleepy. "You hate me," I said. He didn't say anything. "Just like you to not comfort me in my time of need."

He laughed at that. "Comfort is the last thing you need, Wanda."

"Are you saying I'm fat?" I asked.

Max rolled over to face me. He smoothed down my hair and kissed my forehead. "Jack ran because he's a murderer. Why else would anyone run? Find him and turn him in. This whole case is making me nervous. And now you've got innocent bystanders involved."

"Leeza," I hissed. I got a flash: Leeza strapped in a rack. I was standing in front of her, slapping her rosy cheeks over and over. I smiled.

Max watched me. He asked suddenly, "What's the name of the big account I'm working on?" I had no fucking idea. I felt a wave of guilt, which was exactly what Max wanted.

"The Isaacson account?" I tried. I remembered that it sounded Biblical.

Max smiled and hugged me. He said, "I want you to start unpacking this shit tomorrow. And this weekend, we're going away together. I don't care what reason you come up with to stay in New York. If I have to throw you over my shoulder and carry you, I will." I got another flash: Max, carting me like a sack of svelte potatoes, and throwing me down on a grassy knoll somewhere in New England. I kissed him on the knuckles.

He said, "By the way—it's the Jacoby account." We were quiet for a few minutes. Max started to snore in his familiar wheeze. I lay awake feeling like a heel. So I can be self-absorbed. But Max's banking stuff was a killer to feign interest in. I vowed to get up in the morning when Max did. I wanted to shower him with love and affection. And I needed an early start at finding Jack. I had no intention of turning him in. If he was guilty, I wanted to hear it from him. And then I'd skin him with a grapefruit spoon.

I woke up when Otis and Syd had a claw fight on my chest. I was happy to see that Syd was getting out of the bathroom more. Max's side of the bed was already cold. As cold as anything gets in June without air-conditioning. Time check: 10:30 A.M., Thursday morning. Shit, I thought. I missed cuddling Max by two hours. I tried to cuddle Otis, but she'd have none of it, being busy terrorizing Syd.

I took the cordless into the bathroom and called the precinct. I couldn't reach Falcone, but whoever answered the phone said she left a message for me: Watson was still at large. She also wanted me to come to the station by the end of the day or she'll hunt me down, too. Syd jumped in the sink while I brushed my teeth. I felt a kinship with her suddenly. I bent to kiss her little head, but got a blast of her breath. Have I mentioned that Syd has chronic gingivitis? Her mouth was ghastly. I wondered if it'd be better after a little Colgate brushing, so I dabbed some toothpaste on her orange gums.

She hissed, spit and scrambled out of the sink like her tongue was on fire. She darted under the couch in the living room. I found a flashlight and turned it on her. Her little orange lips were foaming with white lather. I would have laughed, except she took a swipe at me and caught me on the tip of my nose. It bled. I made a mental note to pick up a tube of poultry flavored toothpaste at the pet store.

I returned to the bedroom. I had to burrow in some boxes, but eventually I found a cute little sundress from French Connection that would go perfectly with my purple and blue bruises. My shoulder and ribs were still sore. I couldn't find any aspirin. I settled on a few snorts of tequila. I felt all warm and toasty inside. Then I split like a beaver.

The day was sunny. Good thing I wore a sundress. The subway ride to Manhattan was uneventful. My dress wasn't long enough to cover my butt when I sat down. Good thing I wore underwear. I wondered if I could contract any diseases from a subway seat, and then remembered that I was impervious to human strains.

The Number 4 train pulled into my stop—Grand Central Station—about twenty minutes later. I headed toward the Do It Right office in Times Square. A few early lunchers and late commuters sprinted around, fanning themselves with newspapers, trying to cool off and avoid staining their work clothes with perspiration. Along Forty-second Street, on the sidewalk bordering the Public Library and Bryant Park, vendors set up stands selling hippie beads, tarot cards, bootleg CDs and tapes. Three years ago, the only vendors in Bryant Park sold drugs and urine in bottles. The city spent a few million taxpayer dollars to clean the place up. And now, every spring—prime outdoor season—the city puts up big tents in Bryant Park to house the New York designer fashion shows. Of course, unless you're a designer, fashion mag editor or department store retailer, you can't get in to see them. That's what I love about Manhattan's public parks. Either you don't want to visit them, or you can't get in.

Despite my dress, not one guy made any comments along the ten-minute walk. With every year, the amount of street harassment I get drops. I find this puzzling because my breasts haven't. Dropped, that is. I stuck them out and walked the last half block to the

Do It Right office. A bum lay in his own spilled Boones Farm in the vestibule of my building. He said, "Nice stack."

I said, "Bless your alcoholic heart." I walked up the four flights of stairs to my office. I wasn't planning to stay long—just make a few calls, find out when the next bus left Port Authority Terminal for the Ikea outlet in Elizabeth, New Jersey. It'd be useless to use the phone to try and find Jack. If he had half a brain (even one-quarter a brain), he'd be long gone.

I reached my floor slightly breathless. If it wasn't for the broken elevator, I'd get practically no exercise at all. I was just about to fit my office key into the lock when I heard a small moan from inside my office. It didn't sound like one of the mice who lived there. Their moans were smaller and squeakier.

There was no sock on the door handle, so it couldn't be Alex with some chick. We'd made rules about this kind of thing: The sock was my idea. He kept a clean sheet in the filing cabinet. That was his rule: You had to replace or clean the sheet after every use. No problem for me. The few times I've had spontaneous sex on my desk, I've never thought to use the sheet anyway.

Another moan seeped under the office door. It didn't sound like Alex either. I palmed Mama and flung the door open.

Jack Watson was asleep on my desk, his shorts and T-shirt dirty from soot and sweat. His blond hair stuck to his forehead like yellow seaweed. His socks and sneakers were black with grime. Blood was caked under his nose and on his forehead. Despite the sight and the smell (bad), my heart thumped with relief. He was safe. Stinky, but safe. Then I reminded myself of the late-night visit from the cops and the utter stupidity of his breaking out of the joint. I slammed the door shut.

Jack started awake and fell off the desk. He looked up at me with sleepy, swollen eyes. He seemed totally dejected. I felt a wave of pity. I said, "You better have a lot more money hidden somewhere. My fee just doubled."

"The door was open," he said. "I didn't have anywhere else to go."

I closed the door behind me. The room got a lot smaller. I strode across the cigarette burned carpet and flung open one of the windows. The smells of melting asphalt and boiled hot dogs from outside was a relief.

"Aren't you impressed? I got out, Wanda," he crowed. He crawled onto his feet.

"Don't you dare sit down," I said before he lowered himself into the cushy arm chair I keep for clients, the one piece of furniture I actually cared about. He stood upright and grimaced. He put a hand on his back and stretched. "I couldn't take another minute in that cell," he said. "And you were supposed to bring the money back that night."

"Bathroom's at the end of the hall," I said. "Clean yourself up and leave your clothes in the Dumpster in the hall." I found Alex's sheet in the file cabinet under *B* for boff. I threw it at him. "And fuck you for blaming me. I was busy getting my ribs broken."

"You got in a fight?" He seemed concerned.

"Like you care," I said. "Go, before I call the cops." I searched in my desk for something Jack could wear. I found a pair of leggings—Gap black—and a T-shirt with tiny flowers on it from J. Crew. I also came upon a pair of rubber flip-flops I bought when Max and I went to Jones Beach one day last summer. I put sunblock on every inch of my alabaster (white, gleaming) skin, save for the tops of my feet. They got so sunburned that I couldn't put on my Vans without dying a thousand deaths. Jack might have a masculinity crisis, but these clothes would have to do.

While he was, I hoped, peeling off the top layer of his skin, I called for the Ikea bus schedule. We had an hour—perfect. Falcone would never look for Jack in Elizabeth, New Jersey. I'd keep him out of her clutches for the afternoon, but then what? Turn him in? Be done with him and this case? I flashed to the sight of his wild eyes when we found Barney in the Jacuzzi. Then Jack's heaving body when he hurled. I would figure out what to do with my fugitive later. In the meantime, I put $2,500 in my office file cabinet under *R* for retirement.

Jack returned from the bathroom with the sheet wrapped around his slender hips. His bare chest was dusted lightly with blond hair. I could have scrubbed my socks clean on his stomach. If I scrubbed socks. He lifted his hand to scratch his neck. I watched the sinew work in his arm. I said, "When's the last time you gave Ameleth an unsolicited back rub?" I handed him the clothes. "Or cooked dinner for her?"

He fingered my girly vestments. "I can't wear this stuff in public."

"Afraid for your fans?"

He seemed embarrassed. "I'm plenty romantic. Ameleth knows that. She just got distracted." I wondered how Ameleth could get distracted by Barney after seeing Jack near naked. But, I supposed, Barney's big money talk might pull green wool over anyone's eyes. I considered telling Jack about Barney's alleged pimphood, but reconsidered. Jack didn't top my list of people to share confidences with.

I fished around in my purse and gave Jack my pair of two-dollar Batwoman sunglasses. "Just get dressed and let's go. We don't have all day." I turned away from him. He went behind my desk to dress in semiprivate.

"I haven't heard you congratulate me yet," he said. "I was amazing in my escape, outfoxing those idiots at the police station. And once I was free, I ran and ran. Like the wind. I was loose, free, life in my blood. It's exhilarating to break the law. I recommend it. The only bad part was having to hide out under the Brooklyn Bridge for a few hours. I had to lie down in some sludge. The mile sprint over the bridge at midnight was heaven. No one was around. I felt like the last man on Earth. I hope you don't mind that I slept on your desk. You should really do something about that short desk leg." What about hitting him over the head with it? I mused. "Where are we going?" he asked.

"New Jersey."

"Good. No one who matters will see me in this getup."

Having grown up in the Garden State, I took this slight personally. "Would you rather we went back to Brooklyn Heights?"

I heard him groan. "Wanda, these leggings are too tight," he complained.

I turned to look. The sight made me think of bunches of grapes in Korean deli fruit stands. "All the better to see you, my dear." The T-shirt tugged across his chest, too. "You look like a tart," I commented. "It's Times Square, you'll blend."

The homeless drunk was gone by the time we got downstairs. No one commented on my dress or Jack's getup as we hailed a cab. We took it to Port Authority.

I was careful to get a receipt. We picked our way through the throngs of Hare Krishnas and deadbeats to the ticket buyer lines. Jack complained that he had to go to the bathroom. He went. I waited on line. Even for midday, the station was packed with people. A family of European tourists with rucksacks stood in a circle to my left. They were checking a subway map and jabbering in German. I estimated forty minutes before at least two of them were swindled—tourists were easy targets for scams. I turned to see how much progress my line made. Not much.

I turned back to the Germans. A couple of teenagers walked by. One skillfully squirted ketchup from a bottle on the back of the father's pants. The other one tapped the man on his shoulder and pointed to the stain. The father dropped his pack to examine himself, and the squirter snagged the bundle and ran. Needless to say, the other family members couldn't catch him with fifty pounds of miniature Empire State Buildings strapped to their backs. The old ketchup scam. I almost felt sorry for them.

A six-foot tall black hooker walked by just as the family was regrouping. The German jabber was loud and excited. Sensing something was up, she asked if she could help. The mother took one look at her nose ring and pretty pink dress, and spit on her candy-colored pumps. The hooker politely slipped off her shoe and wiped what she could on the mother's David Letterman T-shirt.

I smiled. I liked New York in June. Jack joined me on line just as the Germans slinked off, beaten, to the Roy Rogers on the corner of Forty-second and Eighth Avenue. "What's so funny?" he asked.

"You've got toilet paper stuck to your flip-flops." He actually checked.

Jack said, "I was propositioned in the bathroom. And I probably caught some disease from the urinal."

I sighed. Even I knew not to use the urinals at Port Authority. I thought of the long bus ride. Finally, our turn came at the ticket window.

They were only a few bucks each. I got receipts. I checked the time: too close for comfort. We had to dash to the gate. Jack beat me, even in his flip-flops. It was the middle of the morning on a weekday; the bus was nearly empty. The driver grunted good morning to us, and then gave Jack the fish-eye. I said, "What, you've never seen a former tennis pro before?" The driver ignored me. We took a seat in the back.

The ride took forty minutes. I asked Jack about Freddie Smith. He didn't know him. During our whole conversation, Jack sporadically tugged at the leggings. Two Upper West Side yuppie housewife types sat across from us. The one with the frost-job poked the one with the nose-job in the arm. Frosty then pointed at Jack as he wrestled with his package.

I asked him, "Remember when we found Barney, you got us drinks from that little bar fridge. You didn't happen to notice anything that didn't belong?"

"Like what?" he asked. "These tights are constricting."

"I don't really know. I guess I'm picturing a test tube or some pills."

"Nope, just the usual—beet juice and tomato juice."

"The leggings aren't the problem," I said. "But that dick of yours. We'll just have to do something about that. In fact," I continued, "just think. Once the operation's done, you can wear leggings every day." Frosty, who'd been eavesdropping, gasped.

"What operation?" Jack asked.

"Forget it," I said. The view out the window on the New Jersey Turnpike wasn't what most people would call God's country, unless smoke-spewing factories, polluted marshes (Jimmy Hoffa's final resting place), and the miles of shimmering tar highways were divine. The traffic was spotty, and the air-conditioning in the bus didn't quite filter out the sulfur smell coming from the Tuscan dairy factory outside. We passed the exit for my parents' old house in Short Hills. I hadn't been back since they moved to Florida five years ago. I didn't miss it. Elizabeth, our destination, was only a few exits away. I scanned the passengers on the bus again, looking for tails. Everyone seemed clean—or uninterested. Except, of course, for Frosty and Nosy, now fixated on Jack's incessant fiddling.

We pulled into the massive Ikea parking lot at high noon. The tar moved under my feet as we walked toward the squat, turtle-shaped, blue-and-yellow warehouse. I had the Bjornskinki knife in my purse. I hoped that there weren't hundreds of weirdos like Alex who'd special order bread knives from Sweden. Jack caught some stares from the strictly suburban crowd. The cityfolk usually just come out on weekends.

A kid, maybe nineteen, in a blue apron with the store logo slapped across his chest approached us when we entered the store. He said, "Hello! I'm Branford." He smiled, revealing shiny new braces with rubber bands. I grimaced. Branford kept on grinning despite his metal mouth. He was perkier than my breasts. Not an easy trick.

"Cutlery," I said, hoping he'd just point.

"Kitchen utensils are on the main floor. But you'll have to walk through living room and office furniture

studios to get there." A nice technique. In the event
that I was pining for, say, a coffee table or a new desk,
I couldn't help but pass by.

"Do you deliver?" I asked Branford.

He was staring at Jack, who grew uncomfortable
with the attention. "Yes," he mumbled. "Bedroom
furniture is on the second floor."

Jack said thanks to the kid and turned to go.

Branford frowned. "Pardon me, sir. Don't I know
you from somewhere?" Jack shook his head. A crackling fuse went off behind Branford's eyes. "Yes!" he
almost screamed. "You're Little Jackie Watson. I can't
believe this. You're my idol! I've had posters of you on
my walls for years." He paused, smiling radiantly.
"I've spent hours fantasizing about meeting you. And
to see you now," Branford said, beaming. "Dressed
like this. It's like a dream come true."

"A wet one," I whispered to Jack.

"That's very nice," Jack said to Branford. He put
his arm around my shoulder and steered me away.
Our pace made me glow. I had forgotten that Jack
really was a celebrity. He said, "That kid was trying to
pick me up."

"Were you tempted?" I asked.

"Of course not!" he cried. "He thinks I'm gay
because of these stupid clothes. I knew this would
happen."

I grabbed an oversize cart like everyone else, and we
wheeled it inexpertly along the cart track painted on
the floor. There was a wide selection of wood
furniture—the kind I like. Jack seemed impatient
with my stop-and-go search for a coffee table. At one
point, he hid behind a big red leather couch. I said,
"It's not that bad."

"Have you ever known the pressures of celebrity?"

"So you'll be outed in Elizabeth, New Jersey. That is a sorry fate." I was heavy with the irony.

Jack fumed. His anger rose from his head in waves. "Why don't you just shut up?" It occurred to me that the day in jail might have unhinged desperate Jack. He skulked off down the path marked on the floor with two bright yellow lines. I had to push the cart at a good clip to catch him.

But a vision in oak stopped me and my cart dead in the track. It had short lathed legs and a thick hunter-green stained top. I whipped out my mental tape measure and estimated that it would fit quite nicely in my living room. The price tag read two hundred dollars. Dirt. I sat on the table. I lay down on it. It was big enough for our purposes. I closed my eyes to imagine it. I opened them to see a small gathering of people looking down at me. Branford broke through the crowd.

"Ma'am," he started. "Are you ill? Do you need a doctor?"

Only months ago, I was generally called Miss. "I tripped over this table and hurt myself," I tried for a discount. "I hope I won't have to sue the store for damages."

Branford's lips tensed. "Where exactly does it hurt, ma'am?" he asked.

"My ankle," I whined, lifting it up for his inspection. The crowd started to disperse. Good, I thought. Better to work on Branford alone.

"It looks okay," he said uncertainly.

Jack came sprinting toward us, leaping over tables and shopping carts like a blond panther. He was a stunner in motion. Branford noticed, too. He dropped my ankle with a thud.

Jack stopped on a dime. He said, "Wanda, you've got to come quick."

"What?" I asked, seeing the excitement in his eyes.

"Just come on." Jack snagged my wrist and pulled me to my feet. I tried to pretend my ankle was tender, but it was no use. We rushed up the ramp to the next level. Jack told me to shush, and led me beyond stacks of plastic colanders and salad bowls to the cutlery section.

We were safely hidden behind boxes of two-hundred-piece starter sets before I asked, "What's all the excitement? Forks on sale?"

"Look." Jack pointed, careful not to let his finger protrude farther than the boxes of lobster steaming pans. I followed his finger. Two women were talking at a counter. One woman's back was to me. She had straight brown hair and a tight ass in jeans. Her tank top showed off the taut back of her arms. The other woman, behind the counter, had a fluff of gray hair piled high on her wrinkly head. She was punching keys on a computer and nodding. She groped for something on the counter without looking away from the computer screen. Her free hand held aloft a shiny, sleek object that reflected the track lighting: the Bjornskinki bread knife.

Grandma examined the knife and punched a few more keys. "We already knew they sold the knife here, Jack," I chided.

"Look at the customer," he said. As if on cue, the thin brunette picked up the knife herself and tested the serration on her thumb. She turned profile and made an abrupt chopping motion, splitting the air. Jack drew in his breath so loud that the brunette turned in our direction.

"Molly," I whispered. The waiter/drug pusher from the Slimmy Shack.

"She must be the killer," Jack decided. "Let's get her!" He took a running step. I stuck out my foot to stop him. He fell on his face, cracking my sunglasses. All the customers within earshot jolted at the sound. I dragged Jack back behind the boxes by his flip-flops.

"Billy," I said loudly. "Stop climbing on the woks." It was a terrible cover. Molly would spot us now for sure.

After a few seconds, I dared to take another peek. I breathed out when I saw her back. Grannie finished processing the order. Molly took her receipt and left. I wondered briefly if I looked that good going. I doubted it. A wave of insecurity swept over me like brushfire. I reminded myself that it was unZen to compare myself to others.

I said to Jack, "You okay?" He grunted. I helped him to his feet. I squared him off to face me and said, "Tell me I'm a babe."

He said, "I've got plastic in my eye."

"Are you saying I'm fat?"

Jack did a double take. "I'm saying nothing except that if you trip me like that again, you're fired."

I turned away in frustration. No wonder Ameleth wanted to divorce him. The computer lady had left her post and was helping another customer. I checked to make sure Molly was gone and went over to see if the computer information was still up on the screen. It wasn't. I stepped behind the terminal to try and call it up.

"Excuse me," someone said. I smiled and turned. It was Grandma. I pulled the murder knife out of my pocketbook. Before I got a chance to ask her if it was the same knife, she screamed. Maybe I shouldn't have held it over her head like that. I tried to calm her down, but a small crowd gathered. I hoped there weren't any hero types nearby. I dropped my knife hand and started protesting my innocence.

"What now?" boomed the now-familiar voice of Branford. "Put that knife down!" I dropped it on the floor. Branford picked it up, adding perhaps the hundredth set of prints to the handle. He looked around for Jack. I didn't see him either. Fuck, I thought.

Branford said, "It's okay, people. Nothing's wrong." He squinted at me. The crowd dispersed. This was probably the most thrilling shopping day in Branford's history at Ikea. I said, "I'm not going to make any sudden movements."

Branford slapped the flat blade against his palm. "I think I'd better call the manager."

I said, "Only if you want to see my gun, too." The older woman swooned. Branford's face turned white.

"What do you want from us?" he begged. "We're just simple nonviolent wholesalers."

"You recognize this knife?" I asked Grandma.

She took the blade from Branford. She inspected it and nodded. "It's the same one," she said, and pointed at the sample Molly'd just handled. She gave the knife back to me. I buried it in my bag.

"You have to order it from Sweden, right?" I asked.

She nodded, and then finally said, "It's made with a top-secret Swedish method of tempering metal. It's very expensive—three hundred dollars for this one knife. The whole set costs over a thousand." I wondered where Alex got that kind of money to chop vegetables. Then again, he wondered where I got the money to buy Donna Karan cashmere socks.

"I need to talk to Branford alone," I said to

Grannie. That was fine with her. She scooted over to the shower curtain display in two seconds flat. "I need a record of everyone who's special ordered this knife, or the accompanying set in the last year," I said to Branford.

"Or what?" Branford asked, regaining some composure.

"Or I'll shoot to kill that ceramic pasta server."

Branford seemed confused. He said, "You're a cop?"

"A lawyer," I lied, thinking that more threatening.

"Perhaps we should discuss this in the store manager's office."

"Fine with me," I said. "I'll be sure to mention to him or her that you practically drooled all over my client—Mr. Watson. I'm sure your manager will appreciate the personal interest you show in your customers."

Branford swallowed hard. He growled a bit and stalked behind the counter. He hit some buttons on the computer, and in a few seconds, paper started spinning out of the printer. "This is a personal favor from me to Jack."

With the info in my hand, I said, "Branford. I think Jack might really like you. He thought you were cute. I'd watch that phone." I winked. Branford nearly fell off his feet. I giggled as I walked away. There's no greater torture known to man (and woman) than waiting by the phone.

Jack was in the plants section, behind a large ficus tree. We had what we wanted and we were leaving. Jack complained that Molly was in the lamps section and we could take her down on the Oriental rugs if we acted now. I told him if he wanted to walk back to New York, that was fine with me.

We caught the 1:00 bus back to Port Authority. Jack dozed on the ride. I wasn't sure if we should go back to Brooklyn Heights or try to contact Alex from my office. Jack wanted to sneak back into the club to find Ameleth. He wanted her to know he was all right. I overruled that suggestion. I promised we'd hit the Herman's sporting goods store on Forty-second and Sixth so he could get something to wear.

While Jack napped, I checked the printout from the Ikea computer for any familiar names. The only two I recognized were Alex Beaudine and Molly Mahoney. I wondered why Molly would want to kill Barney. Was there a connection? Jack stirred and then settled. I tried to picture it: Molly, gripping the handle like a lover, slamming the knife into Barney's chest. Her thin-lipped smile and big plans of paradise. I shook it off. I dosed myself. Visions of coffee tables danced in my head.

We made it to the Herman's all right. Jack took a few pairs of parachute material sweats into the dressing room. I hung around the discount Rollerblades racks for a few minutes, then wandered over to examine the skiing equipment. What was keeping him, I wondered. Sporting goods had little appeal to me, except for the cool goggles. After a few more minutes as Superfly, I got a bad feeling. I barged into each dressing room. In the last was a shoplifter stuffing a baseball glove down his pants.

Jack was gone. I ran out of the store and into Forty-second Street. The sun made distortion waves. The bright light blinded me. I wished I had my Batwoman glasses, even broken. I thought I saw a blond man running toward the subway. I ran for the train, too. I hopped on the Number 2 bound for

Brooklyn. I got off at the Clark Street station—only two blocks from the Western Athletic Club.

Ergort stood outside like a cigar store Buddha in blue bike shorts, breathing hard like he'd just pumped some major iron. He had a golf ball-size boil on his cheek. I tried to get around him, but he stopped me. "I got instructions to keep you out."

"From whom?" I demanded.

"Who cares?" he grunted. His arms hung from his shoulders like sides of beef.

"I care or I wouldn't have asked. And obviously you care, or you wouldn't be following the orders." My logic dumbfounded him. His eyes went from comfortable and calm to raging in seconds. "You don't, perchance, suffer from violent mood swings?" I asked.

Ergort's boil throbbed.

I said, "I see you've not quite mastered the art of conversation. Now, if you'll excuse me, I've got an appointment."

Ergort took a step toward me. I got the idea that he'd very much like to introduce my face to the brick facade. Two men in tennis shorts walked up the street. They smiled at Ergort as he held the door open for them. I smiled wide and slipped an arm around one of the men. He nicely escorted me across the threshold. I was in. I wouldn't love facing Ergort when I had to come out. I'd worry about that later.

Janey was at the reception desk. I said, "Janey. How's tricks?" I saw her give Ergort the okay sign. He ducked back outside.

Janey smiled sweetly and said, "You're not supposed to be here. The police are periodically checking the club. Detective Falcone asked that we keep you away for a while."

"Jack hasn't been caught, then," I said. "Not that

you'd turn him in." We stared at each other for a second. She broke the gaze by putting her foot on the counter. She stretched.

"I hear you had a talk with Freddie Kruger last night," she dared.

"We discussed the finer points of sensual massage." I leaned forward to see if the upstairs key was hanging from its peg. It was. Ameleth must have returned it.

"You and Freddie talked about some business matters of mine," Janey said, her head resting on her kneecap.

"You mean how you're the Aerobics Madam?" The elevator dial blinked five, four. It was coming down. I could grab the key and run for the elevator just as the door opened. "Is Ameleth upstairs?" I asked.

Janey switched legs. "Don't involve her in my business. She doesn't know a thing about it."

"Nevertheless, I need to talk to her."

"She's not here." Janey lifted her chin and looked me straight in the eye. "Special discount this week for private detectives who know too much. Six-month membership. Free." The elevator dial blinked, three, two. Janey was too twisted in her stretching position to try and stop me.

I said, "You're pretty funny, Janey. But looks aren't everything." The doors opened. I grabbed the key and made a run for it. The mirrored doors closed just as Janey flung herself against them. I fit the key in the hole, thinking briefly of Max, and whizzed to the top floor suite. I wondered why the cops weren't at the club waiting for Jack. I also wondered how he could get into the suite without a key (unless there was a key I didn't know about).

The elevator doors characteristically whooshed open. Jack sat on the white couch, his head in his hands. The leggings I'd given him were ripped at the knees. Tiny dots of blood were congealing around scrapes on his legs. I said, "The cops are coming." I wondered how he managed to slip into the club during Ergort's watch.

He looked up. The expression on his face was grave. "It's happened again, Wanda."

At first, I had no idea what he meant. Then he gestured with his head toward the Jacuzzi room. I swallowed hard and walked toward the door. I heard none of the gurgles of swirling water. I held my breath and stepped inside.

The lights were on, but at first I didn't see anything. I had to go farther into the room to peer into the tub. With each step, I saw more of the picture. First, a naked ankle, then a leg (attached), a torso. The body—clothed in a leotard and short shorts. She rested on the bottom of the drained Jacuzzi. Her cheeks were blue and swollen. She'd clearly been beaten. My blood turned to slush. I could feel it thicken and struggle to push through my heart.

It appeared Leeza Robbins would never step-aerobicize again.

8

~

Dead Meat

I made my second 911 call in as many days. Then I went back to look at Leeza. She lay motionless in the bottom of the tub, her legs bent at the knee to follow the curve of the Jacuzzi. I touched her throat. It felt warm. I checked for a pulse. Faint. She was still alive but not breathing. I climbed over Leeza and into the tub. I gulped down some of my own breath and bent down to give her mouth-to-mouth. I had to do this to Max one time—he didn't mind.

Leeza's mouth was softer and she had no upper lip hair. I sucked wind in and out of her lungs until I felt a nugget of something hit the back of my throat. I swallowed hard. Leeza's mouth parted slightly and blood trickled from the hole in her gums where her front teeth used to be. I made a mental note to watch for the passage of Leeza's tooth. Despite the gruesome trickle, at least she seemed to be breathing. I'd never be jealous of her sunny smile again. I sat by the edge of the Jacuzzi and cried.

For about half-a-second. Then the wheels kicked in.

What could have happened? Leeza either (1) walked in on something, (2) got walked in on, or (C) didn't know what hit her. Her bruises looked like she'd been pummeled unconscious. I didn't think she was tortured. Just knocked out and dumped in the Jacuzzi. That was the bright side.

Good thing I was not a self-absorbed person or I'd be blaming myself for this. But in my advancing maturity, I knew enough to blame Alex. He was the one who got her involved. I went back outside into the exercise room. Jack sat on the white couch and tugged absentmindedly at his leggings. I slapped him across the face. "What was that for?" he demanded.

"Now my engagement is off," I said.

"I didn't know you were engaged!" Jack said like he was happy for me. "That hurt, Wanda."

"She's alive," I said. "For the moment." I flashed to the times I wished she'd drown in a vat of boiling schmaltz. It was just a whimsical fantasy, I told myself. I never really wanted her to get hurt.

Jack cupped his cheek calmly. "Is this just incredible bad luck, or does disaster precede my every step? My whole life has been spent stumbling from one foible to another. I should make the world a better place and crawl under a rock and die."

I wondered how he had gotten from "it's all my fault" to "kill me now." I said, "Don't flatter yourself, Jack. Your weight to the cosmos is about the same as a snail." I was in no mood to reassure him. "Why'd you come back here after I told you not to?" I asked.

"No reason."

"Stop lying." He looked at me, all wet eyed. "You came up here for a reason, and I want to know what."

"I thought Ameleth would be here."

"Stupid, Jack." I was losing patience. The cops and

paramedics would be here in seconds, and I didn't want to be around when Falcone got a look in the Jacuzzi. I grabbed Jack by the collar of my flower T. "You came here looking for something important." The missing drugs? The hidden formulas? Top-secret beet cocktail recipes?

"A cigarette, really," he said. That *was* important. "I've been so stressed out," he continued. "I really needed one. I'd have bought a pack, but you didn't give me my money."

I slapped him on the other cheek. It felt swell. I said, "Don't move." I left him on the couch and went into the office to hunt in his desk for the stale pack of Marlboro Mediums. Just hearing the word *cigarette,* I felt every pore of my body scream for a drag. The sound was deafening.

Ameleth's office was in order. I half expected to find the computer on her desk humming or clothes strewn everywhere. If I had to bet, I'd say Leeza never even stepped foot in this part of the suite. I wondered if she was beaten somewhere else and deposited in the tub. But it looked like she'd been pushed in there. Assuming the murderer and Leeza's attacker were the same person, then he or she might have a literary inclination toward circular structure. I respected that. I walked behind the partition to get to Jack's cubicle. Squeezing past the school teacher desk, I opened the bottom drawer. I remembered from before that it stuck. I gave it a good hard yank. The drawer popped out, sending me crashing into the cork wall. It shook, but didn't fall. The contents of the drawer spilled all over the golden carpet. I saw a seep stain. I lifted the drawer. The bottle of Bajan brandy lay in pieces underneath it—the metal rollers on the drawer bottom had smashed the glass.

I slurped up what I could and hunted through the rest of the drawer's spilled contents for the pack of cigarettes. Under a stack of press clippings on Little Jackie Watson, tennis prodigy, I found the crumpled soft-pack. All the cigarettes were broken in half. A book of matches was tucked into the cellophane. I fished out the longest butt and lit it. The smoke swirled around my tongue like cotton candy. Stale cotton candy, but just as well. I looked at the mess I'd made. Ordinarily, I'd say fuck it. But the cops would see it and Falcone would think the batterer had rifled Jack's desk. I took a long drag. I carefully picked up the chunks of broken glass and threw them in the drawer. I scooped the papers and pens back in, too. I started to put the drawer back on its rollers.

That's when I saw a green spiral notebook masking-taped to the bottom of the top drawer of the desk. This had caused the jam. I ripped it out and flipped through. Page after page was covered with practically unintelligible scrawl, but I took chemistry in junior high. I knew scientific formulas when I saw them. I shoved the notebook under my sundress. I fitted the bottom drawer back into the desk and I ran into the exercise room. Jack was taking a hike on the treadmill. "Nothing like that good old endorphin rush to make you forget about your troubles."

"Is there no way out besides the elevator?" I asked.

"Not unless you want to take the fire escape," he said, pointing toward the office.

I did. I grabbed my purse, instructed Jack to say he's the one who called 911, and that he'd been waiting here for the ambulance all by himself. I dashed back into the office. The windows faced the front of the building. If I tried the fire escape, any passerby could see me. I crossed my heart-bra, and flung open the window. No time to wait. Falcone's cruiser would be barreling down the road any second.

The black iron planks pinged as I stepped onto the fire escape. I made my way down the five flights as quietly as possible, but the iron bars clanged if I went too fast. I eased around each floor's windows as I passed. I didn't want someone from the inside to see me either. Fourth floor—stationary bikes, step machines, treadmills and aerobics. The room I saw from my perch was full of huffing women (and one man: a geezer, maybe the horny bastard, Van Owen). They had their backs to me. The instructor faced the windows. She bounced something fierce. Her sports bra had clearly lost its snap. I waited for her to do a complicated move and darted past the window.

Third floor was weight room and nautilus. No problem there—the men in the room were far more interested in their own reflections than in some chick in a short sundress on the fire escape. Second floor, racketball and tennis courts. I got a peek into one court. A man and woman smashed the little yellow ball back and forth over the net like they hated it, or each other. I walked casually across the landing, knowing this couple had other things on their minds. One more flight, and I could jump to the street, make a run for it, and . . . shit. That's when I realized my jam. If I jumped, I'd be dropping right into Ergort's gargantuan arms. That wouldn't be a smooth landing. I checked the windows on the second floor—locked. I climbed back up a flight. The third-floor window was open. I climbed inside.

After a graceful spin, I hopped daintily off the windowsill into the free-weight room. I knew how dainty by watching myself in the room's floor-to-ceiling mirrors. There was barely an inch of available self-admiration space, what with dozens of large-shouldered men staring at their triceps in midflex. I dusted myself off and headed out toward the stairs. Maybe I could get down that way, without bumping into Falcone on the way up. How I'd get past Ergort once I hit the lobby was another problem.

"Watch out, lady!" barked a thirtyish man in yellow bike shorts as I walked by. I hadn't gone anywhere near him—he obviously had an inflated idea of how much space he took up. The shock of his bark made me drop the notebook. The guy bent down to pick it up. For all I knew, he was after the damn thing himself. I kicked him in the shin. He stood upright and apologized. I whisked up the notebook. The man nervously smiled. He acted like he wanted my attention. I could still suck them in like a vortex.

I turned to go. In the hallway, I noticed a couple guys in blue run by. Shit, I thought. I had to wait. I stood back in the corner and watched. The guy who tried to touch my notebook was spotting another man—blue and red shorts, white T-shirt—attempting to bench press what looked like ten thousand pounds. The man struggled under the weight. His arms shook violently, and his mouth was turned into a ghastly grimace.

The spotter said, "Your mother wears army boots. You're the biggest pussy alive. You're a faggot, you hear me? A flaming faggot." The man under the weight suddenly lifted the bar and straightened his arms. He tried to smile while his face contorted uncontrollably. Once he'd balanced the load on the bench press bar holders, he sprang off the seat and the two men bashed heads. Then they high-fived and thumped each other in the chest.

Male bonding was an ugly business. The coast

seemingly clear, I made for the door. As I dashed out, I heard someone say, "Hey, babe. Those are the biggest pectorals I've ever seen."

I turned to give the guy the finger. It was Alex Beaudine, pumping his scrawny legs on a Soloflex. His calves were pale. Small rings of sweat stained his white T-shirt. He looked happy. I felt a pang of regret. I should tell him about Leeza before someone else did. I went over to him and put my free hand on his shoulder.

"No touching in the weight room, Wanda, jeez." He shrugged off my hand and looked around the room.

"What, these idiots will think you're a pussy if a girl touches you on the shoulder, but it's acceptable for two guys to tweak each other's breasts in admiration?"

"Don't be a turd," he said. "You just don't understand the code of macho." Alex bore down, grimaced, and lifted about thirty pounds with his legs. "You should see how much I can lift with my middle leg," he added.

"Alex, look. There's something I've got to tell you." My tone must have convinced him to pay serious attention. He knew my tones.

"What happened?" he asked gravely.

Just then a man in sweats ran in, puffing excitedly. He yelled to the whole room, "The cops are here! And an ambulance! I heard them talking in the hallway—some woman got in an accident. She was hurt bad."

The man who'd benched ten thousand pounds said, "An accident? Maybe I can help."

The first guy said, "Are you a doctor?"

"I'm a lawyer."

"You'd better come quick."

The men ran from the room. The other slabs of beef

returned to their preening, grunting and cursing. Alex gripped me by the arms and said, "Where's Leeza?"

I didn't say, "No touching in the weight room." Instead, I said, "She got beat up. She's being taken care of. We can't help her unless we get out of here right now."

"I want to go to her."

"She's unconscious. She won't even know you're there."

He struggled to decide. I didn't give him a choice. I snagged a handful of his shiny brown hair and dragged him out of the weight room. I checked the hallway for 5-0. We took the fire stairs down three flights to the ground level. Along the way, I asked Alex if he knew why Leeza went up to Ameleth's private office suite.

"I have no clue," he said, distressed. "The last we spoke—a couple hours ago—she agreed to just do her classes, look and listen, but to do nothing undercover. Maybe she saw or heard something relevant." I hoped she would remember what it was.

We exited the stairs on the first floor. After a quick right turn, I told Alex to stop. There was only one safe way out. We ran a few more steps. I peeked through the Slimmy Shack's glass doors. I needed to have a conversation with Molly Mahoney anyway. I pulled back the dangling strands of Swedish ivy and took a good gander. Alex said, "For God's sake, Wanda. This is no time for a snack."

I waved my hand to get him to shut up. I didn't see Molly. Maybe she had the day off. I whispered, "The head waiter here just might be the one who forgot to remove her Bjornskinki bread knife after she stabbed Barney to death with it. Jack and I saw her out at the Ikea in Elizabeth ordering another one."

Alex considered that. "Is this the woman who gave you the tussle?"

The tussle. Max gives me tussles. Molly gave me a trouncing. "One and the same," I said. Just thinking about it made my ribs ache. I was pretty sure Molly hadn't seen me and Jack at Ikea. But Jack was hardly discreet. I needed to be sure she wasn't there. I said, "Alex, go into the restaurant and find out if Molly's around. If she is, restrain her. She's got long shiny brown hair and skinny runner's legs."

"You think she's the one who hurt Leeza?" he asked. I had no idea, but after tangling with her myself, I knew she could inflict major damage. "So help me," Alex sputtered, "if she's the one responsible, she's got some bad karma coming her way."

Harsh words from my pacifist friend. "Just find out if she's around." The emergency exit in the kitchen was our only way out of the building. I groped my dress to hold onto the notebook and sent Alex off with a pat on the glute.

Through the cube-glass doors, I could make out the distorted form of Alex moseying toward the counter. I wasn't sure if the man behind the counter—the one standing next to the giant beet juice circulation machine—was Larry the Jehovah. He was tall like Larry. My attention was diverted when I heard a scream. A tray full of dishes clanged and crashed to the floor. I dipped my hand into my bag and ran inside, Mama palmed and ready.

What I saw: Alex lying on top of a woman who had brown hair and skinny legs, but who was most decidedly *not* our bird. The ruckus drew the attention of the real Molly, though, who came running out of the kitchen with a smaller version of the now-familiar

Bjornskinki bread knife. Following her with a spatula was Larry Black. I supposed he could pray for Alex's health after Molly punctured his lungs a few times.

Alex struggled to control the poor woman beneath him, screaming, "I'm fighting the good fight, you wench. You're sure to lose, so just give up already."

Molly leaned over the tangled couple and flashed the knife blade in Alex's eyes. He blinked, then smartly froze. Molly said, "Please get off the customer."

Alex got off the customer. He said, "She was carrying a whole tray of food."

"She was hungry," Molly explained. "And now, she's probably angry."

The woman in question was already gone, having scurried from the room as quickly as she could. All that food. And so skinny. I've heard that ice cream comes up as easily as it goes down. No wonder the bathrooms are right next to the restaurant. All of the other diners had left the cafe, too. I watched them squawk away like frightened geese. I turned back toward Molly.

She was walking around Alex, keeping the knife at his throat. He said, "I know your little secret."

She gasped. So did Larry. Alex decided to take advantage of their distraction. With his freshly pumped mini-muscles, he grabbed Molly by the knife wrist and attempted to fling her over his head. She barely moved. Except when she leaned in with the knife.

Larry said, "Molly, no!" He grabbed the two of them, who were already grappling with each other. The fivesome (including the knife and spatula) fell to the floor in a knot. Alex wasn't doing very well. Molly, however, was getting in some dastardly punches. I lifted my gun and aimed it, fired. Hot lead blasted the beet juice circulation machine. Red liquid splattered all over the counter, the pink walls and the knot of people on the floor. I was spared a single drop; my sundress was unmarked. In their confusion, I took control. I rushed over to the stunned, drenched group and said, "Someone's shooting. Out the back way— fast!" Molly and Larry didn't even flinch. They bolted for the kitchen. I helped Alex to his feet—he shrugged me off again—and we chased after them.

Once in the kitchen, I screamed, "Hold it!" Molly and Larry stopped in their tracks. "Arms up," I said. They put their arms up. "Turn around." They turned. "Now rub your bellies and pat your heads at the same time."

They seemed puzzled. Alex said, "You can't go screaming out of here like banshees. The police are outside, looking for Wanda. Though I have every faith that, should they arrest you instead, Molly, they'll be making a good collar."

Molly pointed at Alex. "I know her, but who the hell are you?" she asked.

"He's my partner." I pointed at her hand with the gun. "You can drop the knife now. And the spatula, too."

Instead of dropping it on the floor, Molly slowly reached over to the kitchen counter to her right and slipped the knife into a big hunk of wood. Seven other knives with white handles poked out of it. The biggest slot was empty (I was wearing my glasses and could see an ant on the moon). I took the empty slot to be the home of the murder knife in my pocketbook. "Missing something?" I asked and pointed at the wood block.

Larry spoke for the first time since I'd liberated the

beet juice. He said, "A bread knife was stolen a few days ago."

I said to Molly, "And you went to Ikea today to see about replacing it."

She stared suspiciously at me. "How did you know?"

"Psychic vision."

"Yeah, well, so what? Is it against the law to order a bread knife from Ikea?"

No, I thought. "We'll be leaving out the back door, and then we're going to have a chat. You might want to grab your stash first. I'm pretty sure the cops will be looking around back here for a crazed gunman. It'd be a shame if they found something more incriminating."

Alex said, "Take them to your place. I'll meet you there later."

"Where are you going?" I asked, annoyed. I needed him to handle both Molly and Larry.

"Leeza needs me."

"She needs a doctor," I said.

"You can be really selfish, Wanda." I needed this conversation now, with the cops up my ass and two hostages? Molly and Larry still had their hands up. I kept my gun level. Alex said, "If I don't go to her, I'll never forgive myself."

"If you leave me now, I'll never forgive you."

He smiled and said, "Sure you will."

I spit fire. My eyebrows were singed. Alex started walking out. I said, "You slimy bastard," and reached for his shirt with my nongun hand. I forgot that I was using that hand to hold the green notebook under my dress. The spiral dropped to the floor with a splat.

Larry yelled, "My notebook!" He dove for it, as did

I. Being limber and possessing uncommon agility, I reached it first. But it was at my feet and he was across the room. Larry stepped toward me to wrench it out of my arms. I reaimed my gun. He backed off.

"If the cops grab us now, they'll impound your notebook as evidence and you'll probably lose it forever. But I'm willing to trade. We can talk over my terms after I've seen a bathroom." I needed to go badly. I didn't think Falcone even knew about the chromium compound/super steroid element to the case, unless Ameleth blabbed. Unlikely. That would cast suspicion on herself. I took a long hard look at Larry. His eyes were riveted on the notebook. "By one theory," I said, "the scientist is Barney's killer." Larry's jaw flapped like a jack. He sputtered for a second.

Molly said, "Jehovahs believe that violence is a sin against God. Larry didn't kill anyone." She said it in a way that made me think she knew who did. I heard voices behind me. Someone was coming. Falcone might know I was there. If Jack hadn't spilled, Janey or Ergort could have mentioned me.

I gestured with Mama toward the Dumpster exit door. Molly quickly grabbed her drug pouch from the freezer and nodded to Larry to just go along. Alex lead the pack outside. I brought up the rear. I wondered if Larry was Molly's drug supplier. If he could invent a compound to make you lose weight without dieting, surely he could whip together some mild speed or a muscle relaxer.

I let the emergency door swing shut behind me. There was no way back in now. I told Alex to steer our captives behind the Dumpster while I checked the coast. It was clear as my conscience. There were about five cop cruisers and one ambulance parked outside. I spotted only one lonely uniform guarding the entrance. I didn't see Ergort—and he'd be hard to miss.

If the uniform just looked the other way, we could make a run for it. I cleared my voice. Then I threw it a hundred feet up the street. "Just smash the windshield. The cops around here are too stupid to catch us," I said. The cop pricked up his ears. Have I mentioned that I'm a ventriloquist? "Go ahead and smash it," I urged my imaginary cohort. "This is the tenth car I've stolen this week. So what if it's a BMW?" I could almost see the wrinkles of concern on the uniform's face. If a BMW were stolen around the corner from where he was stationed—in the middle of the day, no less—it would be embarrassing for the department. He swayed back and forth, unable to make up his mind—leave his post or let a crime happen. I was just about to simulate a shatter sound when he went running around the corner, billy club in hand.

We made a break for it. Molly was the fastest runner so she led the way. Alex did a pretty good job of keeping up. I didn't know where we were running. Anywhere was fine, really. As long as it was toward a bathroom. After a block and a half, I figured we'd run far enough. I was feeling every cigarette I'd ever smoked. And my buffalo shoes had inadequate traction. I got a sudden flash: Falcone sprinting up the street, her fat jiggling and her pores exhaling smoke.

I ran with renewed vigor. That lasted about half-a-step. I was weighed down by my heavy bag, a gun and a very fat notebook. My sundress had to weigh a good, what, five pounds alone. The others—they were wearing workout clothes. Nearly weightless. I got another flash. This one was a blast of red behind my eyes. I know I'd read somewhere that sudden increases in blood circulation can cause clotting.

I slowed down to a limp. I began to feel less like an orthopedic case until someone grabbed me by the arm and tugged me into an alley. I was weak from exertion; I didn't struggle. I looked up. It was Alex. He said, "Your face is the color of lava."

"That exercise nearly killed me," I said.

"The idea is to do it more than once every decade," he said.

I looked over his shoulder. Molly was stuffing her stash in a garbage can in the alley. Larry watched me with a little concern. They were breathing normally. Not a drop of sweat on them. I hated them. I managed to say, "I've got the gun, so I'm still in control."

Larry whispered to Molly. I read his lips: "Let's tell them about the . . . I need to get this off my chest."

"To the river," Molly said abruptly. Alex and I followed her along Columbia Heights. I'd been down the street before, en route to the River Cafe, Brooklyn's best and most expensive restaurant. Max and I went there to celebrate his agreeing to move to Brooklyn. The dining room floats on the East River. The view of the Manhattan skyline through the floor-to-ceiling windows is as choice as the food. Only problem: on windy days, the waves in the river cause the restaurant to rock slightly and people have been known to throw up in their pâté de foie gras.

We passed the restaurant. It was a calm day. We marched toward the massive warehouses that lined the riverbank. Farther down the road—past Atlantic Avenue—you can find the piers where the tall ships from Russia and the Orient park on the Fourth of July. For a buck, you can take a tour of a former Soviet vessel. For two grand, you can sign up to join the crew to sail the ship back home to the motherland. The journey lasts about a month. The people who sign up are mostly wealthy suits who get off on the idea of pretending to be working-class adventuremen for a while. I've never had this fantasy; my life ambition is to do as little work as possible. Also, I look horrible in bell-bottoms.

Molly slowed as we approached a chain-link fence in front of the third blue-metal warehouse. My breathing had settled to hyperventilation. Signs on the fence read: BEWARE OF PIT BULL. Larry said, "This is Jehovah property. We store dry goods and Bibles here for the flock. Before I joined the gym, my job—after completing my chemical engineer training at NYU—was to be guardian of the warehouse. Some lifting, some inventory taking. Some patroling. Mainly lifting."

"That's where he got all those shoulder muscles," Molly pointed out matter-of-factly.

"It took a while before I could lift a hundred-pound bag of dried corn by myself, but before long, I could carry one under each arm," Larry bragged. Remembering that he existed to serve, he said, "Anyway, I've set up a personal space in the back of the warehouse. The only person who knows about it is the new guardian. And Molly."

"How come the new guardian doesn't squeal on you?" I asked.

Larry pondered this. "I bribe him with drugs." He looked heavenward and then said, "Lord forgive me—you know it's for the greater good." Larry's eyes fell back to earth. "I'm a sinner."

"Get over it," Molly said.

"That's a bit harsh," Alex observed.

"I meant the fence. Start climbing."

Was she serious? It was ten feet high. I was in a

dress. I said, "Do you bribe the pit bull with drugs, too?"

Molly said, "The dog isn't let out until after dark."

Alex said, "Perhaps I can help give you a push, Wanda?" He started to hoist me by the butt up the fence.

"I'll do without help, thank you." I put the notebook inside my bag and grabbed the chain link with both hands. To my right, Larry and Molly scampered up the fence and jumped down from the top like they'd done it a thousand times. Which they probably had. Alex set out at the same time I did. I tried to remember climbing trees when I was a kid. But I didn't spend much of my childhood in nature. I was busy shoplifting lip gloss at the mall.

Alex made it up and over fairly easily. Once steady on the other side, he practically fell over from slapping himself on the back. I was halfway up the fence when my arms began to tremble from exertion. I dug deep, and managed to vault myself up. I threw one leg over the top. I wasn't sure what to do next. For a hard guy, I can be such a girl.

Larry could reach my ankle. He encircled it with his fingers. "Just kick your other leg over and I'll catch you."

"A likely ploy. You just want the notebook."

Alex said, "Your vanity never ceases to amaze me, Wanda. You're not even willing to accept help when your physical limitations couldn't be more obvious."

I quickly reminded myself that I was Supersleuth. I laughed in the face of fear. I swallowed hard and kicked my other leg over the fence. I took a few steps down, and then jumped off. I didn't land as gracefully as Molly had. But after a slight wobble in my platforms, I stood up straight, triumphant. I must have smiled broadly because Alex said, "You look like the cat who ate the peacock."

"Tasty," I agreed.

Molly and Larry walked hand-in-hand toward the warehouse a hundred feet away. Alex put his arm over my shoulder. I punched him in the gut. He looked sad for a moment. I wondered if it was for Leeza, or for remembering how good we used to be together. He said, "I hope Leeza's okay. If she's dead, I'll track down her killer and . . . why I'll . . ."

"What? Soufflé him? Leave the hard-guy act for me."

"You can't even climb a fence," he protested.

"Were you not standing right there watching me?"

"I watched you *struggle* to climb a fence. Not the same thing." Somewhere in the distance, I heard a dog bark. I chose to ignore it. We walked toward the warehouse. The blue metal walls were thick and cold. When I got close enough, I said, "Hey, Larry, if you're bribing this guy with drugs, how come you don't have a key to the fence?"

"I do—but if I used it and opened the fence, an alarm would go off at the Jehovah headquarters at the Bossert Hotel. Then the leader would come, and we'd be caught. I'd rather Brother Samuel didn't find out about this. He'd force me to work again for the church and pray until I'd refound my faith."

"Brother Samuel's from Nebraska," Molly shared. "I only met him once. He came to the gym when Larry first tried to leave the church to beg me to release him from my witch's seduction. I told Brother Samuel that if I had any witches' powers, I'd make his hair fall out."

"So do the Jehovah's call you Brother Larry?" I asked.

He seemed perplexed. "Why would they?"

"Nephew Larry?" I asked.

Larry's brain clicked. He shook his head. "Brother is his first name," Larry explained. "Samuel is his last name."

Alex and I looked at each other and silently whistled. Larry led us along a narrow path on the outside of the warehouse. It bordered the water. One wrong step, and we'd be in the drink. East River water was one drink I didn't want to take. Larry said, "I can't unlock the main warehouse door for the same reason —an alarm will go off at the Bossert—so you'll have to squeeze through this hole in the wall."

Squeezing through a hole I could do. Once inside, Larry hit the lights.

The warehouse was the size of two football fields— bigger. I looked up. The ceiling was thirty feet high. A narrow aisle cut through the middle of the space. On either side were mountains of burlap bags. The piles reached as high as the ceiling in some places. "On the left, we have five thousand, one-hundred-pound bags of coffee beans," Larry started. "On the right, two thousand, one-hundred-pound bags of cracked wheat. We've got a few thousand pounds of pepper, dried corn and dehydrated tomatoes. On the far wall, stacked in boxes, we've got five thousand pounds of semolina pasta, ten thousand cans of peas and carrots, and seven thousand jars of baby food. I'm not sure what else they've been storing—except the Bibles. They keep them over here."

Larry walked down the aisle. The giant burlap bags full of coffee beans smelled great, but, as I walked under them, I feared they'd topple and crush me like a bug. The aisle turned and we rounded with it. A few yards ahead stood a twenty-foot-high wall of black books. I looked closer. On thousands of black spines the words *Holy Bible* blazed in gold. Larry said, "Just in case the outside Bibles are destroyed in the apocalypse. That's what the food's for, too. The end of the world as we know it will come. We wouldn't want the chosen to go hungry."

Molly said under her breath, "Stop saying 'we.'"

"I'd have stocked up on Doritos and Diet Coke," I said to Alex.

He grunted and said, "At least some water crackers and anchovy paste."

Larry led us behind the wall of Bibles. We had to squeeze past some sacks of bulgur wheat. Larry said, "This is where I do my finest work."

Alex just said, "Wow!" It *was* pretty neat. A mini chemistry lab, with gurgling test tubes and beakers full of pink and blue liquids on a makeshift table of plywood planks on sawhorses. Not the most sterile environment, I thought. A spiral notebook lay open on the table with unintelligible scrawl covering the pages. A full-size refrigerator (with a padlock on the handle) hummed behind the table and a hot plate rested on a small card table alongside. A bookshelf against the wall was full of mortars, pestles, jars full of liquids and raw powders. A cage under the makeshift lab table housed a couple rats. They squeaked desperately. I fought the paralyzing grip of heebie-jeebies.

"I've only had this space since yesterday," Larry said. "I had to throw it together after, well, after something changed at my last lab. Now if you'll give me my notebook, I can see what I've been forgetting to do in reconstructing my formulas."

I reached in my bag and touched the metal spiral. There could be a free sample of the chromium compound in it for me. But before I handed over the notebook, I said, "First I want to ask you something: Who else had access to the kitchen besides you and the staff?" I asked.

Molly asked, "Why?"

"The knife that was stolen—"

"You mean?" she asked, appalled. I nodded. "Great, now *I'm* going to get pegged for Barney's murder. Well, better me than Larry."

"Molly, don't be silly," said Larry. "You're innocent."

"At least one of us will make it to Hawaii," she said.

"You know I couldn't go without you," he said.

"Honey," she said. They smiled at each other.

I said, "You can kiss now."

Larry shook his head. "Oh, no. We can't do anything romantic in public." Molly rolled her eyes. She must love him a lot, I thought.

Alex said, "And I suppose you'll say that anyone, but anyone, could have gone into the kitchen, taken this knife and used it to kill Barney Cutler minutes later?"

"Yes. It's entirely possible," she said.

"But what's more likely—and allow me to blather on for a bit—is this scenario," I started. "Larry turned over the chromium compound and super steroid samples to Barney in Ameleth's suite as planned." I turned to face him. "Yeah—I know all about it. Barney talked you into turning over your notebook along with the samples, but you didn't mind because you had copies of everything back at the lab they bought for you. You took the thirty thousand and left. But when you got to your lab, you found that it'd been sealed off. Your copies of the formulas were lost. You knew Barney did this to you. You were full of rage. You went back to the club and grabbed Molly's knife. I don't know how you got up there, but you made it to the suite.

"Barney was relaxing in the Jacuzzi," I continued, "He laughed when you demanded the notebooks back. You became blind with rage and killed him. Shall I go on to explain why you had to beat up poor Leeza, too?" Actually, I had no idea how that was related, but I was on a roll. Alex didn't know about the chromium/steroid stuff. He raised his eyebrow. I sent him a telepathic message that I'd explain later.

Larry held up his hand. "You can stop now," he said. "I admit that it sounds reasonable, but the problem is I could never kill anyone. It would damn me to hell."

"Oh, great," I said. "The Christian defense."

"I'm serious," he protested. "I did get hoodwinked by Barney. I admit to hating the man, but I didn't kill him. I forgave him his sins. I was resolved to figuring out the formulas from memory. They were flawed anyway. The samples I gave him might have caused some weird side effects if anyone took them. I warned Barney that they were for the FDA researchers only.

"As far as the money goes, I spent every last cent he gave me to set up this lab and to buy the raw materials to manufacture diet aids for Molly to sell at the club. And to test my new formulas. I realize what I'm doing is wrong—selling drugs, manufacturing steroids without a pharmaceutical license—but I'm doing it to help people. I'm a people person. To see them be the best they can be. I can't let my training go to waste. The Jehovah organization paid good money to get me an education. And I'd rather work on formulas that will improve people's health than do the Jehovah's bidding and figure out how to better preserve dried food for the apocalypse."

A voice from the other side of the Bibles boomed, "Oh, Lord—forgive Lawrence. He knows not what he's done, and, boy, has he really messed up this time."

Larry's eyes went wild. "Brother Samuel!" he mouthed.

9

～

Kiss My God

"**G**osh darn it," said Larry. "Lord, why do you punish me?" he quickly added.

Brother Samuel, a tall man in a short-sleeve, pin-striped shirt and blue tie, stepped out from behind the wall of Bibles. "I've come to pray for you, Lawrence, not judge you. But if I had to judge, I'd say you're acting like a fool."

I'm generally more comfortable with people judging me than praying for me, and I could tell by the nervous sweat on Larry's forehead that he was, too. I said, "Are you the head Jehovah in this operation?"

Brother said, "I would hardly call the Jehovah's Witnesses an organization. More of a following of the Lord's teachings." He spoke matter-of-factly, but without condescension.

"Gary Gilmore's brother was a Jehovah," I shared. (I learned that from reading *Shot in the Heart*.)

Brother ran his hand over his bowl cut and regarded me closely. His eyes never strayed lower than my

182

collarbone—strange. He said, "May I ask who you are and what you're doing here?"

"You may."

He looked heavenward. I hoped he wasn't praying for me. "I've known about this lab since yesterday, Lawrence. I was hoping your foolishness would end—that you'd come to me to explain yourself. But now you're bringing strangers onto our private property. I can't look the other way now." Brother regarded me and Alex. We weren't looking our best. He said, "And the rats. Just stupid, Lawrence. If your rats got loose, they'd gnaw through every bag in the warehouse. They'd breed. I love all the Lord's creatures, but those rats have got to go." Brother looked at us. "So will you people. For all I know, you're the ones who led Lawrence down the wrong path."

"Molly here can take full responsibility for his fall," I said. "We're here for my own selfish purposes."

"Such as?" Brother asked.

"Free coffee beans."

Larry, meanwhile, was hiding under his makeshift lab table. I wondered if he had any formula nearby that would turn him invisible. I took another look at Brother Samuel. What was it about this thirtyish guy with flat hair and geeky shoes that could terrify Larry? In a fight, Larry could succotash him like a squash. Molly stood in front of the table, blocking Larry as much as she could. I wasn't sure how much love it took for her to protect her boyfriend from a man in leisure slacks, but it was probably a lot. Alex stepped toward me and whispered in my ear, "He's packing."

I looked at Brother Samuel's fly. "I know you're not happy to see me," I said. "So that must be a gun."

He patted his pants and said, "The alarm went off at

headquarters, and I had to be ready for action. I'm prepared to fight to protect our supplies. Without the contents of this warehouse, future generations of humanity couldn't survive after the apocalypse."

"I suppose they wouldn't send you alone on such an important mission," Alex asked.

"Reinforcements are on the way." In that blue and white van, no doubt. "And if you even think about stealing any of our coffee, forgive me Lord, but I'll defend our honor. If I don't get you, the dog will."

Alex tapped me on the shoulder and whispered, "I think we should leave."

Molly heard him and begged with her eyes for us to stay. I considered it, but decided they were on their own. Under the circumstances, I figured it was best for me to hang on to Larry's notebook. From the strange grin on Brother Samuel's face, I'd bet that Larry's ad hoc lab wouldn't last through the hour. I sent Alex a telepathic message. He rubbed his left eye—code that he'd received it loud and clear. I turned to Molly and said, "Aloha."

We split like canned peas. At a run, Alex and I vaulted the mountains of burlap coffee bean bags and climbed. A few broken nails later, we'd clawed and scraped our way to the top of the pile. From that high up, I could see that Brother Samuel had male-pattern baldness. Alex said, "Let's fly," and he ran on top the bags and boxes toward the west wall of the warehouse. I liked the sound of the beans and corn crackling under my feet as I ran. The piles were uneven, and I had to make running jumps a few times to keep up with Alex. I was getting more exercise in one day than I had in most of my adult life. I minded.

A shot rang out and ricocheted around the metal

walls of the warehouse. I heard Molly scream. Shooting the rats? I wondered. What a waste of bullets. Alex and I were just at the end of the warehouse. He deftly maneuvered down the burlap bags. I followed and fell about eight feet to the floor. My knee was bleeding pretty badly as we sprinted for the hole in the wall we'd crawled in through. Adrenaline pumped ferociously through my veins.

Outside, we ran along the water's edge toward the chain-link fence. We were halfway to it when something short and brown came flying at us from the other side of the warehouse. As it hurled toward us, I could see the saliva on its pointy white teeth sparkle and glisten in the sun. I would have stopped to admire this vision, if it didn't mean my death. I turned toward Alex to tell him to move, but he was already gone. I yelped after him and pounded the pavement.

The dog wasn't wearing platforms, nor did it carry a heavy purse. He also had two more legs. But, where he had speed, I had motivation. Plump perhaps, but I liked my ass and planned to keep it well into my dotage. I wasn't as attached to the dress, which the dog sank his snapping white fangs into only seconds after I hit chain link. Alex was comfortably straddling the top of the fence. He watched in terror as the dog and I played tug-of-war with my sundress. The angle was right, so I kicked the animal in the chest with my platform. Instead of dislodging its jaw, the dog stripped off a nice chunk of my dress and wrestled it to the ground with his claws. Even I preferred a longer hem than this, although I remained mostly covered. I scrambled up the fence.

I would have hopped off just as easily, but we were distracted by the screech of a blue-and-white minivan.

The Jehovah enforcers had arrived. The driver must have seen us (we were pretty hard to miss—a man and tattered woman straddling a ten-foot-high fence on a sunny June afternoon). We were so noticeable, in fact, that the lunch crowd spilled out of the River Cafe to get a load.

The van slammed into the fence right under where we were straddling it. Alex and I hung on for our lives, and our genitals. Three men in short sleeves, ties and leisure pants dashed out of the vehicle and started to clamber up the fence to take us down. Alex said, "On the count of three, Wanda."

I nodded. Alex counted to three. We jumped over the men climbing the fence and onto the top of their van. I burned my butt sliding down to the street. I grabbed the driver's side before Alex scrambled into the passenger seat. We slammed the doors and locked them. The keys were still in the ignition. We made dust. When we passed the River Cafe, we honked. I thought I heard cheers, but that could have been the roar of exploding blood vessels in my ears.

"Where to now?" asked Alex. He was grinning broadly—with teeth.

"The hospital," I said.

Fear seeped across his features. "Did that maniac animal break skin? Shit, I knew I should have jumped down to wrestle that hell-beast into submission. Why, I ought to have—"

"Spare me a quarter, Alex. I'm fine." He looked puzzled. I shook my head and said, "Hint: I'm glad I'm not the love of your life anymore."

"Leeza," he exhaled. He stuck his head out the window like a dog and yelled, "I'm coming to you, darling." Shiny brown hair blew off his well-boned face. I had a flashback: Alex and I were making love in the dark. The headlights of a car passed through the window of our bedroom, painting a yellow beam across his face. His eyes were open. He was smiling.

The Alex of today pulled himself back inside the van and said, "If Leeza dies, could we be named accessories *before* the fact?"

Instead of hitting the ceiling, I floored the van. We made it to the hospital in seconds. About five thousand of them. Brooklyn General was located on the corner of Hicks Street and Atlantic Avenue, just down the strip from the Detention Center. If Jack really had had a claustrophobic seizure, he could have twitched and crawled his way to the emergency room on one knee.

We parked illegally. We also left the van keys in the ignition and the sliding door open. We hit the emergency room entrance. I was expecting bloodied bodies on gurneys lining the walls, but all I got was a few bored-looking hospital administrators sitting at metal desks. The only sounds were their chatter and the blare of a TV hanging from the ceiling. No bloodcurdling screams, no splatter of gore and guts on a concrete floor. Except for the bullet-proof glass that separated us from the administrators, the space looked just like a doctor's office waiting room. My disappointment must have been obvious.

I visited the can. It was as much of a relief as not getting ravaged by the pit bull. I came back. Alex was rapping patiently on the glass. He was trying to get the attention of a heavyset black woman in bangles and braids. She was typing on a computer. After pretending to ignore us for longer than was polite, I said loudly, "This must be a public hospital."

The woman squinted before smiling brightly. She said, "Sorry to keep you waiting. I was inputting information into our computer system so we could admit an uninsured woman in premature labor." She had a Jamaican accent. "If I didn't get that processed, she would have had to deliver her baby on the emergency room floor. Thank you for being patient." Jamaican, perhaps, but she had the Jewish guilt thing down. One of her bracelets was inscribed with the name Annabelle.

"Is that your name? Annabelle? Very pretty," I buttered her up like a turkey. "I'd like to see Leeza Robbins. She was brought in about an hour ago." This was the closest hospital. She had to be there.

"Family?" she asked.

"I'm her sister."

"You don't look like her sister," she said, checking me over.

I smiled prettily. "I'm adopted." Annabelle shifted her weight on her ergonomic swivel chair.

She toyed with a few of her bangles and twisted a braid of hair. "Well, you can't go into the emergency room." Her accent swung back and forth like her braids.

I said, "I'll give you twenty bucks."

Her eyes flew open and she laughed. "I'd be more than happy to take twenty dollars from you, but you'll have to wait like everyone else. Visiting hours are between three and three-fifteen."

Time check: half past a bug's butt. Shit, I thought. What am I going to do for forty-five minutes? I said, "I'll give you forty."

Annabelle smiled broadly—big tombstones of perfectly white enamel—and said, "I'll take it."

I turned to Alex and said, "Give her forty dollars."

"You give her forty."

"Alex, which one of us gives two flying shits about seeing Leeza anyway?"

She said, "I thought you were her sister."

"We're estranged."

"I'll say," grunted Alex as he forked over two twenty spots. Annabelle nodded her thanks as she accepted the bills. Then she returned to punching keys on her computer.

I rapped on the glass. "What now?" I asked. "Click my heels together and say, 'There's no place like the emergency room?'"

"You can do that," she said, not looking at us. "But you'll have to do it for forty-five minutes until I can let you in like everyone else." Before I got the chance to protest, she said, "And thanks for your donation to the hospital fund. Public hospitals need all the help they can get." She swiveled in her chair over to her printer. She tore off a sheet of paper and handed it to Alex. "That's your receipt. And don't forget—sixty percent of your donation is tax deductible."

I hate do-gooders. I scowled so hard it hurt, and found a seat in the waiting area. Alex joined me. He seemed upset. The room was nearly empty—not many emergencies in Brooklyn Heights that afternoon.

Clang. The outside doors smashed open. Five cops in uniform dragged in a black kid screaming in pain. I'd guess he was about fifteen years old, but it was hard to make a good guess with his face all covered in blood. Annabelle sprang to life and punched through the glass doors. She tried to ask the kid questions, but he was too busy suffering to answer. One of the cops—I thought he looked like the guy I'd used the old ventriloquist ploy on—said, "We caught him breaking into a car on Clark Street. Had to bust him up to restrain him."

Alex whispered to me, "Fancy that." Talk about dumb luck. The kid's, I mean.

Annabelle lifted the kid like a sack of coffee beans. I was impressed by her brute strength. She muttered something about police brutality and kicked a switch plate on the wall. Two double doors burst open automatically. While cradling the kid in her arms, she shuffled down a long corridor into a pen with about forty beds crammed against the walls. The cops looked at each other in confusion. One mumbled into his walkie-talkie about the incident, and the rest of them congregated underneath the TV to comment on a "One Life to Live" scene.

I checked behind the bullet-proof glass windows. No one had come to replace Annabelle. "Stay here," I commanded.

Alex said, "I suppose trying to talk you out of this would be a waste of time."

"You've got to cover for me."

"I fronted the forty."

"You want a medal or a monument?" I asked.

"A simple thank you would suffice, Wanda."

"I'll be back in a flash."

Alex said, "Kiss her for me."

I walked toward the double doors. Alex waited for me to give him the wink, and then he clasped his arms around his gut and screeched in agony. "My valve!" he cried. "Oh, God! I'm dying!"

The cops glanced at him, and then back at the TV set. So much for creating a good distraction. I pressed the wall switch and the double doors popped open. I strolled inside—the cops didn't move a centimeter. I was golden.

A nurses' station was in the center of the pen. I headed for it purposefully, hoping they'd assume I belonged there. I scanned the faces of the patients in their beds along the way. Most were old-timers with IVs, NGs and other tubes sticking in various holes. One painfully thin young man lay on his bed wheezing for breath. Just as I passed, he began a long coughing fit that didn't end even after I'd walked the entire loop around the emergency room. I didn't spot Leeza, but there were a couple screened off beds in the back. No one had yet questioned my presence. I figured I might as well take a look.

The first curtain I peeked behind housed the kid the cops had just brought in. A doctor was attempting to stick a needle in his arm, but the kid fought her off. Behind curtain number two: pay dirt. I recognized Leeza's yellow hair pulled into a ponytail. My first feeling was relief. She was alive and no tubes were sticking out of any of her orifices. She lay unconscious on her back. There were bandages on her throat, and some patches on her cheek. A fiftyish doctor in hospital greens was giving her a chest examination. He seemed to enjoy it more than he was supposed to. He was rubbing himself under his lab coat. I stepped back, shocked by the sight. I looked again, and he'd turned her on her side. He took an anal thermometer out of his pocket. I swallowed hard and threw back the curtains.

The doctor shrank at the exposure. He recovered and looked me over. Okay, so maybe my tattered sundress and sandals didn't project an air of authority. "Cop a nice feel?" I asked. "Is that part of the regular exam?"

His face dropped, knowing he was busted. "Visiting hours aren't for another thirty minutes, young lady."

"That's certainly enough time for you to get a nice long look at my sister's ass. And maybe you might even find the time to fiddle around a bit."

He flinched and I knew I was right on target. "I'm going to call security," he said.

"You'll save me the trip."

The doctor harrumphed and stormed off. I watched him to see if he'd report me at the nurses' station. He didn't. I made a mental note to get his name before I left. I closed the curtain behind me and slapped Leeza gently on her nonbandaged cheek. Her eyes fluttered. I said, "Leeza. Wake up. You're okay. You're in the hospital."

She stared up at me. Her face was puffy and bruised. She eked out, "Hi, Wanda." I remembered her missing teeth. Speaking sounded painful for her. My heart sank. I was responsible. And all she was trying to do was make a few friends.

"You don't need to worry about making friends, Leeza," I said. "You're too good-looking to worry about anything." Even with the bruises and wraps, she looked decent.

"Women hate me because of my looks, Wanda. You do."

Guilt settled on me like a tire iron. I wondered if Leeza had ever met my old friend Santina, a veritable expert at inflicting guilt. I said, "Did you see who attacked you?"

"No."

"Why did you go up to the suite?"

She had to think about that question. "I wanted to help with the investigation. So I agreed to make a date with a john."

Jeez, I thought. Janey worked fast at recruiting. "With who?" I asked.

"Van Owen," she said.

I asked, "How did you get up there?"

"Janey gave me a key."

Another key? "Did Van Owen show?"

"He never did. I felt rejected in a way. I really wanted to be dangerous like you for a while."

Leeza drifted a bit. She wanted to be like me? Poor, misguided fool. Her head rolled to the side. I wondered if she'd been given too many tranquilizers by that molesting doctor. It was enough to make me never want to get sick. Her eyes cleared suddenly and she said, "I think I need to throw up now."

"Relax," I suggested. I found a bedpan on a nearby shelf. I handed it to her. "Use this." I rubbed her forehead and tried to pull her forward so she wouldn't soil herself.

She coughed a little. Over the sound, I heard a voice on the other side of the curtain say, "When I find out who let her in here before visiting hours, heads will roll." The bastard doctor. I dropped the bedpan on Leeza's chest. I had only seconds to hide. With nowhere else to go, I slipped behind the curtains to the third sectioned-off bed in the row.

A man lay there. He looked horrible. His face was broken out in a ghastly rash with red sores and large strips of white skin flakes. A large boil grew mercilessly on his chin, puffing out from his straggly goatee. His hands were meaty, wide and somehow familiar. "Freddie?" I asked in a whisper. His hair had partially fallen out on one side of his head, but those stubborn sideburns and big floppy ears remained unchanged.

He opened his eyes and looked at me. "Wanda?" he asked.

"My God. What happened?"

"I'm surprised you recognized me." His lips cracked as he spoke.

"I never forget a haircut." Well, half a haircut. "I suppose this was your destiny," I said.

"To look like my big screen namesake?" he asked. "You're only the twelfth person to say that. These nurses have a real adorable sense of humor."

I blocked out Freddie's voice for a second and tried to listen to what was going on in Leeza's section. The male doctor I'd thwarted was talking to someone with a Jamaican accent, perhaps Annabelle. He said, "An impertinent young woman interrupted me while administering care to this patient. I'd like to know how you let her slip in here."

Annabelle said, "It must have been when I was saving someone's life." The pause I heard was in its second trimester. Finally, Annabelle said, "I'll find her and be sure she gets what's coming to her."

The doctor said, "Good. See to it this patient gets to X-ray. And she may need a sponge bath—arrange that with those other women."

"You mean the staff of highly trained certified nurses?"

I heard some mumbling, and then silence. I risked peeking out of Freddie's curtains into Leeza's area. Annabelle sat on the edge of her bed, staring right at me. I smiled and pulled back the curtain. "Sorry if I got you in trouble."

"The nurses usually keep an eye on him—especially around the younger, female patients. They're crazy busy, so I'll thank you for your sister's sake."

"Am I hereby ejected?"

"Visiting hours start in five minutes. You can stay

for twenty minutes, and then I'm hoping you'll leave and not come back until my shift is over."

"Deal. Has anyone reported that asshole?"

Annabelle sighed. "He's the chief of staff's son. He's got an 'offspring of God' complex. Whenever anyone says, 'Jesus Christ' in his presence, he says, 'Am I being paged?'"

I gestured with my head for Annabelle to step outside the curtains with me. Once in the main room, in view of the countless beds, I whispered in her ear, "What's wrong with the guy in here?" I pointed toward Freddie's area. Annabelle hesitated. I said, "Turns out he's a friend. Small neighborhood."

Her pause was premature. Then she said, "He came in this morning. Overdose. Anabolic steroids. Only problem is that we have no idea what kind. Until the lab guys figure out what he took, we can't help him much."

Poor slob. "Will he die?"

"He won't die—at least I don't think so. I've never seen an overdose of steroids before—and I've never seen this kind of dramatic facial degeneration either. Whatever he took must have been powerful. He's growing a coat of hair on his back, and his skin continues to peel away. His penis might shrivel beyond repair. I hope for your sake, he isn't a *special* friend."

"God, no." Larry's notebook burned a giant hole in my purse. If I turned it over to Annabelle, I could save Freddie. But the lab people might then take the formula and market it themselves. Then I'll be out my cut of the fortune. Then again, the stuff obviously doesn't work. One look at Freddie was enough to convince me of that. I took the notebook out of my bag and gave it to Annabelle. "Take this before I change my mind."

Annabelle was puzzled. I said, "The steroid formula is in there." I turned to go.

She said, "Wait—what about your sister?"

"She's not really my sister."

Annabelle rolled her black eyes like eight balls. "I know that. But don't you want to visit with her?"

"Not really. Long story." I waved good-bye. I hit the waiting room. It was just time for official visiting hours. Alex was chomping at the bit to go inside. I told him I'd see him later: I was on a mission.

Alex asked if he should call Max and tell him what happened. The words were barely out of his mouth when Max burst into the waiting room. He was wearing work clothes: A blue summer suit with a white shirt and paisley tie. His cheeks were redder than his hair, and from the glisten on his forehead, I got the idea he'd run all the way from the subway. When he saw me, he lunged forward and circled his arms around my waist. He hugged me so hard my spine bones cracked. It felt swell.

"What's going on?" he blurted after he dropped me. "I got a call at the office that someone got hurt and was in the emergency room at Brooklyn General. I thought it was you. I thought you got shot. God, I hate your job."

I loved him when he was desperate and upset. "I'm fine, honeybunny. It's not me. Alex is fine, too." Alex came up behind me and waved sweetly at Max. Max didn't even acknowledge him.

Max asked, "Leeza?" We nodded. I figured he'd last at least a few seconds before erupting. "God damn it. I knew this would happen," he fumed immediately. "And I'd love saying 'I told you so' if Leeza weren't in the emergency room, clinging to life by a thread for all I know. Didn't I tell you to keep her out of this? She was totally unprepared to deal with guns and violence. And look at you—you don't even care."

I didn't know what to say. I knew Leeza was all right. I also knew I wasn't the one who gave her the bright idea to meet a john up in Ameleth's suite. That was her own idea. Sure, I felt lousy that she got pummeled, but I'm not about to forget everything else that happened so I can cry at her bedside. I said, "Hold on one second. If you got a call, Leeza herself must have given them your number. She's pretty bashed up. Most people in that condition can barely remember their own names, much less the work phone number of an ex-boyfriend." Obviously, it was a number she knew well. It must be burned into her cerebellum. "Not to turn this around, Max, but how does Leeza know your number at the bank?" I tapped my foot impatiently and waited for Max to answer that one.

He couldn't. He just stared at me, dumbfounded. My heart sank. That could only confirm that Leeza had been calling Max pretty often at work. And he'd told me that they hadn't seen each other or talked for years before she called him just last week to say she'd be in town. Ergo, Max was a liar. I felt tears rising, but managed to squelch them by thinking about how uncomfortable I felt in my tattered dress and trashed platforms. Was it possible that Max and Leeza had been planning her return? Was I paranoid?

I had to go. "I'm leaving." To Alex, I said, "Try and get some more information out of Leeza." To Max, I said, "Try to get your shit out of my apartment by nightfall." If he really loved me, he'd know that I meant it—unless he made some lavish apologetic display. And came up with a damned good explanation. I wondered, not for the first time, if I were an impossible girlfriend.

I split like a banana for the gym. A slow banana. I took my time walking down Atlantic Avenue. The sun was bright. Some kids rode by on Rollerblades. Max and I had once talked about buying a couple of pairs so we could roll off into the sunset together. That's shot to hell, I thought. I shook off a pang of depression. Max had been talking to Leeza all that time. He lied about it. I remember reading a survey in *Mademoiselle* that said the number one thing women want from their boyfriends was honesty.

I felt a crushing pain where there once was a heart. The feeling was familiar. Shit, I practically wrote the book on heartbreak. I got a flash of Detective Falcone. I wondered how many disappointments she'd had with men before choosing ham sandwiches over hot dogs. Was it possible that I could ever make that choice? I vowed for three blocks to never put myself in the position of being hurt again. This pain was no gain. And there was no way to cure it. I didn't care what women's magazines said. They were all bullshit anyway.

I approached the Brooklyn Detention Center on my right. Jack must be inside. I pictured him, bare chested, running in circles in his cell like a well-oiled hampster, his blond hair cutely matting. I felt a powerful pull to see him. I wanted to find out what happened at the club after I made my break. I trotted up the steps of the Detention Center like a pony and opened the heavy doors.

The guards inside were the same from the last time I visited this fine correctional facility. I said, "Watson. Jack. Now."

The male guard with the short neck laughed at me. "What, you want me to bring him out here like a plate of french fries?"

"Nah. Just bring the fries."

The guard scoffed, stared.

"Then Jack would be fine," I relented.

Another guard, a woman—Officer Martinez, if I remember correctly—wore her shiny black hair twisted in a bun. She approached the desk. "Wanda Mallory?" she asked.

"Ameleth Bergen, actually. Jack Watson's wife."

"Too bad. Detective Falcone said only Wanda Mallory was allowed to meet with the prisoner. You'll have to go, Ms. Bergen."

I stammered briefly. I must be losing my cool, I thought. I regrouped and said, "I am Mallory. It's just that my boyfriend and I broke up, and I wanted to pretend to be someone who's married for only a minute. Not that getting married was ever a goal, per se. But with this guy, this latest guy, I thought I could do it. Maybe I would have cheated a few years down the road—longing for some fresh sex, that initial passion of new relationships—but in the end, I probably wouldn't have gone through with it. I have a particularly keen recall. I could just dredge up a few fantasies about what our sex used to be like. Even the memory of the other night. That would do."

The guards looked at each other, and then back at me. Finally, the female guard said, "I often use fantasy when having sex with my boyfriend."

"Me, too," said the male guard. "With the wife."

We stood silently and smiled at each other. A trio of closet fantasizers, sharing an intimate moment. I said, "So where's Jack?"

Back to business. The woman asked to see some ID.

I gave her my college food card—ten years old at this point. It was the only photo ID I owned. She stifled a giggle (so college wasn't my peak glam period). It was good enough to get me in. She took me through some electric doors to the cell block. Jack was back in his old space at the end of the long row. When he saw me, he said solemnly, "Wanda, it's good to see you."

Martinez hovered nearby. Jack eyed her suspiciously. I said, "Take a hike, okay?" She smiled and didn't budge. To Jack, I whispered, "What happened?"

He approached the bars and took my hand. Closer now, I could see he didn't look good. What I thought were dark circles under his eyes were bruises. I felt a chill. Jack put his hand on the back of my neck and pulled my head toward the bars. He whispered in my ear, "You're not safe here, Wanda. They're after you—the cops, Ameleth. They know you've got some notebook—whatever it is. You've got to run, now." He let go of my neck.

I stared at him. He mouthed, "Now." If what he said was true and Ameleth knew I had the notebook (which I no longer had anyway), she'd come after me with a vengeance. I could always tell her I was on the way to drop it off, but that whole deal I'd made with her was crap from the beginning. For the notebook, she'd have dumped me the same way she dumped Barney. She might have told Falcone I'd stolen it from her. I did, actually, but so what? I tried to organize my thoughts. No wonder those guards indulged me in my heartbreak speech when I came in. They probably had instructions to keep me here, no matter what. Falcone was probably steamrolling over from the precinct this second.

Hell hath no fury like a woman cornered like a rat. I turned toward the guard. I smiled and pointed down the corridor. "Dear God! What on earth is that?" I asked in horror.

Made her look. I stitched my fingers together to make a ball of power, swung at her jaw and hoped. I always close my eyes when I punch—involuntary reflex. I'm often surprised when I actually make contact. My fingers crunched against the hardness of bone. The vandals and drunks in the neighboring tanks cheered. When I opened my eyes, she was out cold on the floor, her shiny black hair knocked loose.

Jack was able to grab hold of a few strands to restrain her. He yelled, "Take the keys and run."

I struggled to work my throbbing fingers, barely managing to unhook the key chain off her belt. Then I was off. I unlocked the electric cell block door, slipped out and closed it as quietly as possible. The cheers from the prisoners must have been audible. I didn't spot the guard with the short neck, though.

Edging around the front hallway, I stuck to the walls like Velcro. I saw and heard nothing. I took Mama from my bag and held her in front of me. I kept moving, slowly by carefully, until I saw the front entrance. I smiled. Just twenty feet and I was golden.

"Don't move a muscle, lady."

I turned around anyway. The male guard was standing ten feet behind me, his gun pointed squarely at my nose. I put my hands up. He said, "Drop the gun on the floor and kick it over to me."

He seemed nervous but confident. For a second, I wondered if I was sunk.

But then, the Goddess smiled.

10

Desperado

Officer Martinez materialized over Short Neck's left shoulder. She ambled unsteadily toward us. He didn't hear her. Her jaw was already purple. A trickle of blood ran from her nose. I stared straight into Short Neck's tiny brown eyes. He drilled his gaze into mine.

Martinez gathered her strength to draw her gun. She screamed, "Drop it!" I did nothing of the sort. Short Neck, confused by the desperate shrill behind him, cursed loudly and let his gun fall out of his palm. It hit the floor with an echoing thud. He turned around to look at who'd challenged him, but by the time Martinez spun past him in the narrow hallway, I was history.

I flew like an eagle as fast as my platforms could flap. I got some bizarre stares from plebes on the street. I thought it was my dress, then realized I was still holding my gun. I crammed it in my purse.

If they didn't catch me within the next five minutes, it didn't matter. I slugged a cop. I was fucked. I kept running—my adrenaline carried me fast and far.

Before I knew where I was headed, I was racing up Pierrepont Street toward the Western Athletic Club. I stopped to catch my breath at the corner of Henry. I weighed the pros and cons of walking straight into bigger trouble than I was already in. The only pro I could think of was Janey. What did I have to lose, anyway? I felt reckless—and single.

Seeing no one on the street, I dashed toward the club entrance. Ergort wasn't standing on guard outside—strange for a sunny afternoon. I walked right into the club. I was shocked by my image in the mirrors on the walls. My dress was in tatters, my right shoe was falling apart, my chin was bruised. I looked a fright—but somehow thinner from all the exertion of the day.

A couple of anorexics passed me in workout togs. I smiled at them and waved energetically. Horrified at the possibility that they knew me, they quickly flip-flopped into the Cut Me store. Acting official, I slipped behind the front reception desk. Janey was nowhere to be found either, so I took the opportunity to snoop around. The video monitors were humming. I recognized no one on the screens. I flipped through some schedules and opened drawers. "Ah-ha," I said. "The key." In fact, there were about fifteen of them, all suspiciously similar in size and shape to the elevator key Jack had used to gain access to Ameleth's suite. I took one and pocketed it. I picked up the intercom. I buzzed Ameleth's suite. She answered and said hello. I thought I heard a voice in the background. Female. High-pitched, hostile. Ameleth said again, "Hello? Jesus, who the fuck is it?" If Ameleth were a flower, she'd be an impatiens.

I tried my best Brooklynese accent. "You order a large with sausage?"

"What?" she asked. "I ordered nothing, simp."

I replaced the receiver and left the desk. I made for the elevators. Still no sign of Ergort. I hit the elevator button. It came. I hopped on. Instead of taking the ride all the way up to the suite, I got off on the aerobics floor. I walked toward the front of the building to find the window that would put me on the fire escape. An aerobics class was in session. The instructor—a neatly packaged brunette with arms the size of breadsticks—shouted over the music, "One, two, three, and *hold.* One, two, three, and *breathe.* One, two, three, and *stretch. You're* the boss. You're the *boss.* It's all you, babe." She faced a wall-length mirror. Behind her, the women panted and fought desperately to keep up. I wondered if this were the beginners' class. The window was in the back, behind the rows of aerobicizers. The only one who'd see me climb on the fire escape would be the instructor. I waited for the right moment.

It came when she said, "And bend. And bend." She had scrunched herself into a tiny ball and rocked. "And stretch. And reach," she continued. She'd buried her head under her knee. I wondered if she too were one of Janey's girls, and how much extra that move would cost her clients. I ran for it. I was safe on the fire escape before she came up for air.

I scrambled one flight up to Ameleth's suite. I carefully peeked inside. No one was in the office space. I held my breath and tried the window. It was unlocked and sailed up easily. I slipped into the room. I heard the buzz of a stationary bicycle and the mechanical whir of the treadmill. Two of them. I tippy-toed across the office and plastered myself against the door to the exercise room. I heard voices.

The tiny baritone was Ameleth. She said, "So what

should I have done? Pretended the samples didn't exist? Mallory would have found out about them anyway. And remember, when I spoke to her, I didn't know the samples were safe. I thought they were stolen."

"Stupid, Ameleth. Let me tell you about people who aren't as rich as you are: If you offer them a lot of money to find something, they'll look damn hard. You shouldn't have offered her a penny. Wanda Mallory would do anything for money. She might as well be a whore like you, Janey."

"Watch that, Betty." That was Janey. But who the hell was Betty? The voice did sound familiar.

"And now, not only does she have the notebook, but we don't even have the samples anymore." The voice was scratchy, smoky.

Janey said, "Yeah, well, you didn't seem to care about holding on to the samples when you gulped down the chromium compound like your life depended on it."

Betty shot back, "At least we know it works."

Ameleth said, "Pull your shirt down, Betty. I just had lunch." The bike sped up. "We've got to decide who will tell Janey's friend Freddie that we lost the notebook." She paused. "I'm the one who had to get the formulas from Barney in the first place. And Janey's the one who was brave enough to hide the samples. All you did was look the other way during the murder investigation."

"Which is still open, ladies. I'm not telling Freddie anything. He's nothing to me. And don't look at each other like that. If you think you can cut me out, I'll throw you both in jail."

Falcone. That bitch. No wonder she'd been giving me such a hard time. Her first name was Betty?

"Ameleth is out thirty thousand dollars," Janey defended.

"And a lover," Ameleth added. "And a husband."

"Like you care at all about Jack," Janey said, the sound of the treadmill speeding up. "It was your idea to set him up for Barney's murder."

"Am I supposed to take the fall myself? I didn't kill Barney. I loved him. Fuck." The bike buzz stopped abruptly. I figured Ameleth was getting herself a garlic cocktail at the juice bar.

The door to the office burst open. It almost pinned me against the wall, but at least I was hidden behind it. I held my breath and waited for her to leave the room. Then I'd get the hell out of there. I didn't like it that this gang of three was on to me. Especially considering that one of them was a gun-carrying cop.

"Guys—get in here quick," Ameleth yelled. Did I forget to close the window behind me? Shit, I thought. You can get your PI license revoked for that kind of sloppy mistake.

I watched through the crack in the door as Janey and Falcone came in. There was a chorus of "What's wrong?" and "Are you okay?" Then there was silence. I saw the image in my head. Ameleth pointed at the open window. The three women putting a finger over their lips to say keep quiet to each other. Then they'd search the room for the mysterious interloper. I was doomed.

Janey threw back the door. My breath caught in my chest. Completely defenseless, my dress might as well have been ripped clean off. I groped instinctively for my gun, but there was no use. I thought to myself, Be cool. I stood up straight, crotch forward. I arranged my arms akimbo. "Jig's up, ladies. I know that you killed Barney, set up Jack and stole the formulas for your own greedy purposes. And, now you're going to pay." I looked at each woman as I spoke. When I got to the end of the line—to Falcone—I was stunned. She must have dropped ten pounds. She still had a ways to go, but damn, she looked good. I never noticed cheekbones—hers were high and strong. And her lovely neck—long and ropey. That chromium was a miracle. The women of America will rejoice. Just as soon as I could get the hell out of there.

Falcone glared with her beady eyes (that hadn't changed). A thin film of sweat covered her forehead and upper lip. She was nervous, but excited. "Where's the notebook?" she demanded.

"I don't have it," I tried.

"We know you have it, Wanda," Janey insisted. She seemed tired. I didn't think she really had the heart for anything crueler than fat jokes.

I ribbed, "Special offer today. Twenty years at Rikers for slutty receptionists." That woke her up. She growled. Smoke billowed out her nostrils, steam out her ears. "You really should do something about that," I offered. "It's very unbecoming."

"Shut up, Mallory," Falcone barked. "Ten guys told police officers that they saw a woman answering your description walk through the weight room with a spiral notebook under your dress shortly after the attack on Leeza Robbins was reported."

"Lies, all lies."

"You dropped it at one point. One of the guys tried to pick it up but you kicked him."

"He was looking under my dress." I turned to Ameleth. "What kind of perverts do you let in here anyway?"

Falcone sighed heavily. She reached into her pocket and pulled out a cigarette. She offered me one. I refused. She lit up. Her secondhand smoke tasted swell—even menthol. Finally, she said, "Are you going to give us the notebook now or will we have to convince you?"

"I told you already—I don't have it to give." It was the truth.

"So where is it?"

"I gave it to AA—Aerobicizers Anonymous." That went over like an anvil.

Ameleth propped her tiny butt on the corner of her desk. She folded her skinny arms across her pink leotard and said, "We've got a lot riding on this. If I don't get my hands on those formulas, this club is ruined."

"What about Freddie Kruger? Has anyone seen his face lately?" They stared blankly at me. "Jack is rotting in prison. Leeza Robbins is in the hospital. Barney is dead. Me and my boyfriend broke up. All so you could make yourselves the richest women in New York? Sorry, but my motivation for helping isn't quite clear."

Falcone said, "How about staying alive?"

"You'll kill me like Barney? Leave me bleeding in a hot tub with a knife in my chest? What'd he do to deserve that, anyway? Try to take over the operation? So like a man," I tsked.

Ameleth sputtered, "We didn't kill Barney. I swear." I didn't believe her. "I loved him," she added, tearing up.

Janey said, "What do you mean Barney had a knife in his chest?"

"Did I say that?" I asked. Falcone eyed me suspiciously.

"We never recovered a murder weapon, Mallory," she said dryly.

I said, "He was stabbed—I assumed by a knife. You pick up on these things when you're a private detective." Janey put her head in her hands at the thought of the stabbing. With her face covered, her blond hair falling over her slender arms, it hit me. She was tall, muscular. Straight blond hair. "The one thing I don't quite get is Leeza's attack," I said. "What did she have to do with any of this?"

"Nothing," Ameleth said. "Absolutely nothing."

"Precisely, Watson," I said.

Ameleth bristled. "My name is Bergen, not Watson. If Jack wanted some chump who'd change her name, he could have married Janey."

"I'm no chump," Janey interrupted.

"Sure you are," I said. "Leeza was attacked from behind, by the way, Janey. Her teeth were knocked out when she fell face first into the Jacuzzi. From the back, you and Leeza have a pretty similar view. Maybe the attacker fucked up. After all, why would he or she hit someone who had nothing to do with nothing." I twisted my mouth like I was trying to figure something out. "What exactly do you, Janey, have to do with this mess?"

"Everything," she whispered. She turned to see the guilt on Falcone and Ameleth's faces. Slowly, obviously terrified, Janey backed out of the room. We watched.

Falcone said, "Go ahead, Janey. We'll find you." Janey didn't care. She jumped in the elevator at a run. It sunk with a whoosh.

Ameleth said, "This whole thing is just so botched. Betty, we need to talk. Maybe we should cut our losses now."

Falcone shook her head in disgust. "Why don't you just tell Mallory everything. That's a great idea." Ameleth flexed her legs compulsively in response.

This didn't look good for me. Falcone removed her gun from her shoulder holster. She walked toward me with the barrel in her hand.

I said, "Before you do anything you'll regret, you should know that there are twenty men with guns downstairs waiting for my word to arrest you all." Falcone leered. The flat end of the black gun butt was the last thing I saw.

I was on a sunny beach in a black tank suit. A skinny boy in cutoffs scrambled up a palm tree in his bare feet. He hacked down a coconut with his machete. After jumping out of the tree, he chopped the top off the fruit, plunked a straw in the hole and handed it to me. I licked my lips in anticipation for the sweet, thick taste of coconut milk. I took a sip. It tasted like sand mixed with paste. I looked up. The little kid was laughing.

I woke with a start. I opened my eyes, but the light was blinding. I had to shut them. I tried to move my arms, but they were immobile. So were my legs. I tried to turn over, but found that I was stuck inside a body-shaped capsule. I was like toothpaste in a tube. My eyelids pulsed with flashes of color and light.

I heard a *click*. The light disappeared. I felt the first rush of panic. Trapped, in a tiny dark place. I squirmed around and tried to thrash my way out. A rush of air blew against my face, and the lid opened like a clam. I must have hit some kind of release. I thanked the Goddess and moved my arms. They felt stiff, but fine. I tried to open my eyes, but I was too dizzy. I touched my face to see if there were any open cuts. Nothing except the egg-size bump on my cheek. I decided to count to ten before I tried to sit up. I folded my arm across my ribs and began counting. Something seemed strange. I ran my hand up to my shoulders. No bumps or tender spots, except for the ones I got with adolescence. I was naked.

I bolted upright. White spots and wavy lines danced before my eyes. I shook my head and they cleared. I wasn't wearing my glasses—I wondered where they were—so I had to squint. The lid of the contraption I'd been lying in was comprised of long fluorescent-shaped bulbs under a glass casing. A timer was attached to the front of it. The highest time was one hour. I stepped out of the machine to get a better look. The glass bottom part I'd been lying on also contained long bulbs. I looked around the room. There were a few facial tables. A steam machine. A shelf full of creams and ointments. A beauty spa room. Mainly skin stuff.

It hit me like a flying pan to the skull. I spun around. A sign on the wall behind the capsule confirmed my fears. It read: DO NOT EXCEED TEN MINUTE UV SESSIONS. The capsule was an ultraviolet tanning bed. I checked my watch. It was gone. For all I knew, I'd been under the light for a full hour. I read once that these contraptions can cook someone from the inside out, like a human microwave. I shivered. I touched my skin. It felt normal. I looked in the magnifying mirror by one of the facial tables. My skin seemed as pale as ever.

As I examined the tip of my nose, I saw him in the mirror behind me. At first I wasn't sure it was a person, or just a person-size shape in jeans and a T-shirt. I made a mental note to consider contacts. I spun around. He stood frozen like a Popsicle. "If it isn't the lascivious towel boy," I said. "Did you turn off the machine?"

He stood paralyzed with fear or lust—I didn't

really know. Finally, he nodded. "Yeah," he managed, his eyes locked on my hips.

"For saving my life, you can have a good long look." I arranged myself in a flattering posture—one leg forward, knee turned in. I sang a chorus of "Rainy Days and Mondays" in my head. "That's enough," I said. "Turn around, but don't you dare run off. I want to talk to you."

My clothes were on a chair by the UV machine. I grabbed my stuff and threw it on. My purse was there. My watch and glasses were inside it. Falcone would be coming back soon to stick a fork in me. I had to get out of the building fast or I'd really get cooked. I said, "Okay, you can turn around."

He faced me. I looked him over myself. He couldn't have been more than sixteen. "As you now know," I said, "I am a natural redhead. That's one you've got up on me. I want you to tell me something."

He eyed me nervously and said, "'Kay." His vocabulary was as broad as his shoulders. He moved his hands in front of his pants. Must have a hard-on.

I smiled and took a step toward him. He took a step back. "How long was I cooking in there before you turned it off?" My skin felt absolutely normal.

He shrugged. I asked, "Did you see who put me in there?"

"Yeah," he said. "I was watching from behind that." He pointed at one of the facial tables. "She took off your clothes." He shifted on his feet.

"You a virgin, towel boy?"

He turned bright red before saying, "Yeah."

"Too bad for you, buddy. Who put me in there? Was it Ameleth?"

"Nah, some cow," he said. I assumed he meant the

slimmed-down Falcone. He shifted uncomfortably. "Look, I'm not supposed to be in the ladies' spa. If anyone finds out I was peeping again, I'll get fired."

"You're not getting fired, kid." I checked my watch: after five. I told the kid to get lost. I split the gym myself—walked right out the front door. I didn't see anyone around. In fact, the place was eerily quiet. Ergort hadn't been at his post all afternoon. I wondered if this was his day off. If Ameleth and Betty (Betty!) Falcone weren't around, they were probably hunting for the notebook and Janey, not necessarily in that order. I felt a chill. The night was nippy. Should I go to the cops and tell them that their crack homicide dick tried to kill me? Go to the hospital and recover the notebook? Hide?

I headed home. I was shivering. I needed warmer clothes before I could do anything. I wondered if Max would be there. It'd only been a couple hours since I accused him of lying. After all that's happened, Leeza knowing his work number didn't seem that important. I turned onto Hicks Street. My skin began to feel prickly as if I'd rolled in salt. I hugged myself and kept walking.

When I got home a few minutes later, Mr. Burpe was at his post on the stoop. I nodded. He grunted and said, "Pretty noisy up there." Was Max really moving out? I ignored him and I let myself in. As I walked up the steps, I heard some thuds and bumps coming from my apartment—the unmistakable sound of furniture and suitcases dragging across the floor. He hadn't even bothered to fight for me, the bastard. Out of the tanning bed and into the fire.

As I stood at the door, key in hand, I vacillated between acting contrite and apologetic or bitchy and uncaring. I decided on restless and annoyed. I pushed the door open and said, "Aren't you out of my life yet?" The cats were nowhere in sight.

The voice that answered was gruffer than Max's. It said, "One more step, and I'll smash your pansy ass boyfriend like an egg."

I looked around but didn't see where the voice was coming from. I nervously said, "Smash like an egg? You can scramble him like an egg. Or even fry him like an egg. But you smash a tennis ball, or a bottle of beer against your forehead." I slipped inside and darted behind one of my large, unpacked clothing boxes in the living room. I said, "Okay, Ergort. Let Max go and I'll do what you want."

I heard Ergort hold his massive, steroidian breath. "How'd you know it was me?" he asked.

"The stench."

"Keep those jokes coming, Mallory, and I'll—"

"You'll what? Whip my boyfriend like a cheeseburger? Beat him like a sponge?" My skin prickled. I looked at my arm. The UV rays had definitely had an effect; I was starting to glow pink.

"Wanda, I think you should know that every time you open your mouth, this man tightens his grip about my neck." Max's voice gurgled. Once I'd killed a man to save Alex's life. And now Max was in danger because of me. I wondered if I, like so many other women, was blaming myself without just cause. I said, "Let Max go and I'll give you the notebook."

Here's my theory: Barney used Ergort as his guinea pig. That's how Ergort got so gargantuan in just one year after quitting the force. For the first time in his life, Ergort felt happy about his looks. He found out somehow about Larry's super steroid, and he wanted to try it. Barney told him no. Ergort was furious—and prone to roid rage rampages anyway from his usual dosage. He stole the knife from the kitchen and killed Barney for denying him. As I now knew, Janey doled out keys to the suite like a Pez dispenser.

Ergort waited a few seconds before answering. Finally, he said, "I'm here for your ass, Mallory."

I scrambled (like an egg) behind another box—one closer to the bedroom. "Don't give me this shit," I said. "I know you're here for the formulas."

"I told you not to move." I heard a crack and gasp. "I'll break him like a stick. Okay? I'll snap him like a fucking twig!"

"Okay. I'm not moving, Ergort." While I dug for Mama in my purse, a revisionist theory occurred to me: If Ergort was going to kill anyone, he'd do it with his bare hands. He might have set out to attack Janey and gotten Leeza but maybe he didn't kill Barney. What was the connection? I couldn't find my gun. The knife was still in there, but Mama was missing. Falcone must have left me the knife as part of her setup of Jack. But she took my gun. Damn her. Mama was like family to me.

"Hey, Ergort," I yelled in their direction. "You took a lot of shit when you were on the force, right? The cops made fun of you because you were scrawny. But there was one cop who didn't make fun of you. This cop got a lot of abuse, too, and the two of you bonded together for protection."

"Wanda, shut up," Max gurgled. "He's choking me."

I tried to get closer. But just as I was about to make a move, Ergort and Max banged out of the bedroom. Max was a fairly big guy—six feet and one-eighty—

but Ergort dragged him along like a rag doll. Max never looked so powerless. I wanted to save him. I cowered behind my sweater box and held my breath as the two men swung past me.

Ergort said, "What happened in the past doesn't matter, Mallory. Betty and I love each other and I'll do anything she wants. Beat up Janey, toss your apartment. I fucked up by hurting Leeza. An honest mistake. But this time, I'll get it right. I'm going to find this notebook if I have to kill you for it."

Jack had said both Janey and Ergort were not at their posts when he got to the club. Was Ergort in one elevator coming down from the suite while Jack rode up? Had Jack really been that lucky? If he'd walked in on Ergort attacking Leeza, Ergort would have killed Jack on the spot.

"Go right ahead. Ransack the place," I said. "There's some rope under the kitchen sink if you want to tie up me and Max."

"What?" Max protested.

"That's sounds like a good idea," Ergort concurred.

I resolved myself to the decision. I had no other option—no gun, no dynamite, no loaded syringes with lethal injections. My skin was beginning to tighten across my face. The pain was minimal, but I didn't want to be touched at all, much less fight Ergort. I stood up, revealing myself. Ergort tightened his grip on Max when he saw me. Max glared in shock. I held up my hands and walked toward the bathroom. I said, "I'd tie us to the sink pipes if I were you. Then you can search the entire place without us getting in the way. You'll want to search the bathroom first, of course."

In a matter of minutes, Max and I were lashed to the sink. Ergort was ripping apart our bed, our unpacked boxes. I wasn't exactly sure what he was doing, but I knew it was loud. That was what I'd hoped for.

"This is just great, Wanda," Max informed me. "Some three-hundred-pound maniac is demolishing our apartment and we're totally defenseless. Is it my imagination, or are you turning purple?"

"If I had my gun, smartass, I would have shot him. He's certainly an easy target." Mama, though, was only a .22. I'd have to hit him in the head to stop a behemoth like Ergort. "Yes, I'm turning purple."

"So what now? We sit here like assholes and wait for him to find what he's looking for? Then maybe he'll go."

"Except he won't find it. The notebook isn't here." I thought I heard voices on the street and the squawk of a police radio.

Max said, "He'll kill us when he doesn't find it."

My skin hurt. The rope around my tender wrist cut like knives. "I never wanted you to move out. I was just furious that you lied to me."

"I didn't ever lie, Wanda. I told you about all those hang ups my receptionist has been getting at the office. It must have been Leeza." I wasn't convinced.

"But you rushed to the hospital. You must have feelings for her."

"What if I totally ignored her and didn't give a shit that the woman I was once close to had been beaten unconscious and was in the emergency room? Would you prefer that?"

"Yes." I smiled at him. He smiled back. We had to twist ourselves into an uncomfortable position to kiss. It was wet and hot and worth it.

Max said, "Is it me or is your skin five hundred degrees?" A knock on our apartment door kept me from answering. Ergort must have missed it, what with his search and destroy mission in our bedroom. I heard the tinkle of keys and then the door open.

"Police!" we heard them yell as they burst in. Mr. Burpe had come through.

I shouted, "In here." The uniform, Frankie, the one who came here looking for Jack, popped his head in the bathroom. I said, "There's a mad giant destroying our apartment."

Frankie spun around quickly. I heard the click of a bullet cartridge. A moment of silence floated over the apartment. It ended with an anguished scream and a gunshot. Cloddish feet thumped across the wood floors. There was a shuffle and then another shot. The silence returned.

From under the sink, our sighs of relief echoed. Max said, "How did you know Mr. Burpe would actually call the cops?"

"I didn't."

"If he hadn't, we'd be dead."

"Possibly," I agreed.

Max shook his head at the idea. "Kind of makes you want to get married and have kids, doesn't it?"

"Not really."

The cops had to call for reinforcements to carry Ergort out of our apartment. He was shot twice— once in the leg and once in the chest. It would have taken a cannon to kill Ergort. He hadn't even passed out. The shooters were pretty amazed when I told them they'd wounded Ergort the ex-cop. Frankie said, "A year ago, you could have knocked him down with a wad of spit." I wondered if they'd put that message on the police report.

Ergort had been crying for darling Betty for half an

hour before the cops made the connection. Then the wounded giant started blabbing his brains out. Falcone had sent him to my place. She'd ordered him to beat up Janey because she was beginning to get nervous about their plot. He fucked up and hit the wrong woman. Not knowing what to do, he just left Leeza in the Jacuzzi and waited for another chance at Janey.

Mr. Burpe acted apologetic for calling the cops on us when he found out about Ergort. I told him to fuck off and that we were moving out at the end of the month. He hung his sorry Irish head in shame. I liked the picture, and filed it in my mental photo album.

As soon as we could, Max and I left. I thought about Jack and how he'd saved me at the Detention Center. I wanted to go to the hospital. My arms were beginning to blister. But first, I had bigger fish to gut. We headed toward the heart of the Heights. I told Max the whole story—that Ameleth and Janey conspired to steal Larry's formula to get rich. Barney was in on it, but he was killed. Ameleth swore she didn't do it. But to thwart a long, probing investigation, she told Falcone about the super steroid and the chromium compound. She wanted in, so Falcone agreed to help frame Jack for the murder. Things went awry when Ameleth told me about the formulas. Had she waited, Janey could have told her she'd taken them from the murder scene herself to hide them safely. I vaguely remembered Janey hanging by the fridge that night. But Ameleth was impatient, and she opened up to me. She should have kept her mouth shut. She had the notebook—she didn't really need the samples. Maybe she was innocent of murder. She had spilled to me because she wanted to know who did kill Barney.

"It's amazing you figured this out. God, you're a lobster," Max observed. "How long were you trapped in the tanning bed anyway?"

"Oh, now you're proud of my detecting skills?" I bet Ameleth went berserk when she discovered the notebook was gone. I pictured her frizzy hair standing on end.

Max asked, "I can't believe Leeza survived an attack by Ergort."

"Glad to hear you're blaming him now."

"It was never your fault, Wanda."

"Easy for you to say now that it so clearly wasn't," I said.

Max shook his head in disbelief. "You never cease to amaze me."

"But if I ever do, you'll let me know?"

"I hope that won't be for a long, long time," Max said. He put his arm around my waist. It felt prickly, but swell. "Where to now?" he asked.

We'd walked a few blocks down Hicks Street to the corner of Montague. "To round up Barney's killer," I said. I pointed at the colossal front doors of the Jehovah's Bossert Hotel. We walked in, getting some stares along the way. I admit that my dress was, by now, unacceptable attire. Maybe they'd never seen a magenta-skinned woman before. But if I were them, I'd be a lot more embarrassed if I had one of those bowl haircuts.

The man at the front desk had one. Around forty, he wore the standard short-sleeved white shirt and tie. I asked him to buzz Larry Black's apartment. He scowled at me and didn't do a thing. I also said that I'd scream at the top of my lungs until I got what I wanted. He nodded and pushed a button on the console. Max and I waited.

Brother Samuel appeared just as I was about to start screaming. I said, "Hello, Brother. We're here for Larry."

Brother smiled brightly and invited us to sit on one of the wooden lobby benches. We sat. He said, "Lawrence has been asked to leave our church. He's currently moving his things out of the building, and we want nothing and no one to disrupt him." He stared at my face. "Are you all right? Your nose is bubbling."

"We've come to help Larry pack."

"That pagan woman is already helping him."

He must mean Molly, I thought. "Perfect. We'll make it a foursome."

Brother blanched. I didn't think it possible considering the already pasty pallor of his skin. He looked at Max. Max smiled his clean-cut American boy smile. "Very well," Brother said uncertainly. "Up the stairs two flights. Third door on the left. I would like all of you out in five minutes."

We followed Brother's directions and found Larry and Molly lugging two large suitcases down the hallway. We ran to catch up to them. Molly's mouth formed a hard line when she saw us. She wore the same black workout clothes I'd last seen her in. Larry had changed into jeans and a clean white cotton shirt. He said, "Thank the Lord. Wanda. Brother Samuel destroyed my lab. You've still got the notebook, I hope?"

"Should we talk in the hallway?"

Molly frowned. Larry shrugged and backed up into his old room. We followed him. I closed the door behind me.

I introduced Max while checking out the room. It was Spartan and clean. The bed was just a box spring and mattress on a metal stand. A convenience kitchen was tucked into a corner—just a half-size fridge and ministove. Molly and Larry took seats on the bed. Max stood next to me. I did a quick appraisal. Max could take Molly if pressed. "I've got a gun," I lied.

Molly's leg muscles tensed. She looked at Max, checking out his bod to see if she could take him. Larry said, "We won't need a gun, Wanda. Brother Samuel has allowed me to leave. As long as I never come back." Larry's voice trailed off at the end. I wondered if he was upset at the prospect of leaving his church.

"We're not busting out of here, Larry," I said. "But this is a bust of sorts, I suppose."

In a blazing second, Molly came at me, her talons ripping through the air. She had her hands around my throat in seconds. We fell on the floor and she began beating my head against the fine, inlaid wood. Max peeled her off me. I regained composure and slapped her across the face. I said, "If I didn't have a client in jail for the murder, Molly, I'd consider forgetting the whole thing." Of course, Jack wasn't in jail for murder. But they didn't need to know that.

Larry sucked in air. "My Lord—Molly? You *did* kill Barney!"

"No, Larry," I said. "You did." Molly went limp in Max's arms and started crying quietly. I went on: "Both of you had the opportunity—that's for sure. And I thought for a while that Molly did it. She probably had a key to the suite from her days working for Janey." I could tell from Molly's dejected face that I was right about that. "But something bothered me about Molly as the killer. For one thing, Barney wouldn't have placidly sat in the Jacuzzi when a strange, crazed woman approached him. He'd try to protect himself. But when he saw Larry—a nonviolent Jehovah's Witness—come into the room, Barney probably assumed Larry'd try to reason with him. It never occurred to Barney that Larry could be violent. It hardly occurred to me, especially after Molly broke my ribs while you stood there and watched."

"You're guessing," Larry said.

"The clincher was the bread knife. Molly was intimate with kitchen cutlery—she special ordered a set from Sweden for Christ's sake."

"Please don't take the Lord's name in vain," Larry said by rote.

I rolled over it. "If Molly was going to stab a man in the heart, she'd take a butcher knife, or something hair-splitting sharp. If she was going to, say, chop off Barney's arm, a serrated knife would be good. You, Larry, a simple chemical engineer, just grabbed the first knife you could reach."

"She could have, too, if she was rushing," he tried. I was amazed that Larry was so comfortable with the idea of Molly taking the fall for him.

"You've got big plans, don't you?" I asked.

Larry smiled and said, "Someone like you could never understand what it means to believe deeply in a faith. I have a spiritual path, and that's the only reason to go on living. Molly and I believe in a fat-free, cholesterol-free, healthy, fit America. It's my purpose to make that happen."

"And that's what you're going to do in Hawaii?" I asked.

"Or Oregon. A lot of fledgling religions find a happy home in the Northwest."

Max said, "Wanda—you're turning fuchsia. I think you need to go to the hospital."

"I've got an idea," said Larry. "You go to the hospital. Keep the notebook. Molly and I will leave quietly, and this whole thing will be over."

"But Larry," Molly protested, "the formulas were our gold mine. If we leave now, we'll have nothing."

"Except each other," I deadpanned. Just turning up the corners of my mouth felt like fishhooks digging into my skin. I fought a wave of nausea and dizziness. I looked at Max. Beads of worry sprouted on his forehead. I nodded to myself. "Okay. If you agree to fly out of here tonight, and promise never to come back to New York, I'll look the other way."

I took a step toward the door, stumbling slightly. Max caught me. He whispered in my ear, "Wanda, you're about to let a killer go free."

"I'm too sick to care," I said, meaning it. My legs were bubbling now with blisters. I must have been in the tanning bed for an hour. Max lifted me in his arms Tarzan-style. Even in my pain, I felt buoyed by the manliness of it. The four of us walked down the stairs. They carried their suitcases. Max carried me. I carried the murder weapon in my purse, but not for long.

Once on the street, Max ran me to the car service on Montague Street. We hopped a hack and sped to Brooklyn General. On the way, I told Max what to do. He took mental notes. Unlike me, he'd keep them. "Remember how you said you wanted to get married and have kids?" I asked him when we pulled up to the emergency room entrance.

"I said that?"

"You bastard."

"Just kidding," he said. "Don't tell me the burns have fried your sense of humor."

"I guess my days as a fair maiden are over."

"Your days as a maiden are," he said.

I was about to say something like, "I'd rather drown in sweetbreads than marry you," when I passed out clean. As I sank down the dark spiral, I wondered if losing consciousness twice in one day could cause brain damage. I wondered if I'd wake up scarred and ugly. I dreamed of caviar on toast and burned onion rings.

11

This One Goes to Eleven

"You have to keep your wrists firm, like steel," Max instructed from the end of my hospital bed. He was explaining to Alex how to bench press properly. I watched them in disbelief.

"Where's the lavishing of attention on me, huh?" I asked. Max and Alex stopped trading pumping secrets for a moment. They each patted me on my precious head and then launched into a hearty discussion of protein supplements. Alex had brought chocolates. I forgave him.

I'd been a resident of Brooklyn General for twenty-four hours. The previous afternoon, I spent four of them in the emergency room. I had first- and second-degree burns on ninety percent of my body. The only part that wasn't fried was the back of my head. Max massaged it hourly. The rest of me was suspended by traction straps. They rotated me like a rotisserie pig every five hours. I got sponged with icy water every twenty minutes. The pain was only bad when I didn't take my Percodans. I never forgot so that wasn't a problem. The doctor didn't think I'd scar too badly. I'd cool off in a couple months.

This was not my idea of the perfect summer. Or honeymoon. That's right. I got married. Max did, too.

But I'm getting ahead of myself. Earlier, in the emergency room, I was taken to a bed by Annabelle. Alex was nearby at Leeza's side. I was never left alone. Once I was settled (and unconscious), Max booked over the Brooklyn Bridge to the marriage license bureau in the City Hall building in lower Manhattan. He made it with nanoseconds to spare. He gave a secretary on her way home a hundred bucks to stand in for me to get the license. (In New York, you don't need a blood test.) By the time he got back to the hospital, I'd been revived. The hospital staff rabbi married us. Max alerted his insurance company immediately, and he signed all the paperwork to have me admitted to a room upstairs. Have I mentioned that I had no health insurance? Not that I married Max for his coverage, but four thousand dollars a day for a couple months was a whole lot of money. I could have only hoped to get that much in wedding presents.

Alex said, "I think she's slipped into another one of those Percodan comas."

I spoke up. "When am I going to get a ring?"

Max laughed. "By the time your fingers have returned to their normal size, you probably won't even want one."

"Oh, I'll want one, darling. And I expect you to wear one, too," I warned him. To Alex, I said, "And you've got three hundred sixty-four days left to get me a very expensive gift."

Alex kissed the back of my head. "Consider it

done." He smiled his big smile—with teeth—and raked the brown hair from his eyes.

Here's how the case wrapped up: As soon as we got to the hospital, Max called the cops. He told them about Larry and Molly. The police didn't believe Max at first. They already had Ameleth Bergen and Janey Johnson in for questioning. Max had to explain over and over again what he'd heard at the Bossert. Finally, the cops agreed to put out an APB for Larry Black and Molly Mahoney. They were caught at La Guardia Airport when the murder knife set off the metal detectors at the gate. A large bag of speed was also found in their suitcase. Once surrounded by security guards, Molly cracked. She told them everything. But she still didn't know how the murder weapon found its way into her suitcase's outside pocket.

Alex helped out with the Falcone bust. While in the emergency room, I begged him to find the towel boy who'd saved my life and get him to talk to the cops. He witnessed Falcone put me in there. Alex didn't want to leave Leeza's side. Apparently, there was some trouble with getting her a room. (I later wondered if the molesting ER doctor had anything to do with that.) Anyway, Alex found the towel boy at the gym, peeping. That kid never gave it a rest. After some convincing and some blackmailing, the horny dork agreed to go to the Brooklyn Heights precinct and tell the cops what he'd seen. After he did, Falcone had attempted murder (mine, that is) added to her list of offenses. When convicted, she'd be gone for a long, long time. I wondered if conspiring to lose ten pounds was worth losing ten years of her life. Falcone was caught by the cops soon after the towel boy gave his statement. She was spotted throwing an unidentified pearl-handled .22 caliber revolver into the East River. I cried when I heard that. I guess it was time for me to put away childish things. My next gun would be a .45.

Jack Watson was released from the Detention Center after paying a five-thousand-dollar fine for his claustrophobic seizures stunt and pulling Officer Martinez's hair. He came to visit me eight weeks after the busts, my second-to-last week at the hospital. He'd recovered from his experiences at the Brooklyn Detention Center extremely well. "I've decided to divorce Ameleth," he announced. "And I'm going back on the tennis circuit."

"Bull," I said, by now resting on the bed comfortably. "You love her. Even if she set you up. And you're afraid to play. You can't even lob balls with a five-year-old."

He sat at the foot of my bed and shook his blond head vigorously. "I've changed, Wanda," he announced. "After all that I've been through in the last few weeks—Ameleth's betrayal, mainly—I realized that my entire relationship with her only served—served, I'm even using tennis words again—anyway, she served to perpetuate my self-doubt. She wasn't exactly a nurturing partner. Now that I've found someone who is more supportive, I can't not try. I'm only twenty-five years old. Jimmy Connors made it to the U.S. Open Finals when he was practically a grandfather at thirty-five. I even hit the ball a few times with my new girlfriend. She was an aerobics instructor at the club before she got in an accident there. Leeza Robbins? Ever meet her?"

Leeza's wounds had healed in a few days. She'd been back at the club for a month and a half already. I wondered if Alex knew about her friendship with Jack. "You should take Leeza on the road with you," I suggested. Just because she wasn't a threat anymore didn't mean I wanted her around.

"You did it again," Jack remarked, slapping the bed. "My God, but you are brilliant. As a matter of fact, Leeza and I are flying out tonight. We're going to London. To Wimbledon. Not that I can get in the tournament, but it'll be good for me to go check it out. I should get back in the scene. Make myself known. Get a new coach. And with all the money, I might as well live a little."

The money. Here's how that happened: Ameleth had to declare bankruptcy to pay for her legal fees. She was forced to sell the club. Jack arranged the sale of the club to Brother Samuel of the Jehovah's within weeks. All was settled by the time my skin healed. Brother planned to keep the club as a fitness center for post-apocalypse survival training. Because Jack was still married to Ameleth, he was legally entitled to half of the sale money. Jack walked away with about a quarter of a million. Dollars, that is.

"Which reminds me," I said. "Don't you owe me a few grand?"

"I thought we were all straight, weren't we?" Jack asked. "The three thousand I gave you should cover it."

"Plus expenses," I said. "About five thousand worth."

Jack wrote a check. He handed it to me and got up to leave. "I hope you'll be happy, Wanda."

"Who says I wasn't happy before?"

"Marriage is hard," he said. "It was for me, anyway."

I told this story to Max and Alex on my last day at Brooklyn General. Max said, "You're going to take marital advice from that guy?"

"He just wants me to be careful."

Alex said, "You don't know how to be careful, though you should. With birth control at least."

"And now that all this is over," Max said, "you'll be hanging up your gumshoes for good. Right, honey?"

"Hanging up my gumshoes?" I mocked. "Please, dear. Leave the witty patter to me." Max left the room to find out what was holding up my discharge—from the hospital, that is.

After Max had left the room, Alex sat on my bed and asked, "What's this about gumshoes?" His jaw muscles were jumping under the skin. Goddamn that husband of mine and his big flapping mouth, I thought. Husband? Did I say husband? How comic.

"I haven't decided anything yet," I lied. "But Max and I were talking about the possibility that I might cool out on detecting for a little while." We'd been talking about it a lot, actually. Every day. For the first time in my personal detecting history, I was beginning to agree with Max about quitting. I got burned in this case—physically and metaphorically. I didn't think I could get it up again anytime soon. It's one thing to claim blithely that I, supersleuth Mallory, laugh brazenly in the face of fear. But this time around, I went snout-to-snout with it. Fear turned out not to be so fucking funny after all.

Alex said, "And you were planning on sharing this information with me, your partner, at some point, I assume?" He was getting angry. I could tell by his nervous hair raking.

"I figured I'd let you know."

"Big of you." He stood up and walked across the hospital room. He stared into the mirror by the sink. "You suck, Mallory."

"Eggs? Meat? Out loud?" I asked, attempting levity.

Alex didn't laugh. "I could have been a famous photographer by now. If I hadn't devoted the last five fucking years of my life to you. To your fucking agency. To this detecting crap."

"Yeah, you could have been a contender." I watched his back tense. "And you know it's not crap. We caught murderers. We protected New York from itself."

"We did some good? Is that what you're saying? Well, in that case, it's fine for you to make decisions about our agency without talking to me first," he said, heavy on the irony. He turned around to face me. "What am I supposed to do now?"

I was beginning to get pissed off myself at this point. "Well, considering that you need me to hold your dick when you take a piss, I have no idea. And if you're really that upset I married Max, then maybe we should part for a while."

"This has nothing to do with Max," he said dismissively. "If you haven't noticed by now, I'm not the marrying kind. I'm happy for you. But I hate you for leaving me in the lurch like this. I had this vision of our future, Wanda. Me and you, solving crimes for years and years. We'd be middle-aged and graying. You'd be fat. I'd be bald."

"That's your rosy vision of our future?" I asked.

"Yeah," he said, crossing his arms over his cute, skinny chest.

I felt a pang. "First of all, I'm never going to get fat. And second, sometimes I forget that you're a big sopping wet Kleenex. I'm sorry. I should have talked to you about this sooner. But I suppose I knew you'd be bummed, and I hate to upset my best friend. Except when you deserve it, of course."

Alex considered my quasi-apology. "This is where we're supposed to hug and say 'I love you.'"

"Let's not and say we did," I suggested.

"Good call," Alex agreed. "And may I also add that when you're fifty and big as a house, I'll remind you of this conversation."

"I'll brain you if you do."

Max returned, unable to locate the doctor who could release me. Alex smiled at me. I felt better now that he knew.

"Let's just go," I said, sick of waiting for some doctor to give me permission to leave. So we left the hospital. It was a Saturday afternoon. I was still kind of sore, but my skin was recovering nicely. I might have some scarring, but nothing a little vitamin E couldn't fix in a few years. We were just outside the hospital, starting our walk home when Annabelle came running after us.

"Wait!" she shouted with her Jamaican lilt. "Ms. Mallory! Hold up."

We held up. She reached us quickly. She was out of breath from the run. She wiped her forehead with her heavily bangled arm and handed me a large manila envelope. "This belongs to you," she said. "It couldn't help us save that man—Freddie Kruger. He was too far gone to do much of anything. But I thought you might want it. I planned to bring it up to you sooner, but things got busy. You know how it is."

"Don't I." My heart started to pound in my chest. I opened the envelope. Sure enough, the shiny green spiral notebook was inside. I quickly closed the envelope and thanked Annabelle. "Where is Freddie now?" I asked, having forgotten about him.

"He's working for the hospital, actually. As a physical therapist for kids with musculature problems. The patients don't seem to be afraid of him, despite his appearance. Some even like him that way. And he does have those magic fingers." That much I knew. We said good-bye. We agreed to have coffee, but we both knew we never would. Once she'd gone, I asked Max, "How much do you think one of those big pharmaceutical companies would pay for this research?"

"A few million, give or take a hundred thousand," he figured.

"That should be enough," I said.

Alex asked, "For what?"

"Whatever," I answered.

Mr. Burpe was stationed on the stoop when we got back to our apartment. He grunted. I gave him the finger. Max and I agreed it didn't make sense to move out right away—we'd keep the place for a year. We'd have to make an Ikea run to replace the stuff Ergort splintered. He unpacked everything and bought a futon couch in the meantime. Alex and I sat on it while Max made us some frozen margaritas.

"You miss that bimbo?" I asked Alex. Leeza told him about her decision to go to London with one foot out the door to the airport.

"What bimbo?" he asked. He pushed hair off his face. His brown pearls seemed foggy for a second. He shook his head to clear it. A pang gripped my chest. I hoped Alex wasn't lonely. I knew things would never be the same between us. The thought made me sad.

"I guess it's good you're quitting," he announced.

"You mean, now that I'm married?" I asked.

"No. I mean now that you got burned physically and otherwise."

I smiled and touched his cheek. "There you go, reading my mind again."

"I'll be okay. Don't worry." He picked at the futon cover. I got worried for him. What would he do? In some ways, he was more alone now than I ever was.

I considered this. "I may be back someday, Alex. Why don't you keep Do It Right going until then?"

He faced me. His eyes seemed eager, but scared. "You think I can?" he asked, uncertain. "Do you really?"

I thought about it. "Nah," I said, and giggled like a girl.